The Coast of Bohemia

By the same author

Stalin's Shoe

THE COAST
OF BOHEMIA

A Winter's Tale

Zdena Tomin

HUTCHINSON

LONDON MELBOURNE AUCKLAND JOHANNESBURG

First published in 1987 by Hutchinson Ltd, an imprint of
Century Hutchinson, Brookmount House, 62–65 Chandos
Place,
London WC2N 4NW

Century Hutchinson Australia Pty Ltd
PO Box 496, 16–22 Church Street, Hawthorn, Victoria 3122,
Australia

Century Hutchinson New Zealand Ltd
PO Box 40-086, Glenfield, Auckland 10,
New Zealand

Century Hutchinson South Africa (Pty) Ltd,
PO Box 337, Bergvlei, 2012 South Africa

Tomin, Zdena
    The coast of Bohemia : a winter's tale.
    I. Title
    823'.914[F]   PR6070.047/

ISBN 0-09-168490-0

Set by Avocet Marketing Services, Bicester, Oxon.
Printed and bound in Great Britain by
Anchor Brendon Ltd, Tiptree, Essex

Bohemia. A desert country near the sea.

Antigonus: Thou art perfect then our ship hath touch'd
        upon
        The deserts of Bohemia?
Mariner: Ay, my lord: and fear
        We have landed in ill time: the skies look grimly,
        And threaten present blusters. In my conscience,
        The heavens with that we have in hand are angry,
        And frown upon's.
Antigonus: Their sacred wills be done!

William Shakespeare,
The Winter's Tale, Act III, Scene III.

I

I watched the moon pale away behind the unwashed window while the night hung on, white and fitful. The boy behind the desk rested his elbow on a hefty typewriter and watched me mournfully; had he been a little younger and had I started early, I could have been his mother.

I longed for the hard plank-bed of the detention cell in the basement; for fidgety sleep; for the tepid brown soup at breakfast; even for the usual team of a bully and an intellectual: for the simple rules of the game.

This boy was far too young for an interrogator. Perhaps they had called in the trainees – the bashful beginners with tough little moustaches and voices that were barely broken – to practise on the meek and the unimportant. He had stopped throwing questions at me hours ago; I had been in good form then and had simply stared him out. The long silence, however, was now stretching thin and uncomfortable.

'My name is Anton,' he said suddenly and loudly, 'but I prefer to be called Tony.'

I gazed at my fingernails, which had gathered dirt and dust.

'We're not supposed to give names, but with you, I don't mind. Nearly everybody speaks well of you, you know. They say you are the only one who isn't in it for money. Why can't we be friends? Why should we sit here like two deaf-mutes, when all this time we could have been chatting over a glass of wine? Or two. Or a whole bottle.'

'Why not two bottles?' I said and bit my lip. Silence, once interrupted, was difficult to restore. And silence was my only weapon of some dignity. Sarcasm was much cheaper and did not last.

1

'Three,' young Anton trumped my aces. 'We could have easily drunk three bottles of wine by now, and had something to eat. Fried liver with tartare sauce. Or Moravian sausage with sauerkraut – but that goes down better with beer. We could have gone to the Three Bears. We still could, you know; they stay open at all hours. You may well say that they are practically our canteen. We service society day and night and they serve us – it's only fair. How about it? Don't be shy, I'll pay.'

I was faint with hunger and thirst. Weak.

'You think that I am a cynic, don't you? Well, I am not. I happen to believe in the system. I may be young, but I believe in human values. I believe that you and I can communicate. Over a meal. You must be starved,' he smiled.

He did have a coffee and a couple of sandwiches some three hours ago. Generously, he then offered me a glass of water which I foolishly drank and which soon made me undergo the ordeal of the open-door lavatory. He was relatively decent about it, kept looking at the ceiling while he listened to my slow painful trickle. The thought of it hardened my will and I turned my eyes to the full moon again.

Anton *alias* Tony gave out a long childish, wistful sigh.

The interrogation room was small and bare like a shabby dealer's office. When the door flew open it nearly knocked over the chair I sat on. Powerful wafts of liquor fumes and cigar smoke filled the air. I knew the smell and rumbling cough; everybody knew them – they were Major Fischer's main credentials. Eyes shut, I waited for the inevitable.

'Pardon me, young comrade,' hissed the major. 'Would you mind telling me what you have bloody well done with my office? Sold all my pictures and carpets, have you? Swapped them for this scraggy whore, have you? I'll have your whatsit for this. Now clear out, both of you!'

Anton blinked nervously. 'This is the fourth floor, comrade major. I believe your office is on the third floor. These are interrogation rooms, as of course you know.'

2

'As of course I know,' sneered Major Fischer. 'As of course I know this dirty bitch. You thought I was drunk out of my mind, didn't you, madame? I am never drunk out of my mind. If I had my way, you'd be whipped to the bone. I'd see you behind bars, in solitary, with nothing to cover your cunt but a pair of filthy knickers. I'd take my wife and kids to have a good look at you. You're the enemy and I spit on you!'

Whereupon he vehemently did so, but lost his balance and staggered backwards out of the door. We could hear his curses fade down the corridor.

Anton handed me a paper towel to wipe the spittle from my cheek. I ran over to a basin in the corner and threw up. I sobbed and choked. I could never stand the sound or sight of spittle; a mere trickle of saliva down somebody's chin would make me sick. I was so feeble that Anton had to support me all the way down the stairs, across the cold street still swathed in moonshine and into the dim and dingy bar of the Three Bears.

And that is how I became a traitor to my cause and met Norma D., a rare light in the winter days that followed.

I drained three glasses of wine in three minutes. I ate a double portion of fried liver with tartare sauce and soggy chips, washing it down with more wine. I talked incessantly and unprompted over the second bottle of wine, and fell asleep in the middle of the third.

Somebody lifted my head by pulling at my hair.

'Wake up, silly,' said a curiously loving voice. 'Joseph wants us out of here.' The voice belonged to a woman with Chinese eyes and a halo of dense curls around her broad face. Joseph, the old barman, was mopping the table; the bar was empty and the thick air tasted bitter.

'I have seen them all,' grumbled Joseph, 'and though my heart never bled when they left, I did not mind them coming in again. Custom is custom. But you're something else. You would greatly oblige me, miss, if you'd avoid my shady

3

parlour in future. If you can't take your drink, don't touch it. Even Norma here knows when to stop, and she is one of God's simpletons.'

She took his hand and pressed it briefly against her cheek.

'My dear Tony,' Joseph mimicked what must have been my voice, 'freedom of expression is your constitutional right!' He shook his balding head. 'Freedom, miss? What do you mean, freedom? You wouldn't know it if I served it to you on a silver plate! Mind you, I wouldn't know what to serve with it and what price to ask. We are too far gone, lady. Far too far. Freedom, indeed!'

My knees shook. 'What else did I say?' I asked through the lump in my throat, as the woman pulled me towards the door.

'Whatever it was, you said it to the devil. Now get out of my sight, both of you! The clock says ten to five and my bones are screaming for bed.'

The dawn was darker than the night. The moon had gone, the black clouds hung low and silently, snow began to fall. Norma stuck out her tongue like a lizard, to catch a snowflake or two. I remembered the spittle dripping down my cheek and was sick again. She held my heaving shoulders and when it was over, gave me a piece of chewing gum – her last. The sharp minty taste sobered me up.

Window after window sprang to light and echoed with the sound of a cough or a baby's wail. Dark huddled figures of factory workers hurried through the snowfall.

'We could go to the Main Station,' said Norma warmly. 'They serve coffee early and beer late.' She laughed at her own words, a high-pitched whisper of a sound.

'We'll go home.'

It was an impulse I seldom regretted.

Norma put her arm around my waist and her cheek on mine. 'I love you,' she murmured softly. 'I really do. I know who you are – you are my Uncle Herman's first wife. My Uncle Herman loves his first wife very much.'

And thus we walked, our hair and shoulders white with

4

snow, our bodies close for warmth. We didn't have far to go, as I lived most conveniently a mere twenty minutes on foot from the police headquarters, but I had to stop by a house on Peace Square and whistle up a signal to a brightly lit window. The lion-like head of Karol, father of six and the soul of dissidency, appeared briefly behind the pane and nodded. I was accounted for and struck off the list of people arrested and detained.

Karol slept only in the politically dead hours of the late morning and the early afternoon.

I slept heavily, missing the early dusk. When I woke up, the sky was pitch-dark but the moon was back, and beneath the moonshine the city lay pale and blurred under a thin layer of quivering snow. Then Norma switched on the light and pulled down the blind.

'I don't want Uncle Herman to watch. He'd move in with us and we don't want to live with dead people.'

'Is he dead?' Lucky fellow, I thought, head in pain.

'He's had a funeral, but he moves about quite a lot. He follows me and sometimes he gives me money. Look!' She opened her purse and it was packed with notes and heavy with coins. Cold fear crossed my heart.

'Norma... you haven't stolen it, have you?'

She gave that thin whine of a laugh which – in the dark – could have been mistaken for weeping. 'No. Men give it to me; Uncle Herman sends them.'

An innocent and a whore. I didn't mind in the least, I needed her badly; she was my absolution. I squeezed her small hot hands.

'Where do you live, Norma? Isn't somebody worried about you not coming home?'

Her eyes were two angry slits. 'You mustn't give me away! They'd kill me with injections!'

'Shush! I won't.'

She giggled. 'You mumble when you sleep. Your eyes are closed and you mumble. It's funny. May I call you "Funny"? I forget names, I always do, but I shan't forget

5

"Funny". I love you very much. *Are* you my Uncle Herman's wife?'

'No, I am not. I am nobody's wife.'

'The wife of Nobody,' said Norma admiringly and kissed my hand. 'We won't tell Uncle Herman though. He'd be mad.'

'Oh, stuff your uncle Herman!'

'Get stuffed yourself, you Funny!'

'Snap your teeth!'

'Eat your tongue!'

'Wiggle your toes!'

'I love you, I really do!'

If I don't lose her out of carelessness, I thought, she'll go on saying it and I'll believe it. I'll be redeemed.

'Would you like to stay, Norma? Would you like to live here with me? At least for a while?'

She nodded earnestly. 'I'll pray for you if you want me to. I'll say "God, be good to Funny." I'll say it every night.'

I gave her my spare keys with an address-tag attached to them in case she strayed. We scrambled four eggs and shared a stale bun. I took her to a pub and she paid for the rounds of beer. Men flocked around her as if she was the magnetic pole. We went home fairly early and I offered, bashfully, to lend her my toothbrush. She bared her perfect sparkling teeth and said she never brushed them. I took a bath first and she used the same water afterwards; it was still quite hot. I fished out an ancient pair of pyjamas for her. For the life of me, I could not remember the man it had belonged to.

'You are my Uncle Herman's wife!' said Norma triumphantly.

We lay, feet to head and head to feet, the way I used to sleep with my numerous cousins behind the chimney-corner in a village with the soft rumbling name of Broumy. It seemed more private, and more appropriate.

'Pray God,' whispered Norma, 'be good to Funny.'

*

6

The cousins poured a boxful of cockchafers down the neck of my shirt. The frantic beetles scrambled wildly and scratched my sunburnt skin, while I yelled and struggled to get from under the eiderdown. It broke in half and the feathers turned to snow. Nimbly, blindly like a mole, I dug a tunnel in it; it led me to a cave full of laughter echoing endlessly to and fro. There were pictures on the walls, huge photographs of young Anton and myself in various stages of drunken camaraderie. The cousins amused themselves by spitting at my face; I pinched their noses but they were rubber – there wasn't a drop of blood; I sobbed with fury.

Then I woke up and found Norma kneeling on the bed, pinning my arms to the sheets.

'You should not drink beer,' she said. 'It makes you mad. You should drink sweet creamy things; they may be bad for the complexion, but they're good for your tummy. It's the tummy that makes people mad, did you know that?'

'No.'

She whinnied. 'See, I *am* important for you.'

I was soon asleep again and dreaming, but mildly.

When the morning came, the city lay paralysed under a foot of fresh luminous snow. The clouds were swimming away, but a new storm was gathering in the west. The glare of the rising sun was overwhelming. Norma said we had better run to the shops while they still had yesterday's goods to sell. For a barmy woman, she was in cunning touch with basic realities.

We were the first to plough a furrow in the snow. Our breath rang loudly in the silence and settled on our brows in tiny icicles. The grocer filled our basket with leftover bread, half a liver sausage and a bunch of overripe bananas. We covered it all up with yesterday's newspaper, against the envy of others, and plodded home. There was a set of deep footprints going our way; we found young Anton upstairs, leaning against my door.

'You must not look on them as people,' Karol had said time

7

and again. 'They're instruments of oppression and as such deserve neither pity nor truth. "Love thine enemy" doesn't apply to non-humans.'

'Will you let me in?'

'Do you have a warrant?'

'Yes, if that's what you want.'

'Let me see it.'

'Listen, I have not come here to play games.'

'Why did you come?'

'Let me in.'

'No.'

Norma giggled. Anton peered at her through the twilight of the corridor and his eyes widened, a slow smile twisting his boyish mouth.

'Perhaps I've come to take her way – I bet the asylum is looking for her. But maybe she'll have to have enforced VD treatment first.'

I unlocked the door; Norma darted to the bathroom and locked herself in. Anton laughed merrily and marched into my neat small kitchen; I winced with the pain of penetration.

'Tea or coffee?' he asked.

'Neither!' But he made two cups of coffee anyway, with the ease of a long-term lodger. He looked in the cupboards and the fridge. 'No milk? Not even a spot of rum? You are not doing very well, are you?'

'I live.' I felt queasy.

'I apologize for Major Fischer,' said Anton, reading my mind. 'He is badly overworked.'

'So you said the other night.'

He smirked. 'I didn't think you'd remember.'

'Come to the point, whatever it is.'

'Relax, this is just a friendly visit. Since you've been put in my care, I need to know everything about you. What do you live on? I mean, what is the source of your income?'

'I have answered that question a thousand times.'

'What's wrong with a thousand and one?'

'I do technical translations. Cold welding. Ceramic kilns. Weaving and webbing. Semi-conductors. Freelance. I pay my taxes to the local council and I keep the receipts. I earn

8

enough to support two people; the charges of parasitism do not apply.'

Anton grinned. 'I wouldn't be too sure of that if I were you.' He was enjoying himself. 'May I see the rest of your charming little place?'

'No. Get your charming little arse out of here!'

He doubled up with mirth. 'Golly! That's insulting an officer on duty, you know. You could be done for it. But I'm not prissy and I like you.'

In the living room, he patted the typewriter and peeped behind the curtain over the niche where I slept.

'What, no proper bedroom? Why don't you buy yourself a larger flat if you say you're such a good earner?'

'I didn't say that. I earn a living, that's all.'

'I bet some of it comes in dollars.'

'No!'

'Don't panic, it's all right with me. Just don't get caught selling them on the streets. And get rid of that moron – I bet she's got lice. Well, I'll be seeing you.'

He held out his hand and I let it hang there. He nodded. 'It takes time, or so I am told. Pity you got so drunk the other night; otherwise you'd remember that we've had a friendly discussion and if we disagreed on some points, we did agree on others. As I said, I'll be seeing you. Watch your step.'

I closed my the door with a louder bang than I had intended and the noise brought Norma out of the bathroom.

'Don't you dare tell anyone,' I said savagely. 'If it weren't for you, I wouldn't have let him in. So keep your bloody mouth shut, do you hear? Don't tell!'

'I'll tell my Uncle Herman,' snuffled Norma. 'He loves me very much and he loves you too. He'll hide us in his grave.'

I could not eat a bite of the scrumptious breakfast, not even a banana. My mouth felt dirty. I had been dined, wined and bribed by a cop. The arch-fiend. The devil. I had to come forward now, or for ever hold my peace.

'Stop stuffing your face, Norma. We have to see a friend.'

In the hall, I discovered that Anton had left his Muscovite

9

fur-hat behind, dangling from a peg, Norma put it on and it suited her beautifully.

The clouds were closing again. It was nearly ten o'clock, but there were still no trams or buses. A solitary old snow-plough moved jerkily down Barley Street, leading a small convoy of skidding cars. A few well-wrapped people shovelled the snow to clear the pavement, but in most places the white menace lay unchallenged. We walked as if our legs were in chains.

The church on Peace Square stood graceful and fragile; the trees and bushes on the green bowed like white-fluffed, frozen ballerinas. I skimmed up a handful of snow and lapped at it, slowly. It tasted sweet and sour, sour and sweet.

Karol was covered in semolina. 'Thank God you're here! The baby won't eat, she screams and splutters. Come in and distract her, will you?'

We left our coats, hats and boots in the hall. At Karol's, everybody walked about in socks.

'Norma, this is Karol. Karol, meet Norma. She is my cousin – we share the same uncle.'

'Uncle Herman,' confirmed Norma. 'He loves babies.'

She miawoed and chirped and made faces until most of the semolina was safely in the baby's tummy.

'Gee,' said Karol, 'thanks! Won't you go and play with the toddlers in the nursery? I'd be most grateful.'

The baby clasped her arms round Norma's neck and cooed in her ear. Karol opened the door for them and shut it firmly again.

'Sweet woman,' he said. 'A bit of a mongol, isn't she? Well, I guess we can't pick and choose our relatives.'

'They choose us,' I sighed archly. 'I need your advice, Karol.'

'Beer?'

'Why not?'

He opened a tall bottle with his teeth. 'Ouch!' I cringed

10

and he laughed. Karol drank beer all the time, without any discernible effect. It's better than sedatives, Marta once explained to me, it just calms him down. He is hyperactive, she said, without it he would be unbearable. And Marta should know, she was an excellent physician as well as a heroic mother of six. Karol had lost his teaching job years ago and became a house-husband, greatly pitied and helped by all. He trained the three schoolboys to do the shopping – their little snouts were popular with the butchers and grocers and every week they brought home things which others had not seen for months.

'Do we need to scramble?' asked Karol.

'I don't know. Perhaps.'

He switched on the wireless, on full volume, and a Strauss waltz spun around the spacious room. Karol did not really believe there was a bug in the ceiling – it was simply a matter of principle with him. The music was suddenly interrupted by a mealy-mouth broadcaster.

'Due to unprecedented weather conditions as well as the chronic unpreparedness of local councils, life in the capital has come to a standstill. Industry, administration, schools and vital services cannot function, as most of the workers have not reached their destinations. All able-bodied citizens are called to report at their nearest agitprop centres, where they will be given tools to combat the calamity. Basic routes have to be cleared for ambulances, fire brigades, the police vehicles to get through. I repeat, this is a call to all able-bodied citizens. We are with you, be with us!'

The waltzes returned. Karol rubbed his hands together, palm on palm; I was always surprised how effeminate his hands were.

'Tomorrow, my pet, the snow might melt away or else they'll send the Army in to clear the roads. Tonight, Cinderella, we can have a ball. Police vehicles can't get through! We'll hold a meeting, play democracy. I want us to elect a proper citizens' committee. It may be beautiful to be vaguely humanistic, but it's so damn ineffectual! I want to see a proper network built up, typing-pools, distributors, education cells, organizers of local-events, police harassment

11

monitors, the works. And I want you on that committee; we need a linguist.'

'I thought you said "elect".'

He laughed. 'Ours can only be a token democracy, child, combined with a bit of straightforward manipulation. Don't forget to nominate me, if nobody else does! I've sent the boys around with the word – no school today – and if the chain works, we may get fifty people where we want them. Hey, why aren't you enthusiastic? What's the long face about?'

'It's about the other night.'

'Was it that bad?' So far Karol had not been arrested and interrogated. Perhaps it was because of the children: as Marta the mother of six was unsackable, Karol the father might be un-nickable. Anyway he had no patience with lengthy accounts of such fleeting torments as a night or two at police headquarters.

'It was... different.' I concentrated on the hole in my sock. 'Slimy. I got pissed on State Security money. Now I think I'm being blackmailed.'

I might just as well have been talking to Johann Strauss. Karol was busy scribbling on a magic slate, the kind that erases words without a trace. It was another principle of his: never utter names of places and dates of events to come, no matter how perfect is your scrambler.

'Old Tavern on the Hill,' said the slate. 'Arrivals between six and seven.' I nodded and the slate went blank.

'Are they open? Nothing works today.'

'Yep. They'll stay open as long as the beer lasts. I phoned from the post-office. The landlord has a pretty thick tongue already. I told him we are a local branch of a dog-breeding society which has decided to have a Christmas party while it's white. He said that was a jolly good idea, only sorry – no dogs allowed. Which was okay with me! So you see, angel, we are all set.'

'I am not. If you won't listen to me, I won't come.'

A cheerful din broke out in the nursery – small voices yelling, little feet kicking. Marta appeared in the door with the baby in her arms and the toddlers pulling at her skirts. Her pretty face wore a frown; she was habitually jealous, and Karol loved it.

12

'The clinic's shut. The janitor and I were the only personnel. It's a real Siberia out there. I am glad you two are cosy enough – but I do object to strange people with practically no IQ playing with my children.'

Norma, terrified, came to hide behind my chair. Karol laughed and showered Marta with kisses and the toddlers cheered. I stood up, feeling fed up with the whole seething family.

'I guess we'd better go now, my cousin and I.'

'Yes,' said Marta shamelessly. 'It's time for Karol's nap anyway.'

'I'll see you soon,' winked Karol.

'Maybe, and maybe not.'

'Nonsense,' he shouted, but Marta closed the door and left us in the dark hall groping for our coats and boots.

We ran down the stairs – flew really, like a pair of heavy Arctic geese with their beaks pointing home, home, home. We hadn't met a soul. The lights were on in the agitprop centre next to the grocer's, but there weren't any patriotic citizens claiming tools to combat the calamity. Ours is such a sad city, I thought, inhabited yet deserted, uncared for, unclaimed. But perhaps it's only momentarily dejected – what's a couple of decades in a city's history? A passing moment, a short winter.

The central heating radiators were lukewarm; the stokers had probably not arrived. We nestled in bed with a book each. Norma held hers upside down.

'For chrissake, woman, don't tell me you can't read!'

'I can. I can read better than my Uncle Herman's second wife. She read all the time – that's why she didn't give him any children. But she only had picture books; I can read words.'

'You can't, not the wrong way up.'

'Yes, I can. Just you listen. This book is called *About Love and Kisses*. It's a sad story.'

'It's nothing of the sort. It's called *Tom Sawyer* and it's funny.'

'Funny you. Do you want me to read you a bit or don't you?'

'Okay. Read.'

She solemnly placed her palm on a page like a healer, and pushed her voice half a tone lower.

'Once upon a time, there was a girl called Funny. She went to school, but soon she was thirty-three and the teachers didn't want her any more. So she went into the fields and sat on a stone. It was winter, and she was hungry. Her shoes had no soles, the snow tickled her feet. So she looked closer and saw a little man with a thimble for a hat, who asked her to breathe on him. So this Funny did so, and he grew very tall. "I am not called Herman," he said, "and I am not a prince, even though my thimble shines like a crown. If you want to know who I am, you must love me and kiss me." Funny did all this and he turned into a stone. She cried so much that she turned into a little wishing-well. But the stone cried too, until there was a big sea in the middle of the snow. A Queen came by and built herself a little castle with ice and pebbles – millions of shiny noisy pebbles she had to dig out from under the snow. She was called Norma but it was a secret. One day she wished she wasn't so lonely, and Funny came out of the sea to speak to her. "You must love me and kiss me," she said. So the Queen did so and they both turned into stones. Then, on a white horse with mighty hoofs and a black mane, came a Ghost called Herman—'

'Stuff Herman!' I said. 'Why should love and kisses turn people into stones?'

'Because this is a sad story; I told you it was. Give me another book and I'll see if it's merry. Tomorrow. I am tired now. Reading is very hard.'

'How did you know I was thirty-three?'

'Joseph told me.'

'How did Joseph know?'

'He knows everything. He told me that I am thirty-three too. Practically a child, he said.'

'You're a big girl now – too big to wear my clothes. We'll have to buy you some.'

Norma snorted. 'I have clothes! I keep them in a locker, number three three three on platform one in the Main Station.'

'All right,' I sighed. 'Let's go and get them. We don't want to spend life in bed anyway. If we're lucky, we can get a hot sausage for lunch.'

The snow grew heavier and wetter. By tomorrow it would have turned into slush. After all, November had only just gone, and there were a good three weeks till Christmas.

It took us nearly an hour to walk to the Main Station. Knee up, foot down, knee up, foot down, we moved like waders in the mud. I was fine in my plastic, padded snow-boots, but Norma's shiny smarties were soaked through. We joined the queue at the sausage stand surrounded by steam as the falling snow met the vapours from the grill. A heavy hand fell upon my shoulder. It was Vlado – an actor, window-cleaner, philanderer and day-time alcoholic. At night, he was as chaste and sober as a priest, and a rival to Karol in political dexterity. He took me to bed once and it was all very gentle; I felt like a child treated to a sweet. Major Fischer was right, I was scraggy; I did not inspire sexual elation.

'Hi there, my favourite sparrow! What a small planet this is. Come here, let me warm you up.' He opened his badly moulted fur-coat and hugged me to his chest. 'Have you heard the news?' he whispered. 'Old Lion-Head is calling a meeting. Are you coming?'

'I don't know yet. You smell of foxes.'

'Vixen yourself! What d'you mean you don't know? Of course you're coming. The earth will move tonight.'

'Not for me.' I blushed.

Vlado smiled. 'My little maiden, cold in the hips. Or did they scare you the other night? How long did they keep you? They let me go at midnight, it was all about nothing. As a matter of fact, the chaps I was with were quite decent. They wined and dined me, would you believe it? At the Three Bears. If they hoped to get me drunk, well, they picked the wrong time. But I suppose they simply wanted a whiff of human warmth – like you, my little blue-tit.'

'Sparrow.' I wriggled myself free. 'And you're not ashamed, I mean that you went with them?'

15

'Only a little. I was hungry. In civilized countries, people under arrest are always fed and watered. But what about you?'

'I came home at half-past five in the morning.'

'You poor darling, oh you poor little kitten.'

'She is Funny,' said Norma. 'You should not call her other names, she doesn't like them.' Vlado raised an eyebrow.

'My Uncle Herman's niece,' I sighed, suddenly very tired. Why didn't I own up? He would have merely laughed, and boosted my ego. But I did get drunk, so maybe he would have turned away with frost in his eyes, satisfied with himself, contemptuous of me. Virtue and vice, who could measure them justly?

On top of it all, my sausage burst and I spilt the grease down the front of my coat. Norma found it very funny; she giggled loudly and could not stop.

Vlado raised his other eyebrow. 'Your cousin's very pretty, like a true daughter of the steppe; those cheekbones are terrific. But isn't she a little weak in the head? Watch out, it may be catching! They say now that everything's caused and spread by bugs. I wish we could start an epidemic tonight. A citizens' disease. A plague of courage. Look at them, just look at them! Mules. Donkeys. Greedy mice. Unconscious. What hast thou done with thy dignity, oh Bohemia?'

'Shut up or somebody'll punch thy nose. You were in that queue yourself, only a minute ago.'

'Ah, but I am different. I have a soul up my sleeve. I am nobody's slave. And I drink brandy, not beer. Beer is debilitating. Won't you two canaries join me in search of a decent bar?'

'No,' said Norma. 'We're going to platform one.'

'What for, my lovely? You couldn't travel if you paid in gold. No trains today. One pinch of salt from heaven and the whole city faints and folds away. But who am I to question your motives? See you very soon, won't I, dear girls? Cheerio!'

*

16

'I hope you girls aren't up to any mischief,' said a guard moodily. 'You don't want to spoil my reputation as "The Man Who Singlehandedly Safeguarded The People's Railway", do you?'

'We're only picking up some luggage from a locker on platform one, if you don't mind.'

'Of course I mind. Why shouldn't I mind? You name it, I mind it. I mind the whole bloody business of living from pay-day to pay-day. I mind winter, summer, spring and autumn. Tell you what – one of you nips over to platform one, the other stays right here as a hostage. That way I'll only half-mind, which is the most I can do at the best best of times.'

The vast hall under the pseudo-baroque dome was monumentally empty. Norma's footsteps bounced off the tiles and echoed like pistol shots between the marble pillars. Or like the hoofs of a colt dancing on ice. The scarlet plastic seats nailed to the floor glistened with damp. A few stranded travellers slept behind the glass wall of the waiting room. The attendant of a small buffet squeezed between 'Gents' and 'Ladies' dozed with her head on the counter. I yawned and so did the guard.

'This,' he said, 'must have been a wonderful place once. Ladies in long skirts and veiled hats, gentlemen wearing dark cloaks and white gloves, porters in gilded uniforms, newspaper boys, pretzel-sellers, nannies, well-behaved children in lace caps or cute little straw-hats, railway guards dignified in their position of tenure and their pension scheme. Well-informed guards, carrying the time-tables inside their heads, time-tables that were adhered to come snow, rain, or drought. Well-fed guards, with tin boxes in their lockers packed with nourishing lunches prepared by loving wives. Of course I mind. I mind the whole twentieth century. I mind my endlessly bickering, greedy family, I mind the lies we feed each other with, I mind the people who blame the Russians for everything. The sods may have started the trouble, but by the burning sun, our own comrades have been quick on the uptake. And if you think about turning informer, it's my word against yours. And I have a clean bill of health.'

17

'Lucky you! I don't. I am what you may call a dissident. A small fish, but still.'

'I mind you people too. Washing the dirt off your hands, aren't you? Flaunting your high-faluting stuff all over Radio Free Europe; that's just more gobbledegook. So you suffer some, so what? Do you have children?'

'No.'

'Are you married?'

'No.

'See?'

'No, many of my friends have children; one friend has six of them – I mean he and his wife.'

'If you are not lying, then they are mad. The children will never thank them.'

'Yours do?'

'No, but they can't blame me either. I didn't make little martyrs out of them. You'd better not marry, you know, if you're inclined that way. Good gracious, do you call that luggage?'

For some reason, perhaps because of her purse bursting with money, I had expected Norma to come dragging a large calf-leather suitcase full of clothes. But all she had were two plastic carrier-bags, not exactly bulging with stuff. I was overcome with compassion. And I decided, there and then, that I would attend the meeting.

It was quite a trek to the Old Tavern: down to the river, across the old bridge, up the winding streets of the Hill. The evening was frosty again and the snow either knee-deep or icy and slippery where it had been trampled. Higher up on the Hill, the steep road was furrowed by sleigh-tracks, but the children had gone home early. An awkward peace and quiet hung over the city.

'It's spooky, said Norma. 'Uncle Herman's second wife is a spook. That's why she didn't give him any children.'

'Fiddlesticks! It was because she read too much.'

Norma whinnied and nudged me in the ribs, which sent me sprawling in the snow. I caught her hand and pulled her

18

down too and we lay there for a while, gazing at the sky. The clouds were floating away, uncovering the stars, feeble yellow specks on the peacock-blue vault of the heavens.

'I love you,' I said sternly. 'I really do. God help you, Norma.'

The tap-room of the Old Tavern was like hell; it stank and smouldered and quaked to satanic sounds of an old accordion. Within seconds, Norma was seated among the locals, who were in various – mostly jolly – stages of inebriation.

'You don't want no dog-breeders, honey! Tell your friend that you'll stay right here with us; go on, say it,' shouted the landlord and banged a pint-pot of beer before her. Norma simpered and wiggled her arse. She stuck her tongue out at me.

'We'll baby-sit for you,' the landlord chuckled in my ear. He pressed a foaming tankard against my breast. 'Here, have one on the house. And tell the dog-breeders not to worry. I'll call in the wife and we'll ship over as much beer as anyone can drink. Spirits by the bottle. No coffee or tea, mind you. Anyone can have their fucking cuppa at home; they don't have to bother me!'

I walked through a swing door and suddenly excitement set my teeth on edge. The clock said a quarter to seven, and the large shabby saloon was packed. Clean, sober people sat or stood around formica tables and rickety chairs, some solemn, some aflutter, but all holding a carbon copy of the agenda for the meeting.

'Hi,' said Anna, handing me one. 'Sixty-two,' she said. 'I counted. Isn't it great? Read and memorize. I'll collect them in a short while and burn them in the stove. Karol's orders.'

'You are almost late,' scolded Karol.

'Where is Marta?' The meticulous typing was undoubtedly hers.

'Home, where else? Mother's place is with her children.'

'Impeccable bastard, Old Lion-Head,' laughed Vlado. 'Come and see the stove. It's a beauty. 1910, I should think. I wonder if they'd sell it.'

I warmed my hands on the glowing tiles. 'Cold hands betray a heart of fire,' recited Vlado. 'And still waters run deep. Smashing turn-out, is it not? But as the proverb says, don't praise the day before the evening's over. Alternatively, don't say hop! before you jump. On the other hand, the more heads, the more wisdom, also applies. *Qui ne risque rien, n'a rien.*'

'Don't be French on a night like this!' Dagmar planted a kiss on his cheek. She was impossibly glamorous and smelled of carnations.

'Why can't you girls all be like Dagmar?' moaned Vlado.

'Attention, everybody!' shouted Karol. His voice did not carry well and he climbed on a chair to gain visibility. 'Please pay attention. Before we begin, in ten minutes from now, I want everybody to get their drinks. Bear in mind that this is a dog-breeders' Christmas party, which means that you have to be generous. Get a bottle of liquor per table and a pint of beer each. We'll order some more beer during the break to keep up the image, but please don't touch the hard stuff before the meeting's over. We'll need clear minds. We also need volunteers to patrol outside the tavern, in fifteen-minute turns. In the highly unlikely event of a police raid, those of you who have a valid reason not to be apprehended will have time to leave through the emergency exit on my right-hand side. The rest of us will make merry, sing and dance. The dog-breeders bit will be explained not as an attempt to deceive, but as a device to organize a surprise party for Anna here, whose birthday it is tomorrow.'

'Happy birthday to you,' intoned Vlado and when others picked it up, he murmured: 'Old Lion-Head should have been an airline steward. I of course am more a pilot than a flight assistant. But he beat me to the chair all right. Still, watch for Arnold, he may well steal the show. The man has a beautiful brain... fe-e-llow, and so say all of us!'

I sat down and hugged my beer.

Faces, faces, faces. Ministers of a fallen government, ministers of locked churches, famous writers of unprinted words, scholars and musicians with blisters and blackened fingernails, stageless performers, muted broadcasters; a few sons and daughters too – street sweepers and cowherders, expelled from schools for their parents' sins; philosophers of all creeds with coal-dust or cement powder in their hair, two-thirds of them men, one-third women. Laughing, frowning, sullen, expectant, pale, reverent.

I had checked on Norma. She was pecking daintily at a plate of thinly sliced brawn with onion rings. The locals watched her with fascination: come on, honey, you can do it, it's the best fucking brawn you can get, hundred per cent homemade. She gave me a wink and a majestic half-smile. It boosted my morale; if Norma can be the queen of all drunkards, I can at least be part of History.

At the stroke of seven, Anna fed the papers to the stove. The flames roared. Karol stood up and everybody fell silent. I could not bear it, I grabbed my coat, mumbled that it was my turn to patrol and tiptoed out. I left my handbag with Norma in the taproom to reassure her that she was not being abandoned.

An aeroplane was crossing the skies just underneath the moon like a wandering star. I flapped my wings and flew, bolder than a hawk, soaring higher and higher, until I too passed under the moon and alighted on the icy wing close to a rounded window. I tried to read its destination from the face of a sleeping child. Paris, London, Vienna, Rome? But soon the mother saw me and opened her mouth in a silent scream. I fell, losing all my feathers, and landed at the feet of a woman called Funny who was too scared for words.

Every shadow took the shape of a man. The bushes had eyes peering through the snow. Young Anton was laughing at me with every rustle, now here, now there. Panic leapt onto my shoulders and drove me hard. My heart galloped. I washed my face in the snow and let my tears flow. Why not, I thought, why not simply tell them the truth?

Weakness overwhelmed me the other day, my friends, in those treacherous small hours at the end of a sleepless night, but hereby I solemnly declare that I shall not be blackmailed, nor tempted again.

21

The door creaked and I jumped and thumped my feet like a rabbit.

'Change of guards,' said Zoe, a beautiful black-haired woman of my age, a waitress with an expert knowledge of Hindi. 'I'm a bit early, but I can't bear it in there. It's worse than a wedding; I want to cry all the time. Go in, I need a private weep.'

She borrowed my coat and wrapped it around her head and shoulders. 'I bet I look like Yasir Arafat,' she laughed. I did not dispute it, although in my eyes she looked more like Mary, the mother of Jesus.

'What are you girls running out for?' asked the landlord. 'Is the john blocked again?'

'I guess we all need a breath of fresh air now and then,' said I. He shrugged his shoulders. 'There is no accounting for tastes. I like my air thick enough to cut with a knife.' He pressed another free pint on me. 'You need fattening up, my chicken! Don't tell the wife. Are you married?'

'No.'

'Good for you.'

'Perhaps.'

His wife came in from the kitchen with a trayful of brand new tankards. 'Don't you believe a word he says, love,' she mumbled. 'He would be after a donkey if the donkey wore skirts. He thinks he is Cary Grant or Clint whatshisname, the fool.'

'Eastwood,' said the landlord. 'Clint Eastwood. Can't you remember a man's name? A man has the right to have his name remembered!'

Yes, I thought, and so does a woman.

'Can I keep your handbag, Funny?' cooed Norma. 'I like it, I like it very much.'

'Keep it. And don't get drunk.' I managed not to blush, though Norma whinnied with mirth.

'What Karol is proposing,' said Arnold in his deep, shy voice,

22

'is of fundamental importance. He wants us to change. He calls upon us to become a cohesive body, not just a loose collection of signatories under an old petition. He asks us to put our individual consciences to collective use. He demands that we create a nucleus of a pluralistic society, living in truth, mutual tolerance and unselfish cooperation, which would run parallel with the official structures of society at large, independent yet interrelated, drawing perhaps more and more people into at least a zone of semi-freedom, creativity and morality. He believes that one day – in ten fifteen, twenty years – this growing parallel society will take over, causing the hollowed-out illegitimate power to collapse. It may not work, dear old and few friends, but it is too powerful a dream to be left untried.'

Karol was watching him open-mouthed. Dagmar's eyes were misty with tears. Anna got hold of my hand and squeezed it so tightly it hurt. Vlado sucked at his pipe, eyes closed in concentration. The distant accordion sounded almost like a harpsichord. Arnold took a jerky pull of beer and dried his lips with the back of his hand.

'We are privileged, my friends. We have been kicked out of tenures, well-paid positions and careers in the subsidized arts; we would hardly have had the strength to leave the slave-market voluntarily. We are able-minded enough to create an alternative community. Please remember that there is no shame in our pride; we are bearers of the nation's conscience, culture and moral integrity. God knows it's a heavy enough burden, so don't let's confuse morality with moralizing. Plain honesty is much more useful – we can't be perfect. Nobody's perfect, if you recall the wonderful crack at the end of *Some Like It Hot*. Therefore, friends, drink away. Skol!'

Some of us laughed, all drank.

'One more thing before I get too boring. Don't let's look with too much awe at the elections Karol wants us to hold. We mustn't forget that there are fifteen times more of us out there in the country than are present in this room. We may, if you pardon the expression, call ourselves activists. To my mind, it would be much more honest if people interested in committee work simply volunteered. They ought to be aware of the implications and consequences and consider well their vulnerability. This assembly obviously has to have a right to raise objections, in which case we should vote. But please don't forget that we have to operate on trust. Sorry to have taken so long. I propose a toast to Karol, to the weather and last but not least to the might of the weak!'

We all cheered. The landlord stuck his head in. 'All right, all right, you thirsty lot! Give us a minute, and bring your glassware back! The wife's tapping like mad, but she needs more tankards!'

'Okay, everybody, take five,' said Karol.

Of course I volunteered. My heart was squirming though, and I did not hurry to put my name down. I was thirteenth on the list and stood a good chance of being asked to wait till next year, decade or century; but Marek, a true-blue revolutionary, got Dagmar voted out. Several apartments had been raided recently, he said, and the raids had one common denominator: Dagmar was never present, although she promised she'd come. Which meant she had the information about people coming together and could easily have passed it on to the police. In his book, that was too much of a coincidence to endow Dagmar with unlimited trust.

Vlado was livid. He accused Marek of being a misogynist, whereupon Marek charged him with sentimentalism. It's always been the sentimentalists, he said, who brought down a revolution. The vote, by a narrow margin, went Marek's way. Dagmar took it surprisingly well, and even bowed ironically to the assembly; but her hollow cheeks and lovely neck went scarlet.

The saloon quivered with murmurs. 'Please,' shouted Karol, 'please! Professor K. has asked for the floor!'

In a split second a reverent silence fell upon the room. The old professor stood up and clasped his hands as if in prayer; his voice was pleasantly dry.

'I am afraid I am on the side of the sentimentalists. Perhaps, at my age, I am weary of revolutions. But that is beside the point. We must, you know – we must abide by the rule that a person is innocent until proven guilty. Trust, however, is a complex notion, often based on emotions and intuitions, even superstitions, as well as facts and logic. Furthermore, however crude our attempt at democracy may have been, we certainly cannot reverse a majority decision. In any case, under point three of the agenda which we shall be discussing next, there is considerable scope for involvement and full use of Dagmar's intellectual and organizational capacities which I personally rate very highly indeed. I suggest she be asked to prepare, perhaps in collaboration with myself and other scholars, a detailed plan for the peripatetic university proposed under section (c) of point three. But before we ask her to do so, the chair should ensure that she receives an apology from this assembly.'

He was seized by a wheezing cough, extracted a pill from an enamelled snuff-box and washed it down with beer. We all pretended not to have watched.

'Finally, my dear friends, allow me to say how blessed I feel by being here tonight – and I would like to thank the young people who pushed me and pulled me up the Hill – for I believe that our modest rebellion against amorality, indifference and corruption, against the dictates of bureaucracy, police despotism and cultural decay, will not have been in vain. We may appear ludicrously pretentious; our numbers negligible; our suffering too pronounced for the masses to follow and too small when compared with those of other tyrannies of the modern world. Still, we have taken upon us the defence, in mutual solidarity, for the inalienable rights of the individual human being, with all his or her faults and weaknesses, in this nation as in all others. Such endeavour, dear fellow citizens, can be overwhelming, but never meaningless. Permit me, however, to propose a slightly heretical toast: to *joie de vivre*, the joy of living!'

Eyes glistened, glasses clinked.

'Will those who feel we owe Dagmar an apology please raise their hands?' Karol stood up and surveyed the forest of lifted arms. 'Our apologies to you, dear Dagmar,' he bowed.

'Don't be a bore,' snapped Dagmar. Her irises darkened to

an ominous royal blue and they stared straight into mine, though I couldn't see why. There was a threat in their directness; my meagre courage ebbed away and I decided not to confess. What was there to confess anyway, compared with the suspicion Dagmar had been under and confronted, proud and snarling like a lioness? I began to edge away from her gaze.

Norma had pushed her chair into a corner and sat there with knees pressed tightly together and mouth moving rapidly in some voiceless complaint. One of the locals held a handkerchief to his cheek.

'She scratched me, the stupid cow has marked me for life!' He snivelled. 'What am I supposed to tell the wife?'

The accordionist made cat-noises on his instrument.

'He groped,' laughed the landlord's wife. 'Serves him right! But maybe you should take your friend away with you now. Poor thing – it's decent of you to give her an outing.'

'She is my cousin.'

The woman nodded. 'God's creation, cousin or not. Like I said, it's decent of you.'

The landlord spat on the floor. 'Are you dog-breeders having a Christmas booze-party or a fucking annual meeting? So far it's been hardly two pints per capita, as the newspaper would say. Tell them to speed up the action! If you get hungry, don't expect miracles, but I do have a barrel of rollmops in the cellar, first class herring swimming in plenty of sauerkraut. Tell them I am willing it part with it, and never mind my bleeding heart.'

'You tell them!' said Norma. Her narrow eyes were drowned in brine. 'You tell them. We're going home. We don't like it here. Please, Funny?' Her burning hands sought mine, her hair bristled against my cheek; I felt that none of my anguish could ever match hers, whatever hers was.

'We have to fetch my coat, Norma, it won't take a minute.' I sighed and pushed her through the swing-door. It was a cruel thing to do to both of us, but I couldn't help it; I was driven by fright, and fury beyond my comprehension.

We certainly made the fur fly.

The saloon was buzzing, faces flushed, drunk perhaps more with the two hours of uninterrupted freedom than with the alcohol consumed. Karol had to shout. 'Agreed, then, we shall keep the constitution of the action committee in utmost secrecy until after its first meeting and the elaboration of a tenable position.' He threw an angry glance at me across the room. 'And where have you been?'

All heads turned to us.

'Who-is-she?' barked Marek, peering at Norma.

'It's all right,' Vlado murmured into the hush. 'She is a cousin.'

'It's not all right!' Marek was pale with indignation. 'I have half a dozen cousins I would not trust with the secret of the hole in my sock.' There was a crackle of laughter; for Marek, that was witty; Dagmar laughed loudest. 'Friends, please! This is not a laughing matter. I know that most of you shrink from conspiracy, and I respect that; ours is – by necessity – an open stand, but please, please, let's at least observe basic safety precautions! We live in an underhand regime, we face a secret police force; we must be cautious, we have to have a set of rules to reinforce our mutual security. Who will vouch for the – ehm – cousin? Apart from her cousin, that is?'

'I will,' spoke Arnold softly. 'Welcome to the family, cousin.' 'Hear hear,' said Professor K.; Arnold smiled at him, walked over to us and shook Norma's limp hand. A mild surprise registered in his eye as he scanned her face close up. If he had a little speech on his lips, he swallowed it. Norma touched his blond moustache. 'You look like my Uncle Herman's younger brother,' she whispered. 'He is nice too.'

'Listen, all,' I called hastily. 'The landlord's getting suspicious. Not enough beer orders. And he wants us to eat up his barrel of rollmops.'

The door swung open and shut. Young Robert, frost in his hair, took a deep breath before he spoke. 'The police are coming. Two of them. In uniform. On foot.'

'So what?' roared Vlado. He kicked the door out and sang into the tap-room. 'Roll in the barrel, landlord! And since when, in this land of beer, has one to order a pint to get it? Get going, man, don't be shy with it!' He grabbed the nearest half-full tankard. 'Prosit!' he shouted through the door, drained the beer, shuddered and grinned at me. 'Everybody has to make a sacrifice, my dear girl. God, I hate the stuff!'

The false merriment soon turned genuine – the two policemen only came for a tot of rum hidden in a mug of tea and soon departed, wistfully, to continue their punishing beat through the frozen night. But much to Karol's regret, the meeting was over; it gave way to hearty, hot, boozy, innocent, irreverent, happy chatter in mingling, excited groups. The smell of the herring stung noses and watered mouths. Norma and I ate a rollmop each, straight from a wooden fork, licking the sharply sour juices off our fingers and palms. A secret whisper went from one committee member to another, and reached me last. I was foolishly glad to receive it from Zoe's lips: tomorrow night, at Marek's place, twenty-six Green Street, third floor. Arrivals at five-minute intervals. I am six-fifty-five, she smiled, so you're seven sharp. Committee members only, she added, and squeezed my arm warmly above the elbow.

Norma and I slipped quietly away, having dropped a tenner in the collection hat. I had hardly drunk a drop, yet I felt dizzy, and guilty all round.

On Little Square at the foot of the Hill, a silent group of old men and women in huge padded jackets moved slowly along the tramway tracks, brushing the snow off the metal with black wicker brooms. Dead people, whispered Norma, and she dragged me on. In the middle of the old bridge, a sudden gush of wind took us by surprise; it tore Anton's furry hat from Norma's hair, lifted it above the stone railing, played with it and dropped it in the slow dark waters of the river. We watched until there was nothing to see.

The wind kept rising, surprisingly warm: the thaw was on its way.

*

'Please Norma, don't sleep; stay awake for a little while; please try and listen!'

'My ears are tired.'

'We hardly spoke on the way home. You have to make an effort, or I'll burst.'

'Uncle Herman says always sleep before midnight, or the soul-eaters will get you.'

'It's only half-past eleven. Don't be stubborn. I have things to say. If you don't let me talk, I won't sleep at all, and the soul-eaters will surely get me.'

'Hold my hand then. I hear better that way.'

'Oh, Norma, I had no business to drag you into my life! It was not your fault: you were only helping a pissed fellow-creature to her feet. But fate ensured that I was shaken and freezing and robbed of peace of mind; I wrapped you around myself for insulation. You know who Anton is, don't you? You thought he was after you when he came here, didn't you? But he was and is and will be after *me*, now more than ever. And there are hundreds like him, hounds who bark and hounds who don't and all of them hunters. I was not afraid of them, but I am now. They can hurt you, simply for being near me, for holding my hand. Tell me, is there nowhere you could go? You couldn't have been in the . . . hospital all your life; there must be a safe bed for you somewhere.'

'Are you a thief?'

'No, I am not a thief. Don't be silly. This is serious.'

'Are you a nun? There was a nun in the asylum. She was in prison first. All nuns are done for.'

'All right, Norma. Think of me as a sort of a nun. I am being done for, yet I've never harmed anybody. I don't want to harm you. You'll have to go home tomorrow. I'll come with you and see to it that you're fine. There must be someone who takes care of you?'

'Uncle Herman does. He'll take care of you too.'

'Damnation, woman! What am I to do with you?'

'You mustn't curse. Nuns don't.'

'What about your parents? Where are they?'

'They live by the Lake. New Village number seventeen.'

'Bless your sweet brain. We'll get a bus first thing in the

29

morning and go and see them. I am sure they'll be glad to have you.'

'No, not in winter. They sleep in winter.'

'We'll get you a pair of proper boots to walk about in the village. And mittens. And a new fur hat. We'll buy a present for your parents – real coffee, to keep them awake. I'll come and see you whenever . . . whenever it'll be safe. Now you can close your eyes and nod off. It's five to midnight, so you'd better hurry.'

'I love you! Please God, be good to Funny.'

I wept in the kitchen. I felt thankful, relieved and brave. Fortified. To forestall loneliness, I thought of the crisp, sunny winter days I'd spent with Norma in New Village, skating on the frozen Lake, cleaning house or cooking Sunday lunch for her frail parents. Maybe they'd have a large dog and a small sleigh; we'd have such fun. There would be no dirty money from the city's perverts in Norma's purse; I'd have to work harder to keep two households. I'd travel by night – there might not be any night buses, but I could take a train and walk. I'd walk through the winter woods, guided by the shine of the snow, by the smoke of the village chimneys, by the lavender smell of tender love.

I made myself a killer of a coffee, brought the typewriter over to the kitchen table and sat till the small hours translating into my best German a tarted-up article about the technical qualities and artistic merit of Bohemian glass. I got the work from a kind lady in the publicity office of Foreign Trade; she didn't ask many questions, as long as I signed my work Veronika Nowak. A perfect name, she said, innocent here and carrying a slavonic chic abroad. You don't look like Veronika Nowak, she laughed; she would have long honey-coloured hair, white languid limbs and a pink round face; but that's all the better, otherwise my boss would start taking an interest in you and we'd be in trouble. She didn't even want to know my real name: funny. Oh, Norma!

The doorbell rang at half-past five, just when I dozed off with my head on the finished pages.

The soul-eaters had come to get me.

They were two young lads in winter uniforms, obviously new to the business, curious and polite; they did not even step over the threshold.

'Looks as if you were expecting us, Miss. Don't tell me you get up at five every day!' said one.

'You're summoned to police headquarters according to paragraph nineteen. You know: citizens are obliged to help with an investigation,' said the other.

'Of what?' I asked wearily.

'How do we know? If you just get your coat and your citizen's passport, please.'

'Don't be cross with us. It's just a job we do. We haven't even had breakfast yet. Have you?'

'No.'

'Tough life, this.'

'If you want to have a quick cup of coffee, we'll wait outside. Five minutes, not more.'

'Thank you, I will.'

Norma sat up in bed, her face all puckered. Like a child, she was truculent rather than afraid. I kissed her on both cheeks.

'You get yourself out of here, do you hear? I want you to go to your parents now – I'll be terribly angry if you don't. Others might come back to search the house: they'd take you away, they'd lock you up in the asylum; you don't want that, do you! Listen, dearest, I love you; I'll be over as soon as I can. What size of shoes do you take? I'll get the boots for you, you'd only buy yourself another flimsy nonsense.'

'Five. But Uncle Herman says I should buy six, five is too small for me. My toes get all squashed.'

'Take all your things with you. Borrow my holdall. Lock the door, my love – you may keep the spare keys, but don't you dare come back. It's Wednesday today, I should be with you in New Village by Saturday at the latest; we'll have a smashing time together. Please Norma, if you love me, do as I tell you. *Please!*'

She moved her lips silently; they said I love you, I really do, and then they went on saying more, but I had no time to read them. A car honked in the street below.

*

31

It was warm in the car, but I still shook with the shivers. Mornings should not be dark; humans should wait till the sun has risen, as the birds do. I was always hooked on birds, I often wished to fly with them and sing or cry harshly high above the humdrum ground. The police car slid slowly through the murky drizzle, wheels splashing and smacking in the grey slush; the roofs, whenever I could glimpse them, were still white, but it wasn't much of a consolation. The lad at the wheel cursed as the car skidded and lightly hit a dustbin; the other apologized for him; tough life, this. Lucky we don't have far to go, he said, and blushed. Just a bit of help with the investigation, Miss, and you'll be back home in no time. After that, why not simply keep your nose clean? Life's short enough anyway, and it could be sweet if only you'd try. Why meddle in what you can't change?

Anton was freshly shaven and beaming. He fiddled with his brand-new polka-dotted tie, until finally – with a sigh – he unbuttoned the collar of his white nylon shirt.

'One size too small. My mum still thinks I am a teenager. You it *would* fit, you have a neck like a . . . Well, well, so here we are.'

I breathed deeply and slowly, anaesthetizing myself. There was no moon to gaze at, so I fixed my eyes on a gothic spire which seemed to be grafted right on top of the square block of police archives opposite. I imagined the snow melting sadly yet gracefully, sliding down the curves and needles of the lacy ancient stone. Thank God this was the fourth floor again; I would have hated to stare at the dirty windows of the archives, cut in half by an uneven whitewash and adorned with last May Parade posters, the colour of dry blood.

'You know' – there was a distinct note of pleasure in Anton's voice – 'you are going to be far more interesting to work with than I thought. I took you for a squirt, but lo and behold – a rising star! You've been quite a brick, haven't you, taking on that committee of yours as if you had nothing to fear, not a worry in the world. I suppose you've given up your pet moron, have you?'

I nodded lightly and dismissively, like a queen – or rather as I imagined a queen would. I was thinking of Marek: poor chap, is he going to try to find out who, out of sixty-two people, had squealed? So quickly, too; hardly a night gone by.

Anton chuckled. 'Golly, you have grown tall! If I don't get a promotion out of you, I'll eat my hat – it's still hanging on your peg, I hope?'

'I drowned it in the river.' I gritted my teeth; clever dick, he seemed to know how to make words pass my lips.

He whistled merrily. 'Now what do I tell my mum? It was her Christmas present; she wants me to keep my head warm. She brought it all the way from Moscow last year – had a hard job finding it, she said, they had none in the shops. Had to ask a rather high comrade for help and he got it for her from a special supply unit. And you drowned it! Oh well, now you owe me a meal *and* a hat; I guess I just extend your credit.'

He rolled a protocol sheet into the typewriter and began to type, now nimbly, tap-tapping like a woodpecker, his left hand rustling with the pages of my citizen's passport.

'She went to see the military parade, my mum did. You know, Seventh of November, the Great October Revolution. When did the Soviets actually change the calendar? I'll have to look it up; it would be a good piece of knowledge to drop into a serious conversation. I have never seen the parade, I'd only been to summer school in Moscow. Good teaching, but not much fun. Nitchevo, tovarich, the world is young and full of sights yet to be admired. Maybe we'll go together one day, eh?'

After that, he settled for silence. It did not seem to bother him this time, but it bothered me.

Two hours passed before a grey light pushed away the darkness outside. The drizzle developed into a steady rain; my spire swayed and quivered behind the splashes pouring down the window-pane. I was thirsty, but certainly glad I hadn't had that morning coffee, my kidneys, if nothing else, were at rest.

Another brief eternity gone, Anton glanced at his watch and stood up. 'I like watching your face and the way your skin stays smooth whatever you do underneath; but all good things must come to an end.' He picked up the phone.

'Two zero two here. How is it going? Right. Tell Comrade Major we're ready for him.'

I looked him full in the face and he grinned. My lower lip began to twitch, but so did his young moustache.

Major Fischer held a smouldering cigar between his teeth and exuded his staple smell of vodka, but he was far from drunk. He too was freshly shaven, though his must have been an unsteady hand with an old-fashioned razor: there were drops of drying blood on the cuts, three on the chin and two on the massive neck. Anton stood to attention and was impatiently waved at ease.

'I like your tie, comrade, but isn't it a trifle loud? And for pity's sake, does the woman never wear a skirt? In the good old days, trousers on a woman constituted an offence, and how proper that was. And she would not be sitting here like a guest waiting for tea; she'd have been shovelling dirt in a labour camp.'

He sighed heavily. 'This is not my kind of day, comrade, make a mental note of that.' His eyes touched me wistfully. 'Rise, Miss what's-your-name.'

The only thing that was rising in me was a foolish yet somewhat fundamental life-preserving anger. 'Why?' I asked, all muscles taut, all nerves on proper alert, not in panic.

'To hear an official warning. Let's get it over with. Rise.'

'I won't. This is not a court. You are not a judge.'

Anton grabbed my shoulder. 'Leave the fuck... leave her alone,' fumed the major. 'So she'll hear it sitting down. So who cares. I don't care about this whole damn thing.'

Anton handed him a solemn-looking folder decorated with the golden coat of arms of the National Security Corps. Red blotches spread all over the major's face. With a quick half-choked voice he read out, from a beautifully printed sheet, a garbled paragraph of a serious warning... hereby given to... known to engage in... anti-state, anti-socialist...

34

alacrity of the State Security and Public Militia... despite... moreover... henceforward. Signed by Chief Commander of NSC. He nearly threw the folder back at Anton.

'And here is what you sign.' Anton's young voice rang clear and important. 'Having heard this official warning, I am aware that my activity in the so-called Citizens Committee, if pursued by me in collision with the interests of the state, and especially in collusion with a group of people known to be in collusion, or intended collusion, with certain foreign groupings, will expose me to just and inevitable prosecution along the line of subversion against the republic.' He placed the open folder on the edge of the desk with respectful care, and held out his smart Parker pen. 'It's clear, short and it doesn't hurt, does it? It's fair and it's the mildest you can get. Comrade Major and I will sign as witnesses. All correct and proper. The others have already signed, I am told.'

'Cut it out.' Major Fischer spoke through lips that hardly moved. 'Give her the bloody pen and let her sign her bloody name.'

'I don't think I will.' I trembled like a pet hamster I once saw, cornered by a big ginger tom, only I didn't have its little whiskers to bristle with. The silence wasn't red-hot; it was burning white. 'I appreciate all the work that went in to this last night, but I don't think it's quite legal.' I accelerated. 'You see, the committee hasn't even met yet, and I personally am quite sure that what little I do is not in collision with the interests of the republic. Not if the constitution is abided by, and that's still valid, isn't it. We didn't have a new one, did we?... I decided, you know, quite early in life, that I wouldn't do anything illegal, and what you want me to sign seems very much outside the law. So you see, I can't and I won't.'

I shut my eyes and waited for the earthquake. I thought of the ginger tom who, after an agonizing minute, crept away defeated by the sputtering fluff of a hamster.

Anton gave me a glass of water and I drank it thankfully. The tremor was still in my fingers and knees and my left cheek smarted from the major's swipe – I dodged half of the blow though I would rather not have done so – and I was exhausted, like a very old wisp of a woman. But I was not, by the goddess of all frail earthly women, I was not humiliated. I felt in fact quite cheekily proud.

Anton said that I had been very irresponsible, what with Major Fischer's temper and high blood pressure . . . he could have had a heart attack, and then what? Also, I had not done his, Anton's, career much good, though luckily Major Fischer was not actually his direct superior, unit-wise . . . He, the major, had had a rather unfortunate attitude to the whole idea of the official warning, mused Anton, and one could say that he almost provoked my defiance. I shook my head and Anton sighed sadly, but brightened up soon enough. By golly, what a spirit in someone so . . . Scraggy, said I and we both laughed, albeit not very loudly.

Blast Major Fischer; before I knew it, I was sitting in the cold cellar of the Three Bears, bare but for the last night's stink. A young waitress, vast around the hips, flirted openly with Anton and served his coffee and soggy croissant as if it was their breakfast after . . . We also had a small brandy each, and she served mine with a hearty scowl.

Anton was doing a good impression of a 'Tony', a young sophisticate knowledgeable of the deeper meanings of fashion. A longish skirt, flared beneath the knee, would enhance my figure beautifully, he said, and express my inner freedom far better than a pair of moulted corduroys tucked in formless snow-boots. I was not to spend all my dollars on good booze; he had seen, in the hard-currency shop on the corner of Old Square and Toll Street, a kind of fur-lined wellington that was slim and smart and looked like real leather – perfect for the city's slush and the type of skirt he had in mind.

I called the waitress and paid the bill; she curled her glossy lips with contempt.

'It's no use, my touchy friend,' smiled Anton. 'You and I are a team now; you owe me more than you think. I'll be seeing you soon, whatever you do or don't do. Why, we may . . . we just may make history together, healing what has been deemed an insurmountable division in society. Tell the Citizens Committee it's safe tonight: no raid. And be careful – one or two of the members are much worse for you than I can ever be.'

'Who?' I blurted, and nearly fainted with shame.

'Have fun, will you – if you can,' Anton called after me as I stumbled once again up the slippery stairs. His voice was brimming with merriment.

'I LUF FUNY', said the mirror in the hall, in bright red lipstick I had not seen Norma wear. 'NORMA + FUNY' proclaimed the white tiles over the sink. The mirror in the bathroom was simply covered in hearts and arrows. I had a weep and a bath and a couple of cigarettes from a packet Norma had left behind. I found the bed far too big and cold; I longed for her so badly I had to weep again, and again. Then the endless raindrops outside the misty window drummed some sense into my brain, and I slept.

I both swam under the ice of the Lake and skated over it, numbed with cold and hot with joy. But somewhere just beyond the Lake, just beyond the planet, a roar of a neigh and a sweet whisper of a whinny seemed to promise the healing of insurmountable divisions. Baloney, said Norma all of a sudden – so real, so near, that I woke up and searched the flat as if I was looking for an elf the size of a needle. The pain of her absence felt like a cruel attack of influenza, the type that twists the bones and will run its course no matter what remedies you take.

I drank a big bowl of coffee, French fashion, and felt none the better for it.

Time, however, had run away like a bolted horse. The clock said four post meridiem and the darkness was already deep as night. Outside, a few golden touches of twilight lingered on the pale, high roofs. The elegant pre-war building of Foreign Trade was only a few blocks away – walking distance in the bounds of my small, aged city.

*

37

'What happened to you?' My kind occasional employer peered over her elegant spectacles. 'Lovers' tiff? Some lover!'

'Slipped in the snow – bumped my face on a lamp-post. I bruise easily. Still, it's better than broken bones.'

'You're plucky. That's what I like about you – no moaning. Ah, you brought me *The Enchanted Glass*. How was it?'

'Gooey.'

'Shush, the writer's a new favourite here. I'll give you an extra twenty per cent for technicality, how's that?' She picked up an elegant lady's pen and wrote me an invoice for the cashier. Enough to keep me... us... going for a fortnight.

'Thanks. You're a treasure.'

'Do you want *New Revolutionary West-Bohemian Hop-Harvester?* Both into French and German?'

'Hop as in beer? Straight technology? Yes, please! When do you want it done?'

'Two weeks will do. Or maybe after Christmas; nobody's going to touch anything before then.' She lowered her elegant voice. 'I could do with a good read. You haven't brought me anything for ages.'

'Nothing came my way. But I guess I can get you some soon.'

'Veronika Nowak, you take care of yourself. You're my favourite freelance, so don't you go bumping into things – in general! You know what I mean. See you, duckie.'

'Happy Christmas!' I grinned, and she waved me in mock despair out of her elegant office.

It was nearly after hours. The cashier grumbled but paid me out, in crispy new notes of paper currency worth nothing in the world at large. Little to worry about; the world at large was locked away, as if for ever.

I splashed out on pork roast, Moravian cabbage and potato dumplings in a steamy little buffet on the corner. I also had a tall paper cup of pungent beer and another couple of fags from Norma's packet. I felt positively rich, intelligent, even devious, and loved.

I still had an hour to kill, so I cruised along the one and only boulevard and bought myself a hot potato pancake for dessert. It was deplorably greasy, stuffed with smelly garlic and utterly delicious.

Marek's place was a little hole off an open landing in a slummy tenement. The huge Che Guevara poster on the wall did little to cheer it up. The twelve of us occupied every inch of space, packed in like sardines; but the mood was jubilant. For had not the stupid, nervous regime given away just how much weight it feared we might carry? Rise and hear the official warning! Sign here, please, and kindly go home – no interrogation, no detention! 'I didn't,' I whispered, 'I neither rose nor signed.' It did not seem very important to anyone and I received little attention; only Zoe touched the purple patch on my cheek with a comforting finger and Professor K. warned me softly and briefly about the treachery of personal heroism.

So they all did sign, even if under protest – I was foolishly gratified that young Anton had not lied to me.

Tea was made, to calm the minds and warm the bodies; I nipped downstairs to the communal pay-phone. Yes, said a surprisingly nice girlish voice, theoretically there is a night train to New Village, one-thirty a.m., but practically – and please, don't yell at me – practically it is advisable not to rely on it. But there is a perfectly good express train at four-thirty a.m. from the Main Station that has an excellent chance of reaching its destination between six and seven in the morning, and if it's one of the villages you want, there might – just might – even be a bus at the New Town station. It is a far more sensible train to take at any rate; I mean, you can't really want to arrive at that God-forsaken place in the middle of the night?

The room was hazy upon my return, rich with the fragrant vapours of the tea, tobacco smoke and heavy steam rising from the wet coats, discarded shoes and damp woollen socks.

'What a restless soul you are,' said Karol. 'Do you have to dash in and out all the time? Sit down, and take the minutes.'

II

All of a sudden – or so it seemed – it was three o'clock. Rapidly, the night began to shorten, like a stub of a candle melting away at double speed. Soon, I felt, the wick would drown, quiver for a while in flameless hot fatigue and then cool off, stiffen, die. I nearly panicked; I had one more page to type but my fingers, stiff already, refused to obey. I took the briefest of showers, switching from boiling hot to brutally cold; the slicked wet hair chilled my skull arched between the sleepy ears, and my spirit rose. I managed to hit the keys again with some dexterity.

I had brought the typewriter back from the kitchen table to my ancient scarred desk in the living room, my heart aching en route and the old thing so heavy in my arms that I almost dropped it; I would have much preferred having to work in the cold airless kitchen with only the blue-flickering gas-ring for warmth, but with the huge comfort of Norma's undisturbed, open-mouthed, child-sweet sleep next door . . .

While sitting at the desk, I faced the window. An ordinary town window, practically blind, merely reflecting the windows across the street set in the same tired brickwork, with only a narrow dusty stretch of sky to look up to, rarely a glimpse of the moon or half the sun, and even less frequently a faint hint of a star. It had never bothered me before, but it began to scare me now. It felt like facing a wall, a solid road-block of thick yellow-dark nothing. Should not the eyes – I fretted – whenever levelled to gaze forward, behold some depth, some space, some open path, at least one route of escape from whatever might be creeping up from behind? Shush, little squirrel, I whispered down my chest where I

40

always thought my soul lived; we'll soon be on a train, going south, not so far away as we might wish but then again we'll be there that much sooner, down by that Lake laced with sharp transparent ice along the edges, out where Norma giggles against those vast horizons, her breath curling white in the air... no walls there, no cages, so shush.

I typed out – last task – the twelve full names and addresses under the citizens committee declaration, marvelled briefly at the line that spelled out mine, and sat back numb with relief and satisfaction. The French and English versions, translated no doubt – I couldn't help but chuckle – by one Veronika Nowak, lay fresh and neat by my elbow. The flimsy carbon-copy of the original that each of us took home from the meeting committee floated in a precious aura of its own, though much soiled and crumpled by constant fingering. I gave in to a big luxurious yawn: it froze on my face.

An ice-cold warning gripped me in the small of my neck – too late, for half a second later a strong hand fell on my left shoulder and another hand, real flesh and bones, shot from behind my right shoulder and moved amongst the pages on the desk. A loud shrill scream filled my brain but nothing came out of my gaping mouth.

'I'll take a copy, if you don't mind,' said Anton's young cheerful voice. 'The mother-tongue one, as I am not much of a linguist myself and as I have certainly not come here to prevent world-wide publicity for your efforts. Heaven forbid! I merely wish to become the best-informed member of the force. It's to your credit too, you know.'

I could not even glance at him. I was shaking with furious, desperate tears which – like the scream – flooded the inside of my head, leaving my eyes dry.

'Oh, come on,' laughed Anton patting my shoulder. 'Don't carry on like that! What's a couple of house-keys between friends? Did you not drown my hat? I've only reimbursed myself in kind! Okay, so I should have coughed or something before I touched you, but it was just too tempting, like playing Red Indians again. You know, at one moment I thought you spotted me; I nearly choked, holding my breath. You have to admit I am better at the game!'

41

'I wasn't playing,' a child said sulkily, using my mouth. 'I hate you!'

'That's only because I scared you. You don't hate me really, you know. Why should you? Turn around and you'll love me – I brought you a present. A rare treat, as a matter of fact: genuine Cuban rum, white as the air above a hibiscus bloom and strong as the god of passion. That's what it says on the label, anyway. Good stuff. You can't say I am not generous.'

'I'll get a chain fixed to the door. You'll never be able to do this again, *ever*.' I even pursed my lips like a child. I did not want to grow up. Into what? A person who has had all her skin flayed?

'Listen,' said Anton severely. 'I'll have to smack you if you don't snap out of this. Be your age! You did not think life would be a bed of roses when you got yourself mixed up in this new folly, did you? Jesus, woman, you ought to be grateful! I could have come with a bunch of the boys and made a real song and dance about this nightly activity of yours, but no, I prefer to cultivate an intelligent working relationship! Now either you summon your wits and show some grace or . . . Don't faint on me, for God's sake!'

I could not help it: I slumped and slid off the chair and sat on the floor in one pitiful heap.

White as the air above some distant bloom it may have been, but the strength of that drink came straight out of hell's furnace. Soon I was up in the chair again with my back to the treacherous window, cross-legged, poised, contemptuous. In my affected, ill-disposed mind, I watched with malicious glee the New Town train come to platform one, linger amidst clouds of steam, swallow a few shivering passengers with dead eyes and smelly breath on blue lips, jerk and shudder off – drunkity drunk, drunkity drunk – where I no longer wished to go. With the same evil mind's eye I watched Marek pacing up and down the stokehole, cheeks already blackened by the few hours of his midnight shift, wondering with fury and fear in his heart why I had not delivered the translations into his hands at the time agreed, at four bloody o'clock, and would I ever... I actually grinned at his anxiety – maybe I will, Marek dear, and maybe I won't.

'Yah,' young Anton said feelingly, lifting a flushed face from a page, 'do you people have to ram it down everybody's throat how noble and principled you are, any time you put a word on paper? Listen to this, just you hear what it sounds like! "Everywhere in the world truth, honesty, moral integrity and human dignity have to be safeguarded and carried out by individual human beings who refuse to relegate their conscience and responsibility to state institutions." Yeh? And who runs the state institutions? Animals? Do I look like an animal to you, or would you say I make a pretty good imitation of a human being? Or here: "It is not our claim to oppose the government: on the contrary, the citizens committee which has been established today and which represents an informal group of a thousand citizens who had already, some years ago, declared their willingness to engage in matters of public interest at whatever personal cost, desires to promote citizens' initiatives that would run parallel to the officially organized activities and strengthen rather than weaken the civic structures of our society." Actually, this sounds rather good, it isn't what I mean. Ah, there it is: "The only livable future lies in the revival, or birth, of a community spirit and mutual solidarity, mutual respect for our human and civil rights and obligations, that is in values capable of counteracting the deadly, consumerist, corrupt, anonymous way of living." What do you mean by "deadly"? And I gave you a name, did I not? I asked you to call me Tony! That's far from anonymous, is it not?'

I stood up, quite sober and rather tall. 'It does not say deadly, consumerist, etcetera. It says deadly consumerist, meaning mindlessly materialistic. Greedy.' I spoke in Professor K.'s slightly pedantic tone of voice. 'And it does not relate to you all that closely. It's addressed to "fellow citizens".'

Anton merely sniggered, springing lightly to his feet from the depth of my one and only armchair. 'I know. I take everything much too much to my tender heart. Time for me

43

to push off – now that you are your old self again. Had me worried, you did. Get some sleep, your looks need restoring.'

The declaration, carefully folded, disappeared inside his jacket; the bottle, still two-thirds full, in a deep pocket of his large coat. Too large and loud: Antonio, *Il Mafioso*.

He patted the bulging pocket. 'To save you the haughty gesture, and myself the embarrassment.'

I stretched out a hand. 'The keys.'

Anton shook his handsome petite head. 'They're safer with me than with you. Mind you, I have a hunch that next time you'll come to me. Ask for two zero two, any time of day or night; I'll never be far away.'

And thus he departed, leaving nothing behind, not even a scent. He was better at the game.

I must have been asleep on my feet, or simply unconscious. The air was but a shade paler when I came to, but down below the traffic screeched and thundered, passing lights splashed slowly across my window which now looked bashful – shamed perhaps, yet as innocent as ever. The windows opposite shone bright and yellow, square electric suns and oblong moons, even – if I narrowed my eyes into slits sliced thinly by the trembling eyelashes – flickering stars.

I set out to complete the night's task – dazed, troubled, but not entirely unhappy.

I knuckled a signal – rap-rap-rap – rap – raprap – on a small back door of an ex-posh hotel where Marek stoked an old-fashioned central heating furnace; waited sixty seconds and repeated the signal in reverse, tapping lightly with the tips of my fingernails.

In precisely thirty seconds, Marek opened the door, scanned the back yard quickly for suspect shadows and took me in, leading the way down a few iron steps and past heaps of damp glistening coal into the hot, clean-swept, ash-smelling stoke-room. He took the typed sheets from me, asked me to stand back facing the door, and hid them swiftly and almost noiselessly somewhere along the solid-looking soot-covered walls. Marek did not believe in sharing vital secrets and it certainly worked – the police had searched the place several times in the past, always in vain. Dear Marek, if only he could put a smile on his face! Women never stayed long with him; who would like to be called 'cohabitant', never hear the word 'love', never see a flower or some other foolish proof of affection, and be ordered about to serve the cause selflessly into the bargain? Not to mention suffering the constant scrutiny of his sadly suspicious eyes...

I expected a storm, but he was not at all furious with me. He said he figured that it would take me longer to do the translations than just a couple of hours, and he wasn't really expecting me at the appointed time. Besides, although he had been rather annoyed with me for that silly cousin business in the Old Tavern, he was a good judge of character and knew that I wasn't one to fail her comrades, so he saw no cause to be unduly worried. Moreover, he said with a proud twinkle in his eye, the domestic chain-distribution was going strong, there had been ten typists at work since midnight and a further fifty since five in the morning, eight messengers on bicycles and four with cars, so all in all – as it was nearly seven o'clock by now – we ought to have reached a good thousand people. And there were copies lying around in bus stations – people had been seen picking them up! Karol phoned the text to a couple of Bohemian broadcasters abroad – from two different public booths – so it should be pouring back into the country soon. It was only fair and correct that the foreign press agencies should not be supplied until after the first domestic round had been completed: Vlado would see to it at eight-thirty sharp. All has gone so well this time, sighed Marek with near-happiness, nobody squealed, the police have no idea that the declaration exists, we've really gone one up on them! He sent me home to get some sleep; we could well expect some rough times by tomorrow, if not by tonight.

I actually kissed him on the cheek, like a true Judas Iscariot. He winced with surprise and walked me up to the door in shy silence.

There was a frosty bite in the breeze, but my lips burned

45

with the piercing taste of sweat, soot and nightmare.

I jogged for a while, alongside the old Jewish cemetery at first, then through the narrow side-streets winding towards the boulevard; I waved arms and shook shoulders as if they were a shaggy dog's pelt full of dead fleas. A nightmare: what else could it have been? We were all romping free, were we not? We'd made our bid to form a warm tea-cup revolution, had we not? By tomorrow, thousands of people might be stirring their spoonful of sugar in it, frowning, wondering ...

I simply must have a thing about young Anton, I thought; he's got under my skin with his clever moustache and boyish pride, misguided ambitions and unrequited sympathies, the little prick. I'd been so tired last night when I fell asleep; my subconscious, fearing the wrath of Marek and the guilt of missing the train to Norma, came up with a vivid dream, a hallucination of Anton's visit, to provide an excuse for all those failures. A cruel way of doing it, yet rather intelligent for such a confused subconscious as mine!

Steel-grey December dawn hung low and cold just inches above the blanched skeletons of trees on the sparsely-lit boulevard. A grim, dense crowd of hurrying clerks and shop-assistants sucked me in. I did not resist. I let myself be elbowed and pushed to and fro, up and down the gritty winter pavements strewn with sand and salt and littered with thousands of tramway tickets – white fresh paper-butterflies one second, torn dirt the next. There was a quiet luxury in the momentary belonging, in pretending that I too would soon disappear – with one of those ant-like strings that gathered themselves together out of the seeming chaos – in a glass-panelled door of an office or a store. Close up, the faces were not grim at all: the men looked clean-shaven and blasé; the women wore elaborate make-up and a certain eagerness not so much in the eyes as around the mouth; perhaps it was the gossip they were after, or flirtation, or some other escape from the tyranny of the apron hanging in the kitchen. At the end of the day, having dodged as much work as possible, having cheated their unfair employer, the state, with a million little tricks, having lied through their teeth to superior comrades and still been trampled upon, having queued on the way home for superior – and sometimes downright ordinary – goods and foods, having quarrelled over the chores and having told the children – for the millionth time – never to repeat in school what they had heard at home, would these men and women switch on a Bohemian broadcast coming from across the sealed borders?

They might, I thought, after the telly.

They probably will, I thought, for a half-hour or so, and they will think us pathetic. Be honest, fellow citizens, you can do it, that's where the salvation lies. Speak a small truth every day – it doesn't hurt that much – if you want the big truth, the instrument of liberation, to prevail before you expire. Gather together in little groups and clubs to learn solidarity, we'll teach you how, and never mind the droves of chaps in police uniforms and the mean, lean leather jackets of the secret force. Always ask a name from whoever hits you over the head in a dark cell; and number. Example: Anton alias Tony, two zero two. Never far away. It's a big help. Oh, crumbs!

Oh, Norma! The longing was so abrupt, so powerful that it jolted me right out of the crowd. I tore a coat-pocket on somebody's zip before hitting a tree and slouching down on the encasement next to a pool of last night's vomit, tidily frozen.

I covered my face and snivelled heartily. I had found myself again, and my soul's desire! Never mind the missed train (and the mean, lean ghost of Anton); the coach station was only a dog's walk away and from there it would be hardly a crow's flight to New Village. I let out the last sob with little inhibition – and felt a stranger's hand slipping into my half-torn pocket.

It was a plump middle-aged woman in a white rabbit fur coat. 'There there,' she muttered, 'take this and buy yourself something nice and hot to eat; it's only a small note, but I am no Rothschild myself; still, it'll buy you a fried sausage or two and believe you me, when the tummy's full, life's not half so bad.'

And she vanished into the frantic crowd. I ought to have felt a complete fool and a fraud – but in fact I felt honoured.

And ravenously hungry.

Making for the nearest sausage-stand, I reflected briefly upon the way in which my body and soul were joined together and found it curiously wanting. I seemed to feed either the one or the other as if they didn't want to sit at the same table.

Then I purchased a large grilled sausage, served on a paper plate heaped with mustard, and ceased to reflect. Happiness, the one of simple breed, was beating her soft little wings somewhere very near; I was in a hurry, though of the well-tempered, measured, savoury kind. My body yielded to the hot spiced juicy delicacy; it seemed to swell into some luxuriant curves. Possibly this was even noticeable, because just then somebody pinched my bottom... in passing, without further commitment.

'You have to watch your back all the time, love,' said the woman at the grill who saw it happen. 'Never leave it undefended, or they'll all but bugger you in broad daylight. Not to mention thieves and stranglers who also come up from behind, murderous sneaks!'

'I know,' I mumbled with my mouth full. 'I have nightmares about them.'

The woman nodded. 'That's indigestion. Have a pickled gherkin; helps to balance the stomach. On the house.'

I took it without fuss – clearly I was on the receiving end of generosity this morning, including Marek's and the pincher's. To crown the feeling, the boulevard lit up with Christmas lights, half their bulbs already missing but still rather magnificent. The shop-windows came alive with plushy pink and green illuminations, the neons flitted nervously over the expanse of paving stone and concrete. An empty expanse now, waiting for the shoppers to arrive.

'Christmas!' snorted the woman. 'I say it's about time the pope and the comrades had it abolished. Prohibited. I watch them run from store to store for four weeks every year, freaked out, debilitated, with murder in their hearts if they fail to snatch up the best, snarling at each other like bloodhounds and bitches. I tell you, if the poor Baby appeared in their midst, they'd trample Him to bits – crib, donkey, and all. Do you pray, love?'

48

'No, but I am not a Christmas shopper either.'

She sighed heavily and rolled a cigarette. 'This is such a shaky time we live in, isn't it just? Downright rickety. Don't go yet. Have a coffee.'

'All right.'

'You look like a Christian.'

'I befriended a woman recently, and she thought I was a nun. Her name is Norma.'

'That's a pretty name.'

'But I am not. I mean, I am not a nun.'

'You have a spirit though, don't you? I know one when I see one.'

'Depends what you mean.'

'Well for example, if someone gave you something... spiritual to read, something that isn't exactly kosher in terms of... you know, but something that's really uplifting, that let's you know that there is a spiritual community in this forsaken country, you wouldn't run straight to the police with it, would you? And if they by some awkward chance caught you with it, you would not tell them who gave it to you, eh?'

'I certainly would not, on both counts.'

'You'd simply say you found it in a public lavatory, wouldn't you?'

'That's a good one to remember.'

She disappeared under the counter. I could hear the sound of her big body folding in two and the soft rustle of her many-layered clothing. When she reappeared, she looked up and down the deserted boulevard and then handed me a carefully folded paper napkin on a paper saucer with the coffee.

'On the house.'

'Thanks.' I pocketed the napkin, drank the lukewarm greasy coffee in one go, gave her a smile and left.

I turned right at the lower end of the boulevard, passed a police car in which two policemen were frisking a boy squeezed between them on the back seats, quickening my pace involuntarily until I reached the public lavatory behind the old Merchant Bank. I ran downstairs, locked myself in a cubicle and unwrapped the napkin.

49

What stared at me from the two thin rather clumsily typed sheets was the citizens' committee declaration, complete with the twelve names and addresses, including mine.

I passed the note the white-rabbit woman gave me on to the lavatory attendant, a dark-skinned elderly gypsy with one large gold tooth among a perfect white set. She embellished her thanks with the promise of a young Adonis with a black moustache and lots of money who was already under my spell and would embrace me firmly in the near future. I know all about him, I said, and would much rather do without; anything else?

She took my palm only to throw it back at me in a well-acted shock. 'Oy oy oy oy,' she wailed, 'great things! Too great to be talked about! But you'd better hurry,' she added soberly. 'They won't wait.'

I caught the sole morning bus to New Village a second before departure – and thought it to be a good omen.

But there was no number seventeen! A thicket of tangled dog-roses, blackthorns, bramble and ivy filled the gap between numbers sixteen and eighteen, the sloes for black beady eyes and the hips for drops of frozen blood. I stood there like an idiot, staring incredulously, clutching a pair of fur-lined boots size six and a pound of fresh coffee to my deflated, aching chest. Norma, you goddamned crook!

Nobody was in at number sixteen. Number eighteen was pig-pink and had shiny ceramic Snow White and the Seven Dwarfs standing about the front garden. The fat woman who opened a window spoke through her nose. Disgraceful, that's what it was, she said. For years and years she and her hubby offered to rent the plot, to purchase it if necessary, clear out the bushes and shrubs and whatever ruins they grew on and build themselves a garage. They would use the roof as a kind of verandah with those white Italian marble pots and statuettes along the front – but no, the council would not give permission. She often wondered why; it wasn't that there was an owner somewhere, for nobody ever came apart from that mad woman who hung about for a day or two each

50

summer, talking to herself and sleeping in the cemetery. Disgraceful, unless of course she was a relation of somebody powerful in the council or even higher! But it might well all change this year, what with the hubby taking over the chairmanship of New Village Soviet-Bohemian hunting club and all . . .

Norma, my moonface, apple of my eye, where are you? Come on out, you twerp! Sweetie, hey, it's only me, Funny, remember? Please, Norma? A flock of jackdaws shrieked angrily, but nothing else moved in the snowbound cemetery. The snow had melted down to a thin glossy sheet that carried no traces of human feet. Mourning angels streaked with the white droppings of the copious birds gazed steadily towards the heavy sky. Minute snowflakes began to dance in the wind. Tears of despair froze on my cheeks.

On the way out, by the sheer luck of a glance, I found the gravestone of Uncle Herman. That's what it said, in bold black letters on grey granite:

UNCLE HERMAN
Who Fell Asleep on July 13, 1970 A.D.

I left the gift-wrapped packet of coffee at the foot of the stone. Wake up, Uncle Herman, for mercy's sake!

I walked four miles along the Lake's shore to the dam, hoping to hitch a ride back to the city there. The wind was bitterly cold and thick with sharp grainy snow, swishing across the vast, man-made trough with increasing speed. At almost regular intervals, the ice cracked with loud echoing sounds. Dead branches, broken boats and blurred skeletons of water-sport contraptions littered the beaches and terrorized my feet: it took me two hours to reach the dam. I climbed up on to the road – blind, chilled to the bone, utterly exhausted. The inn was closed, as was the petrol station. A large metallic sign rattled incessantly on a swaying post. 'WELCOME TO THE COAST OF BOHEMIA', it said, 'THE PEOPLE'S RECREATION ZONE'. The force of the wind pushed me into the middle of the road; a small truck coming down the hill had to stop, skidding dangerously. I was lucky – the driver was an old man, gentle as a lamb.

Part of the canvas covering had torn off the side of the truck and was flapping in the wind. I helped the old man to fix it, thus getting an eyeful of the load; freshly slain geese, their snow-white feathers smeared with scarlet blood.

'Can't pluck 'em,' murmured the driver. 'Can't blinking do anything with 'em, they can't, except kill 'em. The whole flipping farm's got no juice. Happens every bleeding winter. Hop in, duckie. It's all the way to the boulevard, Hotel Moscow International, God help us. Roast 'em they want, pluck 'em they will!'

I fell asleep before we crossed the dam.

Norma put on her new boots and ran lightly down the stairs, beckoning me to follow. Deeper and deeper we went, descending to the bottom of the Lake through a kind of vertical graveyard, a flooded catacomb cheerfully illuminated by thousands of little red bulbs. The water was perfectly breathable and it slowed our progress but little. Finally we reached the bottom strewn with fine white sand: in a shimmering distance lay the Old Village, complete with shingle roofs and flocks of white geese. The church stood proudly erect but when we came nearer, we could see that the bells had gone and the belfry was filled with a much darker, soundless water. As we entered the village, the shingle turned to mud and the geese were but lifeless heaps of plucked feathers tangled with dead soggy reeds.

Uncle Herman wants to see you, whispered Norma, dragging me through a gaping doorway into a roofless room. He loves you very much, so you mustn't mind if he is rude.

All I could see in the murky water was Uncle Herman's gravestone. Then a mouth opened under the inscription and I screamed.

Hush, said a deep guttural voice, and kindly use your brains for a change. First: have you ever noticed Norma wearing not just a bright red lipstick, but any lipstick at all? Second; have you ever seen a cosmetic case or a spongebag or even a proper handbag in her possession? She could have carried a lipstick in her pocket but it isn't very likely, is it, as she never used it? Third: how many sets of spare keys did you have? One, just one, duckie, and you gave that to Norma, did you not? Now, what does it all suggest? She did not leave when you told her to, did she! All those lovely messages in red lipstick were a fake, a very clever fake well designed for your hungry heart! She was led away, captured, look how pale she is; now who could have, who would have...

Anton! I cried. The cold-blooded scheming bastard Anton! It wasn't a nightmare, was it! Oh please, let me go; I have to go now, I have to shake it out of him...

My feet were caught in a heavy fishing net, water was pouring down my throat into my lungs, I tried to scream it out but a hand held my mouth, leather-dry and strong...

'Wake up, duckie! You'll have me arrested for blooming rape, if you carry on screaming and thrashing about like that! You're a strange bird, you sure are. Now hop it, before they requisition you to do the plucking!'

The truck was already parked at the back entrance to the Hotel Moscow International in a short alley parallel to the boulevard. Queasy-faced kitchen boys were unloading the geese, white corpse after white corpse, necks drooping, feathers shimmering in the dark. While I was asleep, another early night had fallen. It was as if sunshine had gone out of my life for ever.

'Who's Anton?' the old driver called after me. 'Listen, duckie, if he makes you flaming scream like that, you'd better get rid of him!'

The dream came back to me, vision by vision, word by word. I started to run.

'Two zero two, please. It's urgent.'

The uniformed guards inside the ground-floor lobby gaped at me with bemused curiosity. Who is it that comes here breathless and eager, all on her own - undragged, unpushed, even unsummoned?

'Your citizen's passport, please, young lady.'

53

'Why? I only want to . . . oh, all right. But please tell him it really can't wait. Two zero two.'

'What's it about?'

'It's private.'

That made them laugh. 'Nothing's private in here, citizen!' But one of them swaggered slowly into an office, my citizen's passport in hand. I bit the inside of my lower lip and tried to look indifferent while my heart began to beat fast with that well-known mixture of indignation, fear and fury. The guard came back with scorn on his face.

'I knew I'd seen you before! She's a dissy, boys, brave soldier dissidentchik with a fanny. Fix her with a seat, will you? She's to wait. Make it nice and proper.'

I was taken into a stuffy waiting room, seated on a stool by a radiator, handcuffed to a hot pipe and left alone. To keep my wrist from burning, I had to pull all the time and hold my arm at an awkward angle, resting the elbow on one or other knee, trying not to fall off the slippery stool. So as not to succumb to useless hatred, I played the face game: painted, with my mind's pencil and brush, every little detail of Norma's features on the bit of blank wall most clearly in view. It was a game requiring maximum concentration, not just to draw the lines but to keep them there, make them grow and assemble, correct mistakes and add a few loving, slightly glorifying touches. I sweated like a coal-miner but, at last, there she was – baring her perfect teeth in one of her whinnies, nose wrinkled a little, eyes slanted and nearly blind with some inward mirth, cheekbones high and forehead flat, broad, windswept and silly . . .

A guard came in and I lost her. He unlocked the handcuffs and handed me the passport. 'Now scram,' he said.

'Beg your pardon?'

'Scram.'

'Have you talked to two zero two? His name is Anton and he . . .'

'He said scram. Beat it. So buzz off.'

'Let me talk to him on the phone.'

'You deaf or something? The comrade is not interested. Now will you get lost or shall I boot you out?'

I dragged my feet through the lobby as if each of them weighed a ton. They all watched me, but nobody laughed. I tramped across the road to the Three Bears and sat down next to two old hookers and a drunken pimp. Why not? I pulled Norma's new boots out of the bag, put them on the table and held them by the heels.

'How much?' asked the pimp, and belched.

One of the hookers touched my cheek. 'What's up, honey? What are you crying about?'

I let go.

Next time I knew anything about anything, I was sitting in a warm passage between the bar and the kitchen, eating french fries and chicken with bare hands and washing it down with swigs of hot black coffee. Nothing else mattered.

But I was aware of Joseph's kind reassuring presence.

'Better?'

I nodded gratefully. My body is restored, Joseph, but now my soul is hungry, I pleaded in silence.

'She is not in the cells.' A faint blush passed across his yellow face. 'Such is the nature of my custom here that I was able to check. Double-check as it were. The gaolers and the jailed both converge in my parlour at the end of each shift. The only other place where our Norma can be, if we eliminate accidents and improbabilities, is the city nuthouse. Which is not as bad as it sounds. It's been her home, on and off, for years. The only home she's got.'

'She lives with me.'

He shook his head gravely. 'Fancy that!'

'Joseph, I love her.'

'Weird thing – love. Don't expect too much in return. She . . . forgets. It's not her fault. She is faithful in her own absolute way. She just . . . goes blank sometimes. She doesn't really need you, you know. She is complete. That's why she warms one's heart so much, I guess. One gets lonesome without her. One's world loses all innocence, does it not?' He gave me a quick, shy smile. 'If you do retrieve her, which you well might sooner or later, don't keep her away from me, will you? Come too.'

'Joseph... how do I deserve this kindness?'

'I know now who you are.'

'I still disgraced myself the other night.'

'Those who walk the tightrope can't help swaying. Sometimes they fall. Strange: if they live, they always climb back. I must leave you now, custom is custom. Wash your face before you go; it tells too many tales. Oh – she'd be on ward seventeen, if nothing's changed.'

Seventeen! I shuddered; what if there is no such ward? Shush, I whispered down my chest. The clock in the kitchen said eight p.m. Washing my face in the loo, I tried to do the accounts: during the last two days and nights, I'd slept some seven hours at the most and lived at least a thousand. Altogether I had spent exactly forty-eight hours with Norma; time appeared to me as the silliest measure of them all. A fraud.

'Frankly, I won't even try,' said Marta. 'But I know who can help: Dagmar's ex. Didn't you know he was a psychiatrist? A consultant, actually. Right there where you need him.'

'I didn't know Dagmar had an ex. But will she ... I mean, would he?'

Marta gave one of her waspish laughs. 'Don't worry. She still sleeps with him. He'll help you if she'll want him to. I disapprove, you know. As a Catholic, I ought to admire you – to care for the sick and feeble in one's own home is a Christian thing to do – but as a doctor I have serious objections. Not only because she is probably better off in an institution, but because it would be a considerable strain on you, and you don't strike me as particularly strong. There is no future in it, surely you are aware of that? She may get worse, never better. Why don't you get a baby instead? Or can't you conceive? It could be a simple blockage, you know. I'd be glad to help you there ...'

'Marta, hold it! I am not married, or haven't you noticed?'

This time, the laugh was warm. 'For a Catholic, that would be an obstacle. But you are not Catholic. As for me – frankly, I would like you better with a child than without. There is something about an unsown woman that disturbs me. I don't like fallow fields either. Now if you were a nun...'

'But I am, Marta. That's what I have recently discovered: I am a nun. Gosh, it's getting late. I do hope Dagmar's at home.'

'Of course she is, she's holding court. Karol's there, flirting away no doubt. No need for you to wince, I enjoy being jealous. Don't tell Dagmar I sent you, you're perfectly entitled to know who her ex is; I mean, everybody does. You're a rum kid, you know. Odd. Still, now that you are one of the twelve apostles, I should show some respect. God knows how long you people will be walking free.'

She shivered, then stood looking at the nursery door. The breathing of the six children was clearly audible and Marta smiled. 'They all snore, even the baby. It's either heredity or pollution, possibly both. There, I gave away my secret – no woman would want to keep my Karol for good, he snores like a circular saw.'

We kissed for goodbyes: something we've never done before.

From Karol's on Peace Square to Dagmar's in Victory Grove, it usually took about fifteen minutes, but I was a woman driven and made it in ten. Father Ignat – a very young priest without state licence and a fellow apostle – opened the door and helped me jump over and between the piles of coats and winter boots in the hall. There were a good twenty people in the beautiful drawing room, all scholars by definition if not by occupation. Nearly all male. My entrance registered on their faces as vast relief and mild surprise. Professor K. gave me a warm welcoming smile, so Dagmar had to wipe away her original frown. She threw me a cushion and I quickly settled down in a little recess by the door.

'May we then assume,' sighed Dr Florian, yet another apostle, 'that my contention was correct? That by no means are we to strive for comprehensive education, but rather for select if fundamental knowledge? Or better still, techniques of learning, or provoking philosophical thirst? Peripatetic university is a fetching title, I allow you that – if you are happy with my conception of the whole business as plain old Socratic midwifery. Most of our prospective students will be pretty ignorant, you know, by no fault of their own. Innocent of all academia. Virginal.'

'It's a challenge,' smiled Arnold. 'I like virginity.'

'Language!' protested Dagmar with mock severity. Her eyes sparkled enticingly and I wished I could like her more.

Professor K. chuckled. 'Dear friends, the hour is late enough for the talk to be light. But before we allow it to fizz, let me congratulate Dr Florian. Plain old Socratic midwifery is exactly what we should strive for. There is no higher achievement in a scholar's life than to assist a successful birth of yearning for truth. Volumes of theoretical work, however splendid, are but a poor substitute for such a gain. And now, dear Dagmar, permit an old man a truly sexist gesture, in gratitude for a perfect evening.'

He bowed over her hand and kissed it lightly, amidst discreet cheers and applause. Father Ignat collected all written notes from people – he seemed to be acting as Dagmar's secretary. I was grateful to Karol – who looked preoccupied, even nervous – for urging everybody to leave now, in twos and threes as usual. In not more than fifteen minutes, I had Dagmar all to myself.

It would have been much easier if I could have told her the whole truth, but I didn't dare. I felt that I had to hack my way out of Anton's web on my own first, before ever confiding in anybody. I stammered a lot and it vexed me, but she was marvellously quick to understand what I wanted. With her bold intelligent scrawl she wrote a note to her ex-husband Dr Burda, urging him to do all he could to get Norma D. released into her cousin's care. Handing me the envelope, she caressed my fingers lightly.

'She is not really your cousin, is she? Are you a lesbian? Don't worry, I won't spread the news. And it's not such news either. I figured you for one some time ago, when you so easily let Vlado slip out of your bed. The best and most chivalrous lover in town! He might have married you, you know; he was very fond of you. And his divorce was just about coming through, remember? I envied you then, but I guess I envy you more now; I wish I could love a woman. I suppose that at best I am a very latent bisexual. She is very pretty, that little Norma of yours. But won't you miss the intellectual stimulus? I get so rapidly bored with handsome idiots! Forgive me, darling, I didn't mean to sound so facetious. I am jealous. After all, you've got yourself on the citizens' committee and I have not. I should have torn Marek to shreds, but my wits failed me.'

Her face darkened and she looked unhappy. I was overcome by compassion. Although only a minute ago I had hated her, now I wanted to smooth her brow – only she made it impossible for me to touch her, she would have taken it for an amorous advance. Christ!

'I would never have been able to take it the way you did!' I said truthfully. 'I would have gone up in smoke! You never fumed, and in the end all that suspicion turned into stardust. You survived beautifully.'

Dagmar slowly shook her head and clenched a fist. 'That's where you were mistaken. I have not. I will yet have to have my vengeance. Off with you now! This is getting too near the knuckle, for both of us. We might regret it tomorrow. Good luck with Norma. I am sure Burda will do all he can, perhaps more.'

She walked me to the door and as she closed it behind me, I heard the chain rattle and click into place.

Back home in my modest Barley Street tenement, I dragged the armchair into the hall and edged it between the entrance door and the airing cupboard opposite. It filled the space completely, thus rendering it impossible for anyone to push the door open. So simple – why have I not thought of it before?

Because I never felt the need for it. Because I believed that people – even police – always rang the doorbell; because I always opened the door for anyone who did. Because I believe that I had nothing that could be stolen or that I should hide, including my own body and soul. I stood looking at the makeshift fortification and mourned the loss of that faith.

Soaking a rag in a sharp-smelling detergent, I wiped the kitchen tiles and both mirrors clean; all that red lipstick gone, my head felt clearer too. I had been dashing and thrashing about in panic, allowing Anton to appear as a Mephistopheles. Wouldn't he have just loved that! He really wasn't after my soul. He knew well enough that even if he had me ready to sell, he wouldn't have at his disposal the price that souls were bought with. Certainly he didn't, when I arrived at his dirty doorstep. He had hidden like a schoolboy. But he was after my spirit and I let him get away with quite a success. If Joseph hadn't been kind... and Marta, and Dagmar... I would have ended up as a shivering wreck.

And how unfair I had been to Norma! Anton needn't have bothered to have her removed from the apartment; I'd sent her away myself! Go and hide, sweet child, wait for mummy; when she can escape the baddies, she'll come and play with you! Norma probably knew more about the big bad underworld than I ever did; she wasn't looking for protection. She loved me. Of course she didn't go when I told her to; she knew better than I that wasn't what love is about. She had nowhere to go; she tried to tell me, but I wouldn't listen. I had been so stupid and conceited – I ought to have sought to have her properly discharged from the asylum the moment I realized that she was on the run! Instead, I took all she had to offer and did precious little in return...

I looked into the clean mirror and thought – what if she won't want to know you, Funny? What then?

Quickly summoning Veronika Nowak, I did a page of *The Revolutionary West Bohemian Hop-Harvester*, German version. Nothing like a bit of German to cool one's emotions... By half-past midnight, I was in bed hugging my old little radio under my chin. It coughed and wheezed – either the European weather conditions were unfavourable or the rotten batteries were getting flat again... Sleepily, I fiddled with the tuning button until I found an unexpected clear wave where a rich male American voice with a confident velvety timbre told me that it remained to be seen whether this latest in the series of moral appeals issued by the dissidents of Bohemia would – or indeed could – have any political effect. Without in any way diminishing the personal courage and bravery of the twelve women and men on the citizens' committee – and the introduction of such an organizational element was indeed a novelty – it was the speaker's opinion that communist regimes could not be reformed on moral grounds, indeed on any grounds, if we considered...

Oh, shut up! I switched him off. That's the easiest thing in the world, thumbing down other people's hopes. And I wonder, I yawned, how much moral integrity, truth, honesty, community spirit etcetera there is where you speak from...

Pray God, I whispered, be good to Norma.

'Why?' Dr Burda looked me intently in the eyes. 'Please explain at length, why do you do it?'

I took my time. I had to sit in yet another stuffy, empty waiting room for two hours before Dr Burda was available. And I did not like him very much. Sleek and sly.

'I can't give you any complicated or interesting explanation, doctor. I simply love her. We seem to make a unit. A family. Not man and wife, if that's what you have in mind. Sisters. Cousins.'

'My dear, that's not what I am asking at all. I want to know what makes a dissident tick – what makes one become one. How does it happen, how can it be justified and sustained, considering the grave existential consequences? Does it feed the ego and in what way? That sort of thing. It fascinates me professionally. Do oblige. It may even help you to clarify things for yourself.'

He smiled encouragingly. I did not wish to antagonize him, but I felt too queasy for words. Dagmar's ex!

'I know just what you are thinking, my dear. As Dagmar's former husband and, let's say, present friend, I should have enough information on the subject for an extensive book, if such ever be written. But you see, she is in no way typical – or so I surmise. With her, it is a matter of a certain... aristocracy. She enjoys standing above the crowd. Her mother was dreadfully common, you see. Fortunately for Dagmar, she divorced the father, married an equally common and loud Australian and settled among the antipodeans. The father lavished praise and affection on his haughty little daughter and died early and nobly, having shot himself – presumably by accident – with a hunting rifle. I am the father now, you see. Dagmar knows she'll always get the alimony whatever she does. Now, doesn't this get you going? You are not really horrified, you know. You'd like to be, but you're too intelligent for that. Now tell me about yourself. Parents living?'

His hand groped in the bottom drawer of the desk and came out with a half-bottle of Scotch. He poured two stiff drinks into a couple of rather scummy tea-cups, still holding me under his gaze. There was something hypnotic about the man; I took a swig obediently, and the nausea subsided. In answer to his question, I merely shook my head.

'Ah. Now let me make a wild guess. You never knew your parents. You've been raised in a children's home – orphanage, to call it by its proper name. Am I right?'

I nodded. Somebody had told him, but who? It's been ages since I recited my life's story to anyone! Dr Burda chuckled merrily.

'It showed, you know – when I was slaughtering Dagmar's parents. Besides, you have a nun's face. It's usually either that or the devil-may-care look with orphanage girls. Still, I am rather pleased with myself. But suppose you take it from here? Was it hell?'

'It was all right.'

'Come on, did you ever run away?'

'No. I didn't need to. I had a place to go to legally. A village. Quite a few aunts and uncles, and lots of cousins. My father was unknown, my mother died in childbirth and her family hardly ever spoke of her, but they took me in each summer. I was neat, docile and hardworking.'

'And?'

'There is nothing spectacular. I was never raped, battered or otherwise mishandled.' I was getting angry and words suddenly rushed into my mouth. 'I tried a little prostitution at around fifteen – we all did – but wasn't very successful. Too scraggy. Went to work in a dye-factory instead. Did evening classes and got myself to university. Modern languages. Never married . . . nobody offered. No abortions – no pregnancies. Did some teaching – we all did – but hated it. Couldn't grasp the principle of exerting authority. I don't know why you should want to listen to this.'

'I wasn't very good at teaching either, mainly because I disliked the students profoundly. So what did you do then?'

'Got lucky, or so I thought. Sat next to a man in the theatre – that's what I did with my nights, I was a theatre-buff – and whispered some translations into his ear. *Die Bühne* was visiting, and the poor sod had no idea it would be in German. He landed me a job in the International Trade Union and that's how I got to know how the other half lived. The playboy comrades. Went on a study-delegation with them to West Germany – they loved it, but I found that I didn't like capitalism either. That's one thing a children's home does teach you; you become a primitive communist, share and share alike, no privileges. Began to believe that the answer – and change, if any – must come from within the people, not the system. Came back, clashed dreadfully with the comrades, and returned to the dye-factory. Idyllic – until I opened my mouth at a few meetings and got sacked. God, I didn't know where to turn.'

'One can adapt, you know. Private decency and public ambitions don't have to clash. But I suppose you never developed the private sector around yourself, so to speak. One probably does need the nuclear family for that. Interesting. Drink up, there is no harm in whisky. Or do you find alcohol disgusting?'

'Lord, no. Do I look that prim? I would drink like a fish, only I can't take much. I blab. I like good drinkers though, they are . . . generous.' I found myself thinking of Vlado and of what Dagmar had said. I could believe he'd been fond of me, in his big sweeping way, but that he'd ever have thought of marrying me... sheer nonsense. Yet I felt warm sweet blood in my temples for a few seconds.

'You didn't know where to turn,' prompted Dr Burda. I took another sip of the Scotch. Now that he suggested it, it was rather disgusting. I had decided to end the conversation as quickly and as gracefully as I possibly could when he said something which yanked me up on the chair. 'Was that when you became a dissy?'

'Don't ever use that word! It's obscene!'

He seemed mildly surprised. 'But my dear, Dagmar uses it all the time. Dissy friends, dissy evening, dissy literature, dissy children – I seem to recall even a dissy dog. "Don't forget I am a dissy," she'd snap when I'd suggest some frivolous entertainment. But I suppose it's like the Jews telling hilarious Jewish jokes and resenting anybody else who does the same. I am sorry.' He peered at me almost pityingly. 'Do you get a lot of bashing? Nasty characters, the secret police, or so Dagmar tells me. It's not the twisted arm that hurts, is it? It's the chipped dignity, is it not? Or so I imagine. Our patients suffer from it too if it's any consolation; some of the nurses just relish the power to humiliate. Human nature – can't be helped. Such people should not be employed by state institutions. I give you that, but it's hard to avoid them. They appear highly principled. But you still didn't tell me how you got yourself into it.'

My head felt light as a balloon. Had he doctored that drink? I wouldn't put it past him, I thought – and winced with shame. I was beginning to be as suspicious as Marek!

'There isn't a coherent story to tell, really there isn't. You just... meet people. I met a window cleaner who wasn't a window cleaner, his friends and his friends' friends. People who were all out in the cold after a lifetime of great achievements and good positions, and some who'd rejected official positions in the first place; they'd all done nothing more than refuse to say or write or paint YES where the only answer was NO. I mean where there was no ambiguity, no compromise possible. The bottom line. Truth or lie. Right or wrong. They all ought to have been bitter – but they weren't.

They went on pursuing the truth amongst themselves – there is no such thing as a solitary dissident, you know, it only works in community – and when they thought eventually that they'd come up with something generally useful or important, they made a few hundred carbon copies of it and sent them around. They scraped a living as best they could, in menial jobs mostly, or doing dictionaries and translations, under pseudonyms to shield the people who gave them work. It was like coming home really. Finding the kind of inner freedom which wasn't lonely – which actually had to be shared to make any sense. That's it – it all made sense – still does. It's a wonderful relief, you know, when your life suddenly makes sense. You asked about feeding the ego – I suppose that's what does. Sense. A meaning to your scraggy little life.'

The doctor nodded, then looked at me keenly. 'Tell me one last thing, though. Would it work without the persecution? It's an old question, you know. The torturers and the tortured, don't they make a unity, without which the human spirit would go puff out into the void? Don't you actually need your secret policeman, your devil, lurking in the dark yet close at hand, to remind you of the good you're purporting to achieve, to reinforce the meaning of it? I am not suggesting that you indulge in perverted pleasures like some of my paranoics do, but isn't it a thought worth exploring? Maybe those of us who – admiring you as much as we do – don't feel like joining the dissident troops, are not so much cowardly as unwilling to enter this daily relationship with the devil. Maybe you have the strength not to succumb in the end – to me, it smacks of vanity. Mind you, you yourself are a most intriguing specimen. I cannot detect any vanity in you – more like a teeny weeny bit of an inferiority complex. But then again, isn't inferiority a sister of vanity? Do pardon me, I get carried away with idle theorizing. The question was, would that community of yours work without the harassment? Would you personally be able to uphold that meaning you spoke about without being hounded?'

While he talked, I had an enormously vivid vision of him and Anton playing a game of chess together, bending intently

65

over the board, their eyes flickering with guarded amusement at each move. It was so life-like I had to shake my head to get rid of it.

'Don't dismiss it so lightly,' said Dr Burda, sounding hurt. 'It's better to be aware of one's frailty.'

'I am well aware of it, thank you. It still doesn't give the police any excuse to trespass illegally on citizens' rights. To sneak up from behind, without a warrant...'

I checked my breath. This was neither the time nor the place.

'Listen,' I said unhappily, 'this isn't fair. I don't know how you got me blabbing, but you did. Now you'll think that I am some kind of a fanatic or something and that Norma shouldn't... But it's not like that; most of the time it's simply a life, good and fairly quiet. I can give her a home. Please, if she wants to, let her come. I'll have her properly registered as a lodger, and if you discharge her officially, the police won't bother her. You know she doesn't have to be in an institution. She copes with everyday life and she isn't a public nuisance. Please.'

'But that's all been arranged, my dear. Norma is being discharged on the understanding that she'll reside with you. I saw to that the moment my secretary handed me your – Dagmar's – note. Ward seventeen is one of mine. We're only too glad to recoup a bed. This is a very crowded hospital with a long waiting list. We always lose her in summer and never bother, but when she runs away in winter, it's a worry. We didn't keep her under lock and key or report her missing because she is dangerous or because we are evil, simply because she had nowhere to shelter and we didn't want her to perish. We thought she had no living family – now that a cousin's been found and claims her, that's fine with us. I don't care how removed a cousin you are, my dear. As far as I am concerned, you are perfectly suitable. I am fond of Norma, and wish you two lots of luck. If it doesn't work, she can have her bed back.'

He rose and I jumped to my feet, still disbelieving, afraid to breathe it in.

'But... does she want to come?'

Dr Burda gave me a wry smile. 'She raised no objections.'

'I don't know how to thank you.'

'Don't try. You've paid me in pure gems. I would not have missed this conversation for the world. It's going to be very useful for me. I taped it, you see – I hope you don't mind. Strictly confidential.'

This time the nausea was for real. I nodded a quick goodbye, ran out of the office and found a lavatory just in time. There I threw up the whisky and some bitter liquids and splashed my face with hot water, prohibiting myself all thoughts other than those of Norma waiting for me on ward seventeen.

It was a short walk across the park. The midday sun – sun! – shone ferociously, the grass sparkled with hoar-frost, patches of snow lay golden in every ditch and shallow and the air felt like ice against the cheek. There was nobody in sight. From all sides, through the barred windows of the wards, came the clanking of ladles, pots and spoons.

Ward seventeen was locked.

'Norma's at lunch,' said the nurse who came to let me in, 'though we can't get her to eat anything. It's nice today, chicken and chips – won't you have some? Maybe she'll have a bite then, seeing you at it.'

'Thanks.'

'She's all packed; the discharge papers have arrived ... How come we've never seen you before?'

'I only discovered she was my cousin a few days ago.'

'And you're taking her home. Fancy that!' She beamed at me, but I could sense suspicion lurking behind her smile. 'Now don't get upset – we have some shifty characters in here. Not that Norma's been a darling, she's been banging on doors, kicking chairs, yelling – calling the doctor a shitface! – ever since the police brought her back. In the end, we had to give her an injection. Nothing to worry about, she's quite chirpy this morning. It wears off, you know, while they sleep.'

We walked through a broad corridor painted in dark shit-yellow, past empty doorless dormitories and bleach-stinking toilets, and across a vast day-room where the air pouring in through dirty windows in heavy shafts was alive with dust and cigarette smoke. The green carpet was scarred with a thousand burns and the dented iron buckets were half full with stubs and wet litter. The ping-pong table lacked a net and there were no bats or balls in sight; a handful of broken pencils were strewn on it. A cupboard in the corner labelled 'GAMES' was secured with a large rusty padlock. There was a pulsating lump in my throat; the orphanage had been pretty grim, but this reeked of despair.

We entered the dining hall and my heart leaped. Norma sat in the first row facing the door – I saw her hands tighten around the holdall on her lap. Her nose puckered a little and her lips parted but she didn't move; she sat there, stiff against the wriggling, shuffling, shoving background of some fifty bodies in grey-striped cottons, never letting me out of her gaze. I took a place on the bench directly opposite, which left but a narrow square of table-wood between us. Presently an orderly banged a plate of chicken and chips before each of us, although the other women were already twisting their spoons in a grey, lumpy rice-pudding. A vast girl next to me began to laugh, pitching it higher and higher into a wailing shriek.

'Shut up, cunt!' barked Norma and the girl swallowed and hung her head in silence. 'I know you,' said Norma severely to me. 'You are my Uncle Herman's third wife. He only married you yesterday and he doesn't know yet if he loves you very much.'

'That's fair,' I nodded, 'but I love him a lot. He's helped me to find you.' I forked a chip and Norma did the same. I dared a tiny smile and her lips twitched too. We ate without a word for a while, with Norma imitating – exactly and mischievously – every move of my hands and mouth. My eyes were smarting with tears of delicate joy. Never in my life have I tasted a more wonderful dish of chicken and chips.

A thin white-haired biddy shuffled over and tugged at my sleeve. 'Give us a fag, Fräulein, for services rendered to the Kaiser and *Gott im Himmel, bitte schön.*'

'Fuck off, you fucking old Hitler!' screamed the big girl.

'Fuck off yourself, fat arse!' Norma winked at the old woman. 'I'll send you some. I am going home, see?' She produced the spare keys, my address-tag still attached to them. I gulped and Norma giggled.

'Uncle Herman sent them. The cops stole them, but Uncle Herman can pick the pocket of any cop. He sent men to give them back to me.'

'When was that?' Dear Norma, we'll have so many traps to avoid, but never mind.

'Before lunch. Nurse said so. Tall, handsome men they were. She saw two, but there may have been more. My Uncle Herman has a whole army of them.' She suddenly gave me her brightest, broadest smile. 'I know who you are. You are Funny. You are the wife of Nobody, but my Uncle Herman loves you very much.'

Making her sit down on a chair in the day-room, I pulled the boots out of their bag. Norma held them to her breasts while I unzipped and peeled off her paper-thin shiny old ones. Her feet were terribly cold, as if she had been walking in the snow.

'Size five?' she enquired with a flirtatious little smirk.

'Size six,' I said sternly. 'I won't have your flaming toes all squashed.'

'I love you so much,' whispered Norma, touching my cheek. 'I really do.'

I would have settled for less. The world had come full circle and I was so grateful – come what may.

The same nurse came to let us out, clearly intent on an emotional farewell, but we didn't give a damn.

'Let's walk,' said Norma. 'I know a way. It's very beautiful. I want to show it to my boots.' She looked down at them. 'Boots, you're lucky.'

'And so are we.'

'No,' corrected Norma. 'We are happy.'

She led me by the hand. Past the central kitchens we went, and pathology, across a shrub-infested tennis court, over a dump overgrown with bushes and out through a hole in the wall.

We stood on top of a steep hill. Open heathland sloped down to a lower hill on which lay the city's zoological garden. The river shone deep below on our right, disappeared further ahead under the rocky side of the zoo and reappeared again in glittering patches amidst the buildings and bridges of the distant city. The sun was already turning pink, but the azure hadn't paled yet; the scarce snow reflected all the colours of opal. 'Yahoo!' yelled Norma and threw the holdall down the slope; it rolled away with increasing speed, thudding softly and flapping the handles. We ran after it, sliding and skidding, waving our arms for balance, shouting and hiccuping. Then we crossed a narrow road, climbed down and up a ditch and crawled into the zoological garden through another hole in the wall hidden by bushes.

We tiptoed past the cages with sleeping owls, slouched along a fence on the other side of which the wolves were doing the same, raced by a paddock with three galloping bisons, scurried past the stinking foxes, badgers and skunks and ran down a thousand stone steps alongside a huge *volière* with hunched eagles and gawking vultures. We dodged out of sight whenever we saw a keeper; the zoo was closed on weekdays in winter, and this was Friday. At the foot of the hill, Norma turned right and led the way past the waterfowl ponds and children's playground into a maze of small glass-fronted cages full of shrieking parrots, then out on to another dumping ground. Having trekked over it, we faced a high fence with barbed wire on top; I must have looked worried, for Norma doubled with silent mirth. She just poked about a fence-post with her nimble fingers and soon unhooked a whole portion of the mesh; we slipped through easily, and repaired the damage together.

We spent a while throwing pebbles into the river and licking bitter-tasting icicles which we broke off a small frozen waterfall of an in-flowing brook; then we turned left again and walked swiftly up the rapids on a firm but slippery bank. The river branched here – one branch wild, one tame, with a small island in the middle. There was a pontoon bridge first, great fun to cross if one cared to stamp one's feet – which Norma did and I imitated – then a boring broad bridge across the tame water, and we were on the main road. There was a bus-stop and an empty bus with its engine running. We ran and caught it just in time.

'Lucky for you,' announced the driver, 'that I am two minutes late – had to obey a sudden call of nature here in the wild. There isn't another bus due for an hour. Lucky for me, too, for there is nothing like a couple of young women with cheeks the colour of a polished Christmas apple to warm a man's heart.'

Norma chuckled and pinched his nose and he seemed even more delighted. We went to sit in the back where it was warmest.

'Are your boots happy now?' I asked. 'It was a very beautiful way you took me.'

'They are only boots,' corrected Norma. 'They don't know much about much, once you make them walk.'

'I am happy though. Are you?'

Norma nodded earnestly. 'We are very lucky, you know. Very lucky to be happy.'

And that brought out a whinny – and another pulsating lump at the back of my throat which had nothing to do with despair.

Laws and regulations! We'll stick to them, I told Norma, and let's hope they'll stick to us too. The housing department of the local national council, located half-way between Peace Square and Barley Street, was crammed with nervous, worried, angry people. We queued for over an hour at a window, only to be told that I couldn't possibly have a lodger in such a small apartment and that it was window twenty-one we needed – the flat-sharing register. The clerk there was elderly, grumpy and suspicious. He could not understand, he said, why anyone would want to share a blinking studio flat, and if we thought we'd be back in a week's time applying for larger accommodation, we had another think coming, seeing that comrade chairman of the council had been extra strict with cheats and schemers lately. In the end, he took our citizen's passports – I was strangely pleased to note that

Norma's was as worn, greased and thumbed as mine – copied my address into hers and stamped it with official vigour and vehemence.

Norma kissed the wet stamp, staining her lips with the blue-black ink; she looked like the innocent maiden who found bilberries in the middle of winter on a fairies' hill. I told her the whole fairy tale while we queued in the invalid pensions department. There the clerk was a kind young woman who promised to give Norma's case special consideration. She marvelled at the fact that Norma had never received any money from the state; the hospital should not have kept it all, she said, and if we wanted to make a complaint... We did not and she quite agreed; complaints were lengthy and cumbersome affairs and often worked against the complainants, though she could not rightly say why and it did not seem right. Anyhow, Norma should be receiving her pension at her new address in a few weeks' time; she was sorry, but the window dealing with emergency payments was closed on account of flu; and would we girls manage? I said yes, thank you very much, and just about prevented Norma from showing off her mighty purse. Merry Christmas to you, cheered the woman and we wished her the same and departed, as set in proper citizens' ways as we could ever be.

We had lost the sun while doing it; it was dark again outside, and awesomely windy. Our caretaker, Mrs H., watched us approaching the tenements from her ground-floor window and when we entered the hall, we found her there lying in wait.

I introduced Norma as my cousin and new flatmate – registered and all – but she was clearly brimming with some other excitement.

'I'm sure that's fine, Miss, two single girls in one apartment is ever so much nicer than one, even if it's a bit of a squeeze... But, Miss!' She lowered her voice to a hectic whisper. 'You gave us a right jolt, you did! Heavens! There was me and my Rudi listening to the radio... you know what I mean... taking it easy like; I mean, it's much the same most of the time if you don't mind me saying so, neither here nor

72

there, but then it came like a bolt from a clear sky... Gracious! I says to Rudi, listen! That's our Miss from the second floor, and that's this very house they are announcing to the whole world – right street, right number and all! Seeing as we're the caretakers here, it's our pride, and that's for a fact! We're famous like, that's what we are, Rudi, and none too late for us to enjoy it... on the quiet, mind you, but still! She would not expect us to wave a flag or something – never did, did she, seeing as we're not cut out to make a spectacle of ourselves. But I'll go and shake her little hand the minute she walks in tonight, says I, respectful like and no more said. Or maybe just a little, seeing as we owe her an apology... God help my stupid soul, Miss, but we thought you might be one of them hard-currency racketeers or something in that line, knowing you was not into whoring or thieving, bashing that typewriter of yours most of the time. But we could not help noticing, now could we, the police coming into the house like and taking you away in the small hours... Come to think of it, this here your friend, was she not...?'

'That wasn't me,' said Norma. 'That was my Uncle Herman's second wife. She runs away, see? But she won't be a bother any more. She's been fixed good and proper.'

I quickly put out my hand for the caretaker to shake. 'Thank you very much, Mrs H. It's nice to know that you think kindly of me. And your husband. I won't presume on your good nature, don't worry. I'll keep this handshake a secret – a good thing to remember. Moral support.'

A door creaked upstairs. 'That was very nicely put, Miss,' whispered Mrs H., 'and it's good to know that there are people with a conscience in this here country.' And she hastily retreated behind the door of the caretaker's flat, where her husband Rudi was having a bout of chain-smoker's cough.

Norma made a face after her, hanging her tongue out and wagging it like a lizard's; I found it greatly refreshing.

It didn't take long for the door-bell to ring, with the familiar

73

loud insistence. We'd had our tea and were in the middle of reorganizing the closet and the chest of drawers to accommodate two women instead of one, a delightful serious activity which we both enjoyed very much.

I gave Norma a lighthearted peck. 'Sit tight, sweetheart. Don't fret. I'll be back presently – tonight, tomorrow, or the day after at the latest.'

'Sit tight, yourself,' sniggered Norma. 'I'll be on the town.'

But when I put on my coat and was about to open the door – the bell was ringing angrily – she ran lightly over and gave me a powerful hug. Her quick whisper was inaudible, but I knew well what she was saying by reading her lips.

'I'll pray for you. I'll say please God, be good to Funny. I'll find Uncle Herman too and he...'

'Oh, stuff Uncle Herman. You're all I need,' I said, pushed her well back and stepped out into the arms of two uniformed youngsters waving a summons calling upon me to help the police with an investigation.

It was the simple routine, the tough guy and the intellectual; young Anton was nowhere in sight, nor was – bless my lucky star – Major Fischer.

Having duly enquired what crime had been committed in the investigation with which I was supposed to help, and having received no answer apart from a rude rebuff, I sat tight. Tight-lipped. Indignant and angry – automatic reactions, really – yet fairly relaxed. My intelligence and reason were called upon, my utter stupidity and wretchedness sneered at, names of the persons who copied and distributed the declaration required, threats issued in terms of ramming the entire citizens' committee down my throat until I choked and begged to be allowed to peach on my own grandmother; admiration expressed as to my endurance and determination and gentle prodding applied to make me see how misguided it was; scissors produced and snapped over my head to evoke the close-cutting of hair awaiting me in prison; apologies proffered for the overworked colleague and

74

assurance intimated that I would at least sign, using my aforementioned intelligence, the pre-prepared protocol in which it was stated that I had voluntarily taken part in an 'official conversation', being aware that my activities were bordering on the criminal offence of anti-state agitation, eventually subversion, as had been made clear to me by the official warning delivered by Major Fischer on behalf of the Commander-in-Chief of the Security Corps. It was suggested I signed bloody fucking quick or else, and offer made of an addition to the protocol declaring that I had refused to answer any questions, using the citizen's right to remain silent.

I declined to sign and that was that. They both discarded their guises, said it was time to go home – for them, not for me – and transferred me, amidst rather good-natured if slightly vulgar jokes, to the cells for preliminary detention in the basement. The familiar red slip did not even describe me as a 'suspect'; I was merely to be detained until my identity could be fully established. This was heartily laughed at by all and sundry, including the woman guard who gave me a brief and kindly frisk.

She said it was a merry night and I was in good company – if 'good' was the right word for such a crazy bunch as you people were, she added.

The corridor between the cells resounded with a Moravian folk ballad sung in a straggly chorus. I recognized all the voices – and the addition of Karol's!

'Karol! Et tu, Brute?! Hi, everybody, sorry I am late!' I called out, waiting for the cell to be unlocked.

'Marta and the kids are awfully proud of me!' shouted Karol.

'You're spoiling the tune, my sweet chatterbox!' That was Vlado and I blushed; it was just as well he couldn't see me. 'Get settled in quick, will you? We'll start again and this time, Marek – please! – sing, don't roar!'

I found myself sharing a cell with Zoe, Anna and a friendly prostitute called Manon, as in Lescaut.

'Not really?!' I cried.

'Cross my heart,' said Manon. 'Mum thought the poor

wretch was a romantic heroine pure as snow, and when she found out the truth it was far too late for both of us. At least she doesn't fuss. Fate, she says, and gives me kinky underwear for Christmas.' She giggled to herself.

'Professor K.?' I asked.

'No, thank God. They pulled him in all right, but drove him home again. Respect for old age – I hope,' said Anna.

'How was it?' Zoe peered from her upper berth.

'Normal. Better than usual, actually. Short and rather toothless.'

'The same here,' said Anna. 'I wonder.'

'Ready, everyone?' Vlado's rich voice carried easily through the partitions. 'One, two, three!'

The ballad regretted, in wistful tones, the freedom about to be lost by two young lovers preparing for a wedding; a white rose she, he a green tall tree.

We were thrown out, without the bonus of the tepid brown soup, at five o'clock in the morning, Manon included. She couldn't believe her luck and invited everybody for breakfast at her place down by the river, a mere five minutes of brisk walk and that, she said, might be stretching it.

A shadow peeled hesitantly off the wall by the entrance to the Three Bears. I would have known it everywhere – in the dark, by broad daylight, in the desert, amongst the crowd of ten million. I ran over and hugged the bearer of that shadow.

'Silly twit!' I scolded. 'What do you mean, standing out here in the blasted cold?! You'll catch pneumonia, or else get yourself pulled in for loitering!'

Norma whinnied happily. 'Silly yourself! Joseph said wait, after he locked up. It won't be long, he said. A man called Anton told him; he loves you very much.'

'Anton? Don't, dearest. Don't ever believe that. He was the handsome ugly who bothered us the other day, remember? When you locked yourself in the bathroom? He is a baddie, Norma, we don't want his love.'

'I'll be blowed,' said Manon. 'If it isn't that nut Norma! Come along, sweetie, we'll have a massive fry-up in my old dump.'

Norma got a frankly cordial greeting from everyone, even

76

Marek. At Manon's place, which wasn't a dump at all, she curled up on a fake tiger-skin sofa and slept like a baby. The twelve of us – Manon unknowingly filling Professor K.'s boots – each ate a hearty dish of eggs scrambled with bits of bacon and onions, swamped our stomachs with good strong coffee and opened an ad-hoc meeting which, as we all later agreed, was one of our best.

'Ouch,' said Manon. 'All this hurts my dainty ears. You won't mind if I scamper to my sinful bedroom, will you? There are gallons of vodka in the fridge – help yourselves if you feel like it. I might not know you next time I see you, so don't be surprised. A girl has to live. But it's been an honour, cross my heart and mum's knickers.'

'Madam,' cried Arnold, kissing her hand, 'it's we who are honoured and infinitely grateful!'

'God bless you,' said young Father Ignat.

But it was Vlado who sent her away chuckling happily, all blushing and youthful, having whispered God knows what into her ear. He then came to sit next to me on the rather incongruous antique chaise-longue, snuffling close in an imperceptible cuddle. It all made wonderful sense.

'Who's going to take the minutes?' asked Karol and they all looked at me.

'Be fair,' protested Zoe. 'She did it last time. And in case you don't know, my shorthand is impeccable. No one can read it but me!'

'Dilly-dally, dilly-dally,' grumbled Dr Florian. 'History's stampeding away, you know.'

'Hear, hear,' said Marek. 'The people out there are waiting.'

'Oh, dry up,' exclaimed Vera, his present co-habitant and co-worker. 'It'll be the day when you offer to take the minutes!'

Norma stirred in her sleep and everyone lowered their voices. Life, I thought, life!

III

The weekend was spent in quiet domestic activities, as if there was nothing the matter with the world. The weather, as it often does in the quirky month of December, turned mushy again, wet and dim, endowing the indoors with a special comforting glow. I fiddled, lazily yet fairly efficiently, with the *New etcetera Hop-Harvester*, amusing Norma with long harsh-sounding German words which she repeated with perfect ease, adding a peal of laughter at the end of each. The flat smelled of soap and polish; Norma gave every object, small or large, a thorough wash whether it was needed or not. She wouldn't hoover, though, and watched me doing it with a frown upon her face, keeping well out of reach of the nozzle.

'It killed Uncle Herman's wife,' she whispered. 'She tripped and fell and it sucked her soul out.'

'The first wife or the second?'

'The third,' said Norma, mischief returning to her eyes, 'so you'd better watch out too!'

We developed a habit of sharing the occasional cigarette; it felt wonderfully wicked, like smoking dope behind a supervisor's back. Neither of us seemed to be hungry at mealtimes; we ate a huge plate of nibbles at midnight between Saturday and Sunday.

'Did you have a mother?' asked Norma late on Sunday morning.

'Twit, I must have done, mustn't I? Everybody has had a mother,' I said unfairly, and owned up. 'No – not one to remember. She died before she could give me a cuddle.'

'You can borrow mine,' smiled Norma shyly. 'She won't

78

mind. Uncle Herman said never to show her to anyone, but he can stuff it.'

From the depths of her purse she fished out a cracked, passport-sized photograph of Elizabeth Taylor, lips pursed amiably above a slightly doubled chin, eyes beaming with motherly love. We pinned her on a shining yellow bloom, one of the Van Gogh sunflowers on a framed reproduction Vlado had once brought, using it as a lid for a crate stocked with booze. He hung it up for me on the wall opposite the window, where it immediately caught light and brightened the room considerably. Somehow, I thought, one love brings out the memory of another, perhaps in a greater glory than it ever possessed.

We did not discuss Elizabeth Taylor, Norma and I. We were both happy with the pretence, though I suspected the star would have been shocked to find herself an adorable mother of two thirty-three-year-olds in wintry Bohemia.

'What shall we do about father?' I asked.

'Nothing,' Norma replied vehemently. 'Uncle Herman wouldn't like us to have one. He is jealous.'

'Who needs a father anyway – so late in life,' I said wisely, and attacked the *Hop-Harvester* with the approaching Christmas in mind. We might want to do something really nice, like going to the mountains for a few days, perhaps stopping on the way to call on my large – so distant, so long unvisited – family in the village of Broumy. I chuckled at the thought of Norma facing all those cousins.

'What's funny, Funny?' asked Norma, upon which we both had another round of giggles in the teeth of doom.

Robert – the youngest of the committee members, though Father Ignat wasn't much older – rounded off the Sunday by bringing us a heart-shaped box of chocolates. A whole stack of these, twelve to be precise, appeared on Karol's doorstep, he said. They had not been poisoned; Marta let the neighbour's dog have one chocolate, and he was still fine half an hour later. So it had to be a well-wishing gift from an unknown fan of the citizens committee; Karol sent Robert to distribute the boxes as a reminder to us all of our accountability to the people. And would I please be at Arnold's in Ponds Road by eleven tomorrow morning? A journalist from *Le Monde* would arrive at midday; and while Arnold, Professor K. and even Marek didn't need much help with French, Karol and Vlado certainly did. Not to mention that a woman was needed to make up the balance, and as Zoe and Vera held daytime jobs and Anna said she hated interviews, the joke was on me. We treated Robert to hash'n'mash, which he said was just like his mother's although usually avoided on Sundays in his family, and to a can of beer we were saving for a night-cap. I would not have been so generous, but Norma took it from the fridge and poured it out for him. Mother, she announced, liked her beer warm, having been brought up amongst foreigners, see? But we believed it was ever so much nicer ice-cold and Robert agreed. Oh, he remembered, leaving, these I found on your doorstep! And he pulled two envelopes out of his pocket, one white and one brown, with neither a name nor an address on them.

Norma begged me not to open them before daylight returned; we didn't want to sleep with ghosts of bad people's words, she said. These might have come from good people, like the chocolates, I argued, but she shook her head so fervently and looked so anxious that I ceased to persevere and we went to bed in peace, lying toes to chin and chin to toes – cousins behind a warm chimney corner.

I read the letters by coyly quivering daylight at seven-thirty in the morning. Norma slept: I knocked on her forehead, not very gently.

'Wake up, you witch!'

She gazed at me, a slow sleepy smile lighting up her eyes. 'I love you so much,' she sighed. 'I really do.'

'You're still a witch,' I grumbled, kissing her nose. 'Sit up on your arse and keep me company. Have a chocolate – there isn't much else for breakfast! Eat the crispy ones with nuts and things and leave the soft centres for me. I haven't got cutting diamonds for teeth.'

Norma searched first my face for reasons for such grumpiness, then the room. On the floor by the bed lay the letters, all crumpled by my angry hand. She leaned over and picked them up disdainfully, her lips curling as she peered at the lines.

'I don't want to read them. They're very bad.'

'Oh, stop it. Nobody asked you to.'

'I want you to read them to me. I'll hold them up for you. That way, it won't hurt so much.'

I let a long sigh escape from my chest; I knew she would retrieve my peace of mind. 'No, sweetheart. They're just stupid. We don't want the nasty cretins in bed with us. Forget it! Look, the weather's turned again. The sky is pink: it'll be a sunny day. Cold and sharp as a chisel, but sunny. Tell you what – you read something for me. You promised me a merry story, remember? Pick a book while I make the coffee; but make sure the story has a happy beginning, middle and end.'

Being quick and nimble at forgetting, Norma did not give the letters a glance as she scrambled out of bed; I scooped them up and went to the kitchen to tear them to pieces and flush them down the sink – but not before re-reading the malicious lines. They were brief enough to take no more than the kettle's boiling time.

The letter that came in the white envelope went straight to the point: 'Watch out, you bitch. You are nothing but a filthy swine, and if you don't stop your dirty tricks, the boys will beat you to a pulp, you cunt. Don't think your imperialist friends can help you, you silly cow. GET OUT of the fucking citizens' committee NOW, or ELSE.' It was signed 'true citizens of Bohemia'.

The brown envelope had yielded a more circumspect typed note: 'Miss, it has come to our notice that you profess to be one of twelve leading authorities on how we want to or should live. We have never heard of you before and we don't want to hear a word from you AGAIN. As far as we are concerned, you are NOBODY, and if you don't stop your undesirable activities, you may well become NOTHING. Think it over quickly, or expect MORE.' Signed: 'Guardians of peace'.

81

On second reading, the two letters were remarkably similar, which took a lot of edge off the first impact. Red lipstick, I thought; Anton's fake-factory all over again. The only thing that worried me now was the mention of 'imperialist friends': did it mean that the meeting with the *Le Monde* journalist had been set up by somebody careless? The quiet bliss of the weekend had made me vulnerable; the mere thought of the police busting up the meeting sent chills down my spine; I wished for the day to end in Norma's company, not in an interrogation room and a detention cell. But there was so little I could do, apart from keeping the letters and showing them to Marek!

My spirits rose with the same exuberance as the whistling kettle, leave it to Marek, he'd know what's what and would not lead us where we didn't want to go.

Norma was back in bed nursing an old leather-bound volume of *War and Peace* on her lap.

'Fat things are merry,' she declared.

We drank the coffee in companionable silence, each gobbling up a few chocolates in the process. Soft centres for me, nuts for her. Then the book fell open in the middle and Norma's palms smoothed the pages.

'Once upon a time, a mother had three ugly coppers for sons. She was also an ugly stepmother and had two pretty stepdaughters, but they couldn't stand it and ran away. They were very happy in the woods eating bilberries and things, and there was a fat white cow who lived in a cottage and gave them milk, so it was a merry time. But they got lost. One went one way, and the other couldn't find her. The ugly stepmother was happy about this, she was so hateful, so she sent the coppers to keep it that way. But the coppers had a bad time of it, falling about and breaking their legs and growing warts on their noses, because they tried so hard. People laughed at them and that made them mad. In the meantime, one girl grew up big and pretty and the other stayed small and skinny, and when the coppers knew that they were glad. They thought this was the end of the story, but it wasn't. A man called Uncle Herman' – she glanced at me coyly, but as I didn't protest she went on at the same breathless speed – 'he drank milk from the same cow and there was a medication in it and it told him where the girls were and he sent men to bring them together. The stepmother knew this from some hookers, and she puffed up all big and round like a balloon and they had to give her an injection and never mind if it killed her. And then the coppers did it once more; they took one girl one way when the other wasn't looking, and a fat man helped them, and they brought the girl where the stepmother was and the stepmother wasn't dead yet and gave her an injection. But the tall, beautiful man called Uncle Herman sent men to give her milk from the white cow, and the girl drank this and went to the loo and peed all the badness right out. It was very loud and the other girl heard it with her magic ears and came to take her home and they lived merrily ever after. And the ugly coppers and the fat man were punished by Uncle Herman—'

'Stuff Uncle Herman,' I said, as was my due cue. 'What fat man? Norma, dearest, was he with the cops when they came here for you? A plain-clothes man? What did he do?'

'It was a merry story,' whimpered Norma. 'Why don't you like it?'

'It was a wonderful story and I love it, and I am sorry to be such a fuss, but I really want to know about the fat man – unless you made him up.'

'I made nothing up, silly! It's all in the book. Can't you see when a person is reading?'

'Norma, please.'

'He laughed. He said he was a doctor, but wasn't. I know doctors – they don't laugh. He was a queer.' She blinked with sudden tears. 'He messed things up with his lipstick. I told him you'd be angry!'

'I should have been, but I was such a stupid fool. It's all right, sweetheart. I got rid of it... eventually. Forget it. They just wanted me to think you ran away from me. As if... have you forgiven me, Norma? For packing you off?'

She seemed not to know what I meant. 'You never read to me,' she complained.

'I will, I promise. Tonight.'

We dressed warmly and went to the corner shop to get some provisions.

'Did you have a grandmother?' whispered Norma while we were queuing.

'Never.'

For some reason, that made her giggle and the women in the queue looked at us with cold, unkind, hungry eyes. I put my arm around Norma's shoulders and drew her close. When it was our turn, the shopkeeper patted Norma's cheek and gave her an iced bun, all squashed and torn along the middle. We fed it to the pigeons.

'Of course she can't baby-sit!' cried Marta, pulling on her boots. 'Be reasonable! It does require intelligence, you know. Besides, my Auntie's here. But she may stay, if she is ... quiet.'

Norma peered at her defiantly. 'My Uncle Herman's first wife gave him so many children that he had to call in all his men to baby-sit. But I watched over them most of the time. And I am more quiet than you are. You shout.'

'I do?' Marta seemed surprised. 'Gosh, I am late! Well, see how you get along with Auntie. If she doesn't want you in the nursery, ask Karol to give you something to do. He is the organizer around here. But don't hang about him too much, he's preparing a statement.'

That was probably directed more at me, so I said I wouldn't dream of disturbing him and walked with Marta half-way to her clinic. We parted on a busy corner.

I pushed on towards Green Street, wondering about the strange strength of the woman. I hope it's not just vanity, she had said, squeezing my hand with her firm fingers. I hope to God it is His will that my Karol becomes an instrument of Christian love and justice. I may wish He hadn't chosen him, but I guess I shall bear whatever comes with pride. And I trust I won't sin by wishing it had been me whom He chose. I suppose being a doctor and a mother is a task honourable enough for a woman. And she gave me a stern look of

84

disapproval! I still chuckled under my breath when I rang Marek's bell.

I rang and rang, thinking he might be fast asleep after a night-shift, but had to give up in the end. By the dustbins in the courtyard, I tore up the letters and lifted a wistful eye to the sky. Thus I stood for a while, but there was no message, not a wink from the feeble morning sun, not one meaningfully shaped cloud, not a word.

'You barmy or sumpin'?' cried one of the small boys whose football hit my knee.

'And how!' grinned I, and vacated the courtyard which filled with their shrill, victorious little voices.

Half an hour later – after a bumpy ride in an overheated tram – and still half an hour early, I surveyed the neat pre-war villas of Ponds Road with faint misgiving. It all seemed too friendly, too content, out of place in this grumpy city. What's more, there actually were two small ponds at the end of the road, willow trees and all! Barley Street was a dust-bowl without a single stalk of living grass; Peace Square was as noisy as a steel-mill with tramways and buses; Green Street was a disconsolate row of sooty nineteenth-century workers' tenements where no tree ever lived; but Ponds Road had to boast real live ponds! Just like Arnold, I thought – so genteel, so genuine. I tramped up and down the road in a morose mood, until it was eleven; a window opened in the upstairs of a villa and Arnold asked me to come in with an equally morose nod of his finely shaped head.

Dagmar opened the door.

She led the way with nonchalant intimacy, as if she were the mistress of the house. I'd never been there before; Arnold was a distant land on my map of visitable people. Not that he was an inaccesible legend – parties he gave were the talk of the town – but although Vlado often asked me to come along, I never dared.

An attractive man with longish hair sprang from a sofa. *'Enchanté, Mademoiselle! J'espère que vous allez bien? Pas de difficultés? Pas de flics aux environs?'*

No, I haven't seen any police around, I replied, puzzled. Wasn't he supposed to arrive at twelve? Judging by the empty tea-cups, half-eaten cake, full ashtray and discarded miniature batteries next to a miniature tape-recorder, he must have been here for quite some time.

'It was Dagmar's idea,' murmured Arnold, helping me out of the coat. 'She brought him early. I couldn't very well not talk to him. General stuff; I told him he must do the main interview when you folks arrive. I only hope he still has some tape left. I am a terribly slow speaker in French.'

Dagmar smoothed my hair. 'Don't fret, darling. I am leaving, I know when I am not wanted. Committee members only and all that. *Au revoir, Pierre, et merci beaucoup.*'

'*Merci à vous, Dagmar. A bientôt.*'

'I wouldn't if I were you,' I said slowly. 'I mean, why don't you stay.'

'Absolutely,' said Arnold. 'Where is everybody?'

'It's only ten to eleven,' smiled Dagmar. 'And I am going, but thanks anyway.'

I looked at my watch. 'It's nearly ten past, actually. It's certainly not like Marek to be late.'

Dagmar started; she didn't recover quickly enough for me not to have noticed. 'Oh well,' she said lightly and walked over to the window. 'Oh-o.' It sounded rather casual. 'The police are here. *La police est arrivée, Pierre. Je suppose que notre amie ici a due être suivée.*'

'*Merde! Pardonnez moi. C'est affreux.*'

'I don't think I have been followed, Arnold. As a matter of fact, I am pretty sure I was not.'

Arnold sat down on a red-leather pouffe, looking more tired than scared. He disregarded my protest completely. 'Have they only just arrived? What are they doing?'

'Standing about, hands in pockets.' There was definitely a note of amusement in Dagmar's voice. 'The car's yards away on the corner. They could have been here a few minutes. I guess the committee members turned on their heels and ran home.'

I fought an urgent desire to slap her face. Arnold tugged at my little finger. 'Go to the kitchen and have a look at the back, will you? There's a good girl.'

86

The kitchen window overlooked tidy gardens and a narrow snow-powdered alley, sleepy and deserted.

'Seems okay.'

'Get out then, all of you, while the going's good.' He, too, looked sleepy and deserted; even shut his eyes.

Dagmar led the flustered Frenchman out by the hand, throwing me but a cursory ironic glance. I gathered the three tea-cups, plates and ashtray and went back to the kitchen to wash them. The frozen alleyway resounded with two sets of footsteps only: I almost wished to hear them being followed by heavy boots. On the tram, I went through the whole catalogue of my books, trying to pick the right one; I so wanted my first reading to Norma to be a success with her. Now it seemed rather improbable that it would be tonight. Forgive me, pet, I whispered into the air, hoping she would hear me with her magic ears – but you see, don't you, that I can't very well leave the man alone?

The two miniature batteries, loudly foreign, still lay on the sofa; I flushed them down the toilet bowl in the striking black and white bathroom. All that time Arnold never moved, but when I sat down in an armchair next to his pouffe, he took my hand and placed it on his knee. An antique clock, ridiculously noisy, ticked away through another eternity. How many yet...? Bracing ourselves against the shriek of the door-bell, we kept the precious silence intact.

It was two minutes to twelve when we heard a distant engine start, roar up and fade. Arnold ran to the window.

'They've gone! They just up and went!' He was like a schoolboy who, by one chance in a million, escapes the headmaster's cane. The clock chimed a few bars from Mozart's Eine Kleine Nachtmusik.

'Somebody must have fiddled with it,' complained Arnold. 'It used to chime only at midnight. Or maybe it's decided on its own that what we live is one long night, with midnight striking every twelve hours. You never know with old clocks; they may well have a sense of history. Listen, I am aware that we don't know each other very well, but would you mind awfully getting blind drunk with me? Or simply keep me company while I...?'

'I thought you'd never ask.' I leaned back in the armchair,

uncrossing and stretching my stiff, aching legs.

The sunny afternoon swayed gently and without haste in the quiet room which was expensively furnished but covered in fine old dust. Arnold talked and I listened, though my own thoughts strayed now and then to where the absent friends were... and Norma.

'Tell me, are you naturally brave or were you just being womanly? Taking care of a hapless male, that sort of thing? You don't look womanly – take it as a compliment. I am a dreadful coward, you see. I don't know what to do about it. Not a coward-coward; I would do what I consider right or simply normal and in keeping with the truth, fully conscious of the probable unpleasant consequences. I am fine and quite collected once I am in; it's the process of getting there that screws me up. It's to do with my upbringing; I can't bear being impolite. But how do you remain polite with people who have rudeness in their job description, without denigrating yourself? They open the car door and I say "Thank you", while they shove and bundle me in! They cut their fingers on an old razor while searching for God-knows-what in the bathroom, and I apologize profusely. They laugh at me behind my back, but that's not what gets at me. It's the self-humiliation. I don't seem able to avoid it – as if humiliation wasn't hard enough to cope with. You saw me; it's always like that. I nearly die between the door-bell and the moment when I am finally seated in an interrogation room. Answering or not answering their questions can be done with perfect politeness – I am at ease there. It's the physical element of behaviour, I suppose, that... they hurl me across my own living room, I tread on someone's foot in the process and say "Excuse me, please." And I cringe with moral pain. Maybe I would not do it in gaol. Maybe it's because it is my own living room. Or a friend's apartment. Or an open street, familiar café – benign, normal space. You're not like that, are you? How do you cope?'

'I get angry. But I have other...'

'Yes! Yes! That is the correct reaction! Spontaneous,

perfectly human, befitting one's innocence. Why can't I do it?'

I nearly told him the story of the spittle, and how I followed Pied Piper Anton, two zero two, and virtually asked to be humiliated; but he was so self-absorbed, so in need of a listener that I remained undeclared. Womanly.

The sun shifted westwards, leaving the room in sudden deep shade: the bottle of cognac – levels of the dark-honey coloured liquid sinking fast – shone like a seaman's lantern in a brewing storm.

'I wish,' sighed Arnold, 'that I hadn't been born a solid bourgeois. If I had lived in deprived conditions as a child, I might have grown up with more understanding of the cruelty accompanying every Utopia, as I might have been a Utopian myself. Striving to reorganize society, life, according to a strict arbitrary plan; accepting the pain of it as a necessary ache en route to a new order which would provide justice, and even happiness, for everyone. I might have been a reformed Utopian by now, overwhelmed by the collapse of it and sorry for the pain it's caused, yet still nursing the dream. Like Vlado. I abhor poverty and the exploitation of the disowned poor by the owners of wealth as much as he does; I despise the very amassing of wealth; but I never possessed the Utopian dream. It's not just that I fear and reject revolutionary terror; I simply don't believe that life can be planned, organized in every detail, regulated, purged. I am merely vaguely religious – believing in a higher-than-human horizon – and I am certainly not sorry I've never been a bigot. But I do wish I'd been a comrade. I might have been able to understand better what's going on. Here and elsewhere, where the comrades believe they can have the future without the past. My humanism might have had more cutting edge. I wish you hadn't such sincere eyes: they invite confessions.'

Vlado had said the same thing once. And if my memory wasn't deceiving me, he wished he'd never been a comrade and envied Arnold his unsoiled humanistic vision!

All I want, I thought rebelliously, is an upright life and the warmth of love – for everybody, true, but first of all for myself. I was beginning to feel fidgety – what had happened to the others? How was Norma doing in the nursery? I drank but little; I sniffed at my second tot of cognac in the beautiful Napoleon glass and found the powerful scent too rich, alien and sad. I was ill-disposed towards sadness; I reached back for the anger.

'It's a dreadful thing to say, but I bet she knew – Dagmar, I mean. She knew the police would arrive at eleven; she expected them. Arnold, forgive me, but she must have arranged it.'

Arnold scrutinized my face for a while, then chuckled. 'So my sexual life is an open book, is it?'

'I don't understand.'

'Come on, why else would you apologize to me while accusing Dagmar of something she is perfectly capable of? Not that I would think for a minute she was an agent – Lord, no – but I wouldn't put a prank like this past her.'

'A *prank!*'

'Why yes, a prank, a caper, possibly a stink. Firstly, she has a natural grudge against the committee, as you well know. Secondly, she likes her lovers to be of importance, to get a larger slice of fame and fortune... Listen, she did go to bed with a plumber while he was re-doing her bathroom, but then she ransacked the town for rich customers and landed him the poshest, hard-currency-paid jobs which he reaped long after she parted with him and without even knowing who had arranged for them. By which I also want to say that if indeed you are right and Dagmar did pull a trick to secure a solo appearance in *Le Monde* for me, I knew nothing of it. I disapprove. I am also amused, but that's because I am drunk. You mustn't tell on me. Please?'

'I won't if I can help it. You know, I think I'll go on the wagon. Shouldn't we all...?'

'Utopia! Besides, the important question isn't do we, or don't we, want a drink. The important question is, do we want to go on living?'

We sat silent for a short while. I watched Arnold's face

with a quiet and slightly queasy fascination: it frowned and
un-frowned, lit and un-lit, like moody weather. The eyelids
went heavy and the lips quivered like any other drunkard's,
but the forehead retained its nobility. I could not resist
touching it. We could make love, murmured Arnold, if
you're in an erotic mood; that's one thing in life that's never
disappointing. Little do you know, I thought, but said
nothing and watched him some more, until he drifted into a
solid, untroubled sleep.

I let myself out by the back door and walked straight into
the arms of young Anton. The question is, my head
screamed, do we want to go on living?

'You took ages,' Anton complained. 'Has he been screwing
you or what?'

'None of your business. What do you want?'

He grinned merrily. His teeth sparkled, nearly as white as
the snow. 'I thought you might appreciate a ride.'

'No. Thanks for the trouble.' I hoped I sounded ironical.

'No trouble at all. The car's at the end of the alley – you
can't, in fact, miss it.'

I braced myself. 'You'll have to use force to get me in.' I'd
had enough of tricks and games.

Anton nodded. 'That's the spirit. But, my dear, this is
neither the time nor the place for it. Wait till you see who I've
got there already.'

Not Norma, I pleaded; dear God, let me eat dirt or walk
barefoot on ice and snow, but leave Norma in peace. I almost
ran, Anton's ringing footsteps and boyish chuckle on my
heels.

The car was a grey, private-looking Lada; there seemed to
be no other policemen around, secret or otherwise – apart
from a man lounging on the back seats, contemplating an
elegant, slim, palm-hugging flask of brandy: Vlado.

He smiled warmly and beckoned me in. My stomach was
turning, I felt sea-sick. Something was hugely wrong and I
couldn't find my options within it. Meekly, trembling with
confusion, fighting an urgent smarting in the eyes, I climbed
on the front seat through the door held open by Anton with a
politeness that was either completely mocking or utterly

sincere. Vlado leaned over and kissed me lightly below the ear. His breath smelled of fresh mint.

'Sober,' he confirmed. 'Miracles happen. Cease trepidating, my little humming-bird. Rest your wings. You make me dizzy. What took you so long? Knowing Arnold, it was either a lecture on existentialism or an erotic experience not to be forgotten.'

'Stop it!' The shout brought my stomach right into my mouth; I retched.

'Golly,' said Anton admiringly and swerved the car in what I thought was the wrong direction, 'you ought to have been a nun. I often wondered if prohibiting nunneries was such a good idea. I have a cousin like that, she is so chaste she can't go to the movies any more; she throws up when they do anything below the neck. Speaking of cousins, yours is just fine. She was last seen bossing a load of children and an aunt. Your alleged relative is a protected species now, so – please! – relax. When you vibrate like that, you interfere with my driving.'

He was clearly heading out of town. Westward: what for? There was the Wild Rock Park only a few miles ahead, but that was absurd... Of course, the West Prison! The infamous old brickwork that people used to disappear in, never to return; I had been taken there once before for an interrogation, with the intent to scare the daylights out of me; I was so angry it didn't quite work. A second visitation should not be more frightening than the first; I relaxed. Only a few seconds later, I was furious with myself – why didn't I at least try to walk away from the car? I turned around to Vlado who was still contemplating the flask – the seal unbroken – as if it were a crystal ball filled with amber genius.

'Have you any idea where we're going?' I asked angrily.

'More or less, yes.' He didn't take his eyes off the flask. 'A little late for lunch, but better late than never.'

'Ha ha! I suppose Karol, Marek and Professor K. are already there?'

'I certainly hope not, my little chicken. This is a private party. It may appear as a bit of a *divide et impera* operation, but even if it is, it's for a good cause. Or so I believe.'

I gaped and Anton burst out laughing. 'I get it!' he guffawed. 'You know what she thinks? She thinks we're taking her to the West Prison! Oh my, isn't that rich?'

I couldn't hold the tears any longer. I felt so raw that I winced with pain when Vlado squeezed my shoulder.

'I am sorry.' Vlado's voice was very gentle. 'I had no idea; I thought he told you. What a pair of pigs we are. We're really taking you for lunch, a cordon bleu venison feast in the Wild Rock restaurant.'

'It's closed in winter,' I said, as if it mattered.

'So it is,' chuckled Anton. 'That's why we're going there.' He switched on the radio and a syncopated polka swiftly extinguished any thoughts left in my brain.

Stark black vertical rocks streaked with blue ice. Green ice over the brook, dark water bubbling underneath. Purple snowdrifts in the shade of the gorge, a glimpse of a lilac sky. Then a blue-white meadow on each side of the road, glittering trees – and rocks again, a couple of rugged pyramidal towers and the Wild Rock itself, its sharp peak veiled in a small cloud of smoke escaping from the tall chimney of a pseudo-Swiss cottage. A tamed miniature wilderness at the foot of the city: wild enough for me.

With a twinkle in his eye, Anton introduced the robust manager as his cousin; the man seemed cordial enough. Its windows shuttered, the main dining room lay in a dusty twilight; the legs of the chairs resting on table-tops pointed to the ceiling like a forest of dead forefingers. The vast wooden floor creaked as we crossed it, pushing through the cold stale air, a small fleet of ice-breakers. A broad rustic door marked 'Private' opened into a cosy wood-panelled room lit by candles and logs blazing in a rustic fireplace. Stuffed glass-eyed trophy-heads of Bohemian deer gazed sadly upon the table laid with chipped rustic china, sharp knives, bread-baskets, bottles, tumblers and cold meats.

Vlado sniffed at the plates and sighed. 'Venison it is, cordon bleu it ain't. I guess I'll roast mine in the fire.'

'Well, Mahlzeit,' said the manager. 'If you need something, yodel. The wife said you can have coffee if you must, but don't expect any other favours. No pudding.' The door shut behind him with a thud.

'Exit bear,' nodded Vlado. 'Do they live here all year round?'

'Yup.' Anton was taking the coat off my shoulders. 'I suggest we don't want any coffee. She is a dragon, my cousin-in-law.'

I'd been determined not to touch anything, but my mouth felt so dry that my eyes kept falling wistfully upon the dewy bottles of beer. Vlado opened one, filled a tumbler and clasped my fingers around it.

'For pity's sake, woman, drink!'

I drank, and I ate too. Not much of either, but enough to revive the spirit. My cheeks flushed; disdain and puzzlement began to turn into curiosity. I looked at Vlado, willing him to explain.

'*Ave femina!*' Vlado said with a bow. 'What distant land does she hail from?' He sounded tense.

Anton, I noticed, was drinking rather heavily, chasing brandy with wine. His youth suddenly appeared worn and tight, like a jacket he'd soon have to throw away. The candles flickered, the fire hissed and crackled, behind the window the daylight was dying rapidly – and so was my patience.

Vlado's fist thumped the table. 'Okay. Here goes! Things are happening at the top. At the top of all tops, so far and yet so near, if you get the meaning. There is a decent chance of democratic reform, if things at the bottom are handled with care. If there are no attempts to put the cart before the horses. People like Arnold and Karol, not to mention Marek, might do great harm by shouting what needs for the moment to be whispered. Professor K., Florian and most of the others are naturally cautious, though they could be swayed the loud way. In other words, we have to put a brake on the committee. Don't look so alarmed; I am not saying we should dismantle it, just slow it down. We don't need martyrs now; we need quiet, diligent, inconspicuous workers: bridge-builders.'

94

Cold- and heat-waves were passing each other along my spine. Why me? 'What's he got to do with it?'

'Tony? Sweet skylark, he is the bearer of the news.'

'His name is Anton and he runs a misinformation factory.'

'I should have said one of the bearers. I am not a meathead. It trickles through all channels. And you're not being fair to Tony; he's got to appear as filthy as they come in order to do some clean work for us. *With* us. He's been testing you and found that you're much stronger than you think you are. Well-liked, yet nobody's fool, emotional yet practically incorruptible. And you can keep your secrets to yourself.'

'Amen,' muttered Anton. 'She learns from her mistakes – a rare accomplishment.'

'So what do you say, my favourite sparrow?'

'What do I say to what?'

'To working for a real historical chance instead of a series of ephemera. You have courage; your heart may be too big for such a small body, but you have a good head on your shoulders. You never say much – that's to your credit, or has been so far. I'll do most of the talking, but I'll need you to back me up, in both words and deeds. We'll have to start with a little white lie, I am afraid. You see, Marek and Karol were taken down to the police headquarters. Professor K., thanks to Tony, was merely prevented from leaving his house. Tony went to your flat, but you were already gone; so you'll have to say, more or less truthfully, that you got picked up after having made it to Arnold's. I nearly made it – I got nicked on the corner of Ponds Road. They kept me in the car and then drove us away together. It's authentic enough. And don't worry, they'll all be free by the time we get back to town.'

'How does Dagmar fit into all this?'

'Dagmar?' Vlado looked blank.

'She ... does not,' hiccupped Anton. 'She's the cat walking by himself. Herself. Rudyard Kipling. Isn't she lovely? She makes a lovely scapegoat. Everybody thinks she is the tipper off-er. As it is, I tip her off. She thinks I am a cute bastard. Am I cute?'

'You're drunk. You'll need that blasted coffee after all.' Vlado clearly dismissed Dagmar as a side-track issue; he ruffled Anton's hair with chummy kindness. His own breath still smelled of mint, in the teeth of all those bottles on the table; I found it amazing, and profoundly disquieting.

'Keep the glass out of the man's reach,' ordered Vlado, 'or vice versa, while I slay the dragon to make her surrender a mug of her strong vile brew. If I can find the kitchen.'

With Vlado gone, Anton appeared remarkably less drunk, almost sober. His handsome head tilted towards mine. 'Beware, my friend. You're now knee-deep in the quicksand; don't try to wriggle out on your own, you'd only sink. This is a dangerous game and a sensitive person like you may get hurt – on the other hand, the odds are not entirely against us and the rewards could be high. I remember telling you before that I am not a cynic; I like power, true, but I like it to be intelligent, enlightened and progressive, not torpid and tyrannical. I suspect I've never been really young – I never toyed with anarchy, always believed in organization and firm control. But then I met – inevitably – the Major Fischer types, both the full-scale animals and the embryos, and realized that these ineffectual brutes can only breed more dissent in a modern society. They won't retire, they'll have to be pushed off the stage; I'll do nearly anything to see them go, even siding with you lot.'

He blew me a kiss and I instinctively jerked my head aside to avoid it.

Anton winced. 'Come, come, don't scorn a genuine affection! I may flirt with Dagmar, but I am not flirting with you. People don't, do they? Listen, tell me, how do you get on with women?'

'Not famously.' The man always drew words out of my mouth, as if he knew where the tap was.

'I thought not.'

'It's not that I have anything against women. They usually have something against me. I don't know why – I don't compete.'

'That's why. They must be very suspicious of you. I am – sometimes. You are a rather suspect creature, you know. You're so silent – or are you? Maybe you're sly. You don't get on famously with women, yet you set up a household with—'

'*Don't!*' I snapped so hard that my teeth clicked audibly. It made me laugh. The whole affair was laughable if not merry, a pretentious farce complete with medieval props – melting candles, spilt wine, abandoned food, dying fire, Mephistopheles turned Faust.

I opened my second bottle of beer and took a hearty pull, relishing the strong bitter taste, the tingle of the froth around the mouth. I borrowed Norma's husky 'reading' voice – it scratched my throat comfortingly: 'I don't really know what this is all about. I can't see what good can come out of you siding with us – or rather with Vlado – forfeiting your policeman's soul. I don't understand why you or Vlado have chosen me to play the game; I am terribly bad at games. I am not cut out to be a winner – but I also make a very bad victim. Oh, I can be pushed all right, but there comes a certain point from which I bounce back. I think that point's coming up right now. I am walking out of here; I am not afraid of the dark and a long march can only do me good. I shan't do anything to discredit Vlado; I used to love him and I am faithful, so whatever story he chooses to tell about what happened this afternoon, I won't dispute it. I'll keep mum, but I shan't actively lie. As for the committee – if what Vlado says is true, if there is a good wind blowing, then I am sure that people will only be eager to discuss it in all earnest, and see for themselves whether or not different tactics and strategies are required. I'll be eager to discuss it – any which way but this. I don't know what role you've devised for me, and I do not wish to know. You tell him I am going and don't bother to leave any more stupid letters at my door step: I won't read them.'

I snatched my coat and ran for the door, expecting Anton to have a grab at me; he didn't move. 'Beware of the quicksand,' was all he said, in a quiet mildly amused voice.

I zigzagged between the tables in the dark dining room, bruising both thighs. It was much lighter outside, white clouds cruised under the black sky and the snow gave out enough pale glow for the feet to be placed safely on the road. I looked back only once, just in time to see – in the brightly lit window of what must have been the kitchen of the Wild Rock restaurant – Vlado kissing a plump, yielding redhead. He had slain the dragon all right.

The car caught up with me after I had walked about a mile and reached the gorge; I hid behind a loose boulder and watched it pass. Then I scrambled up a ravine, found a rambler's path I'd walked along many a summer and plodded toward the main road, carefully avoiding looking down the sheer rocks. I'd never suffered from vertigo, not particularly, but tonight my balance was... felt... precarious.

Finally there was a ploughed field, its soil frozen and solid under the feet; I whistled with relief, ran, tripped over a clod and fell, bruising a knee, an elbow, a cheek. I wasn't in a weeping mood – I laughed my way out of the pain, waking up a flock of carrion crows roosting on a nearby tree. Life, I thought, life!

The first three cars I thumbed didn't stop; the fourth had Anton for a driver and Vlado for a passenger.

'What took you so long?' asked Anton. 'We've been cruising here for an hour!'

Vlado opened the door and pulled me in unceremoniously. His breath smelled of brandy and his hands were hot. I huddled by his side, my head in his armpit, and dozed off almost immediately. I had a brief dream about being a trooper in a marching army, the last in a line, pulling a rope at the end of which was a hee-hawing donkey – now visible, now lost in a rolling mist. A drum was beating; the beat was irregular and miserably slow, yet somehow the whole dim affair was steeped in hope – I awoke refreshed and chirpy just as the car pulled up in a short, unlit street by the embankment.

'See you,' Anton said curtly and drove off in a whirl of mist that might have come straight from my dream.

Vlado sighed. 'You've upset the man. He was worried about you.'

'But you were not.'

'Of course not. I know what a trooper you are.'

'You don't see a donkey anywhere, do you?'

'Are you calling me an ass? Listen, ruffled feathers, let me explain. The whole idea with Tony is quite simple: he'll tell us as much as he knows about the police actions and intentions so that we can minimize the risk of raids, and we – that is you and I – will—'

'No. Don't! I don't want to know more than I do already. I am not playing. I am sorry, officer, you've picked the wrong trooper. A sissy.'

'I have not. But I've picked the wrong psychology. I'll revise my approach and talk to you soon. Maybe later tonight, after closing time.'

'I don't feel like going to a pub, Vlado. The Wild Rock was quite enough for me, thank you.'

'Have you forgotten? Or has Robert forgotten to tell you? If things went wrong, we were supposed to try and assemble in Café Bohemia, the whole committee. Things did, didn't they, and that's where you and I are going. You promised to back up my story and it's the least you can do, my little parrot: be my little parrot.'

'All right, I'll give it fifteen minutes over one cup of coffee. But I won't be your little parrot. A mute swan, more likely, the dwarfed variety.'

My joys were few and far between, but they hit the heart straight on, like a sudden splash of cool dancing water on a hot day. The first thing I saw behind the pane of Café Bohemia's panoramic corner window was the halo of Norma's hair next to Marta's sleek black waves and Karol's mop. Professor K., wearing dark glasses, impassive but for a benign curl of the lip, presided over the bobbing heads as a godfather over a family mob. Anna had on her broad-brimmed purple hat, adding a touch of festive glamour to the occasion.

Vlado and I hurried towards the entrance, the harsh cold wind from the river in our backs. In the light of the vestibule, I saw that his face was set in preoccupied, purposeful, optimistic lines: once a comrade, I thought, always a comrade. It ceased to worry me.

They had pushed three tables together and were feeding on open sandwiches off a huge glass plate.

'Have one,' said Norma magnanimously, with the tiniest twinkle in her eye. 'It's real Hungarian salami. You-know-who got it for us; he sent men to bring it from Hungary.'

'No thanks. I've eaten.' Oh heck.

'Where?' Marta was instantly suspicious.

I looked her straight in the face. 'I feasted on Bohemian deer in the Wild Rock restaurant.'

'It's closed in winter,' drawled Marta, disappointed. Everybody thought I had made a hilarious joke. Amidst peals and snorts of laughter, Marek – who liked code-names for everything – proposed we should call the police headquarters the Wild Rock restaurant from now on. Between them, Arnold and Dr Florian delivered an ad hoc disputation on the colloquialisms of *rock*. It would seem, they concluded, that we must be off our *rockers* trying – in a *rock*-bottom situation – to *rock* the boat. They were about to do the same with *wild*, when Vlado cleared his throat loudly. Being a sensitive bunch of people, they all looked at him expectantly.

'The question is,' he said in a low urgent voice, 'do we want to rock the boat just now?'

Marek's eyes narrowed. 'If you're hinting at certain whiffs about certain let-ups . . . warm easterly winds blowing across the steppes . . . brother, if that proves true, let's rock, and how!'

'Shut up shop,' murmured Anna. 'We've had enough for one day. This place is full of ears and eyes. I want to sleep in my own bed tonight.'

Instinctively we had moved closer together, shoulder to shoulder, buttock to buttock. Professor K. lifted his white well-groomed hand. 'Dear chaps – ladies – I don't know what this little exchange was all about, but I can work out the conflicts behind it. It smells urgent and important. However, even if history moves fast these days, it doesn't move all that fast. Moreover, we don't want to project ourselves in this old-fashioned pleasant haven as a nest of conspirators. Let me remind you that over the years we have cultivated an art of communication quite rare in this electronic age, namely

100

that of correspondence, the written discourse, the ... round robin. I suggest that the two contenders do us one each, so that – when we are in private surroundings – we can discuss the subject at length, and well-prepared. But now let us sit back and indulge in the art of witty converstion, a rare treat at any time.'

Norma tittered prettily and clapped her hands. 'I like you. I know who you are. You are my Uncle Herman's teacher. Uncle Herman loves his teacher very much.'

'*Beata simplicitas*,' sighed young Father Ignat and blushed. 'I didn't mean it as a witticism.'

'Okay, professor,' grinned Vlado. 'That's fine with me. I'll jot down a little analysis when I get home, though some things I'll have to leave a bit vague – until we talk, that is.'

Marek stood up. 'You people may go on enjoying civilization, but it's another night in the wilds for me. The stokehole's calling.' He turned to Vlado. 'I'll expect the robin to hop in by tomorrow afternoon – I'll hatch one myself after I've heard it sing.' He smacked a quick little kiss on Vera's forehead.

'He tries,' said Vera wistfully. 'Sometimes he is almost human. What happened to your cheek?'

'I tripped and fell. Cross my heart!' I added hastily. 'You should see my knee.'

'Too true,' nodded Vlado. 'The knee's much worse. She walks too fast and would not take a man's arm.'

Zoe took it up in terms of male chauvinism and soon the talk began to flow – now smooth, now sharpish – just like the tangy black coffee which, according to Professor K., in Café Bohemia has retained some of the pre-war quality long lost elsewhere. In the mornings, the café overlooking the river belonged to students and artists; in the afternoons, it was full of behatted old ladies nibbling on a piece of cream cake; at night, it turned into a smoke-filled den visited by shadier characters – old ballet-dancers, speculators, adulterers, writers, has-beens. Anyone out on the street, passing by the panoramic window, could have taken us for any of these, wondering perhaps what were we so merry about. Or thinking what lucky sods we were: the blasted Christmas approaching, we didn't seem to give a damn. Only Karol's brows were knitted together in a fierce frown throughout the evening.

The two secret policemen who sat some four tables further down the room looked bored to tears.

'Wake up, lazybones!' I pinched Norma's big toe. 'It's your turn to make the coffee. Make it tea, will you? I don't think I can stand another coffee for a month. You did enjoy yourself last night, didn't you?'

Norma's head vanished under the sheet for a second – she bit my little toe.

'There! That's for breaking my dream. It was lovely; it was all about apples. I was in a castle and the apples just came rolling in through a tall door, millions of them, all over the shiny floor. I never ate any, because of you.'

'I'll buy you a bushel today.'

Norma whinnied. 'I made it up, silly. It was a stupid dream, so I didn't want you to know. I forget now.'

'I'll buy you a pound then.'

'I want to do the shopping. I have a better head for it than you do.'

'All right, all right. Just remember to buy some apples – you've made my mouth water with your dream, true or false.'

'I lied. I didn't forget. D'you want to hear about the dream?'

"If it's not too long. I am dying for tea.'

'It's short, but maybe you shouldn't want to hear.'

'Okay, I don't.'

'I was in a castle, but you were in the clink. I had a snake in my pocket, with a little crown on his head, so I sent him to bring you home. He did it, but you were dead. I didn't want you dead.'

Last night, when we came home from Café Bohemia, I'd read Saint-Exupéry's *Le Petit Prince* to her; she had insisted that the snake returned the prince to his little planet alive and well. Death has caught up with her overnight.

'Sweetheart, you and I are only thirty-three. We shall live for a long time yet.'

'I don't mind about you being dead. I mind about me not wanting you dead. I shooed him away, I told the stupid snake to drop you back in the clink. It was very bad of me. He gave me an apple, but I couldn't eat it. I thought that you wouldn't want to love me any more.'

'And so I won't if you don't make the tea right now.'

'I am afraid of dead people. Uncle Herman always used to bring them around.'

'But he doesn't now, does he?'

'No, he doesn't want to scare you. He likes you. But he thinks that perhaps you don't like me so much.'

'Stuff Uncle Herman! Besides, he is lying through his teeth. Not only does he know I love you, he knows very well I wouldn't know how to live without you. All right, you have a lie-in and I'll make the tea. And if you've made all this up just to get me out into that freezing morgue of a kitchen, I don't want to know.'

Norma shrieked with laughter, but there was a deep sea of worry in each of her eyes.

The days that passed between then and the twenty-second of December were just as I'd promised Dr Burda they would be: simply a life, and fairly quiet. The snow fell every day in measured, well-behaved quantities, covering up most of the shabbiness and some of the raw places, yet creating neither chaos nor special opportunities. Events, accidents, bickerings and celebrations took place, but in bearable numbers and a manageable manner.

The peripatetic university attracted mainly the school-banned offspring of the dissidents, with a few courageous 'real' students thrown in for cheers; apart from Father Ignat's Latin class which Dagmar housed in her apartment, none of the lectures and seminars were raided – a noticeable progress compared with a similar attempt some years before when the police had hounded the participants to exhaustion. Dagmar, of course, wasn't at home at the time, and there was some more tittle-tattle as to her credentials, but nothing serious, especially as one week later the Latin class too was left in peace.

Arnold's interview in *Le Monde* was a great success; even Vlado was happy about it, for it was erudite yet accessible, articulate yet tolerant, philosophically sharp yet politically vague. It was followed by an hours-long but not particularly nasty interrogation, from which Arnold emerged with a huge headache yet otherwise unharmed. He started a passionate if platonic love affair with Zoe, to the great sorrow of young Robert who felt that it was unfair competition and told everybody so. Zoe came to supper, which Norma insisted on cooking, and bravely polished it off – earning my admiration and Norma's devotion – and spent the evening pondering whether or not she should commit herself all the way to a relationship with a man who is a worldwide celebrity and a Narcissus if she ever saw one. Which meant that I had to climb to the top shelf for Greek mythology and read the story of Narcissus and the nymphs to Norma at bed-time. She said it served him right.

Anna broke her right arm slipping on a patch of ice and drove everybody crazy by dictating whole chapters of her new novel to them. Anna was a writer, and we all agreed she was one of the best, until we had to take down her latest effusions. But Rohwolt and potentially even Gallimard and Penguin, not to mention the samizdat readers including my kind employer in Foreign Trade, were waiting impatiently, so who were we to grumble? I promised to type it all up, but then I had a vested interest, hoping to get a foreign translation contract or two. I liked Anna – on the whole – but Norma could only find fault with her. I read better than she writes, she said, and there were times when I felt inclined to agree.

Speaking of my kind employer in Foreign Trade... I finished both the French and the German version of the *New Revolutionary West-Bohemian Hop-Harvester* five days before Christmas and she paid me handsomely and instantly, overcoming considerable resistance from the morose cashier struck with a pre-Christmas malaise. I slipped her Professor K.'s vastly amusing *Fictional History of Bohemia* signed by the author as all samizdats, and she slipped something into my pocket – it turned out to be a US fifty dollar note. Norma and I were rich beyond all expectations, and we were all set to meet my cousins in the village of Broumy in style: a letter had arrived inviting me – and 'partner if any' to spend Christmas with my 'loving family'. Loving family?

Speaking of money – it was trickling in from all corners. Members of the committee received at least a couple of envelopes every day, without or with a covering letter, unsigned or signed. Here is a little something, keep the good work going, get yourself a decent meal, get us a good read, get your kids a Christmas present, get on with it. Vera and Father Ignat agreed to be co-treasurers of the unexpected fund which was, of course, a blessing, as it meant that more typewriters could be purchased and financial support provided for the most hard-up families. Vera even bought a second-hand automatic washing machine for one of our dedicated typists who had three small children and a useless husband.

Dr Florian's fiftieth birthday was the celebration of the season, complete with live rock music, visual arts, declamations and famous monologues performed by Vlado and Kristina – who had hitherto been a recluse, after a lifetime of theatrical stardom. We all travelled to an empty boathouse – formerly a barn – by the Lake, not far from New Village; Norma was delighted and quite high, though she wouldn't, or couldn't tell me what exactly New Village had meant to her. There were two barrels of beer – plus whatever people brought and about fifty guests whose combined breath was the main source of heat. Around midnight, the police arrived in God-knows-how-many vehicles, surrounded the barn and hailed us to disperse, using several loudspeakers and powerful searchlights. By that time, however, everybody's courage had been heightened by the arts, the drinks and the communal spirit; we simply went on dancing and the police gave up on us. In the morning, hung-over and fretfully sober, many people claimed that it must have been a collective hallucination, until someone found a truncheon on the beach with a police number on it and gave it to Dr Florian as a belated birthday present. The best he'd ever had, he declared, and we believed him.

105

As expected, the main continuing event was the saga of the round robins. There were three of them – one by Vlado, one by Marek written as a response to Vlado's, and one by Karol tearing them both apart. Many more were announced to be hatching, so the strategic meeting kept getting postponed until the last and ultimate date was set – six o'clock on New Year's Eve, the time when even the political police were likely to take a night off. I was toying with the idea of writing a briefish discourse myself, but soon abandoned it; I was too happy to have been left more or less alone though Vlado – trying out his new psychological approach – dropped in every other day between his rounds for a cup of tea laced with brandy. Norma loved it; she often sat on Vlado's knee while he lectured on the practicalities and impracticalities of politics in our part of the world. Marek was quite wrong, he said, if he thought that we could agitate amongst the factory workers and persuade them to take up arms, however metaphorically. They knew by now that change, if any, must come from the top, otherwise there would only be bloodshed and/or a deep plunge into yet more disappointment. Besides, though the workers weren't happy with the way things were going, they weren't hungry; in fact, they made quite an easy living and would not jeopardize it for some voice calling in the wilderness. Marek's demand for radicalization would not speed things up, it would hinder them; but at least he was a socialist, which to a degree meant being a deep-down realist, in our part of the world. Karol, of course, was quite a different cup of sorrows; by rejecting the system completely, in whatever mode, he has shown himself as an idealist but of a dangerous kind; he was, if you read him properly, calling upon the people's lowest and readiest instinct – that of revenge. On the whole, however, Vlado was contented and praised Professor K. for suggesting a written discussion which, in our part of the world, was bound to take weeks if not months and prevent any rash actions. In the meantime, our own top comrades were seething with trepidation at what was happening in the big brother's house; the hidden reformists amongst them had already begun to send out feelers seeking new alliances in the moderate opposition. The

106

only feasible road forward, said Vlado, was that of social and political reconciliation, but the way things were, some underhand manipulation to that effect would be needed, and some peculiar affiliations. Actually, it was nothing new – it has happened many times in history, one way or the other. Neither he nor Tony was going to hurry me and push me into doing things I wasn't ready for – they've made a mistake here – they just wanted me to know that the time might come when I would be needed as an active element or at least as a witness.

Gossip had it that Vlado and I were back in bed together, or about to be; a threesome, as far as I could tell, has not been suspected. Norma went 'on the town' a few times and I had massive problems with this; I even sought advice from old Joseph at the Three Bears. He told me off rather severely: who was I to judge?! I wasn't judging, I protested, just worried. Same thing, he said, it implied superiority on one side, inferiority on the other; couldn't I just enjoy happiness while it lasted? Was a bit of simple generosity too much to give in exchange? He had me shamed; but he also promised to keep an eye on things and give me a ring if anything went wrong – which, in this mean world, could not be entirely ruled out even with such blessed innocent creatures as Norma.

That certainly had been an event: two days after the Wild Rock adventure, our telephones – dead for five years – came alive! I was having a bath when mine rang and at first I didn't know what the sound was. Norma would not pick it up; dripping wet as I was, I lifted the receiver with an unbelieving hand. 'Hi, beautiful,' said Anton's voice, 'this is your friendly neighbourhood watchman calling: welcome back to modern civilization; use it in moderation, if you know what I mean; don't call us, we'll call you.'

I would have much rather gone on without the phone, it felt like having an intruder in the house, but Norma soon learned to draw amusement from it. She'd dial for today's recipe; the weather; she'd listen for long minutes to the golden voice speaking the time; but it was the daily bedtime story she liked most. I loved watching her when she listened to it; it passed across her face in soft waves, like a breeze across a field of young corn. She'd then tell it to me, greatly embellished, full of twists and verbal pirouettes that would have made every storyteller's mouth water. Eventually, she came round to answering its ring: 'Norma here,' she'd say, 'what d'you want?'

In the afternoon of December the twenty-second, just after dusk, Norma went to bed with pre-menstrual pain and a hot-water bottle, while I walked to Café Bohemia for a pre-Christmas round of coffee and cakes. For no apparent reason, I was jumped on in the street by two plain-clothes men, bundled into a car, blindfolded, manacled and – judging by the sound and time of it – driven some twenty miles out of the city. I was then led across a snow-crisp squeaky yard into a hollow-sounding building and an overheated room. The blindfold removed, I found myself face to face with Major Fischer. He sent the men away and bade me sit down on a straight-backed chair without ridding me of the handcuffs. My arms, folded awkwardly behind my back, hurt already.

'Well, well, well, look who's here,' he mused and hit me across the face with the back of his hand. It wasn't an unbearable blow, just hard enough to make my nose bleed. The blood trickled warmly and stupidly down my lips and chin, making me feel undignified, like a child with a heavily running snout. I wasn't ready for this, it didn't make sense; I began to shake with a desperate, uncontrollable fear, my knees jumped up and down and my feet thumped the floor.

This pleased Major Fischer no end. 'Look at the scared little rabbit,' he told the four blank walls. 'We'll soon have her shitting out the truth.'

The truth about what? I nearly asked, but bit my tongue just in time with all the tooth I could muster; it tasted of a better, angrier blood. When I saw his hand poised for another blow, I stopped shaking. He hit me still but with much less relish, or so I imagined; then he went to sit behind a desk with nothing but a single typed sheet on it.

108

He tapped this with his stout forefinger. 'This, Miss Brave-Pants, will cook your goose. It's inflammatory, seditious and libellous. We can prove it's been done on your typewriter, so you'd better tell me all I want to know. Save your neck.'

From what I could see of the text, it could have been typed on my old machine, though I certainly never did it – the margins and paragraphs were not in my style. I tried to summon my wits, at least some intelligence, but all I could really concentrate on was my physical appearance: the nose that had stopped bleeding but felt as if it was swelling up, the blood caking on my upper lip, chin and neck, the armless torso with the bust sticking out of the half-open coat on which two buttons were freshly missing. The sweat: I could picture it gathering all over my skin.

'Dear fellow citizens,' the Major read with a snarl, 'let this Christmas be a spiritual preparation for a time of reckoning and hope. There are signs that the evil empire is crumbling at its very core. The bolshevik leaders are reaching for the old promise and last resort of "democratic reforms". In our beloved country, many lesser comrades in the official structures, including the police force, are giving out signals that they wish to reconcile the party with the people whom they have betrayed. Let us wait and see how far they are prepared to go; let them open the gates for us, and then let us stand up as one man and take over the factories, the farms, the town halls like the true rulers of the country that we are. We can afford to wait – what we cannot afford is not to exercise our human and civil rights when the time is ripe. Be with us, who are with you. True members of the citizens committee.' He pushed the sheet aside queasily and lit a cigar. 'That's easily ten years, Miss True Member. I'll give you five minutes for a think.'

Pulling a half-empty bottle of vodka out of a drawer, he swivelled the chair around; I gazed at his broad muscular back and wondered what a swig or two of vodka would bring.

By and by, in an almost absolute silence indicating that we were either in a village or somewhere yet more remote, I forced myself to think. The text was clearly a fabrication though fairly cleverly done, using authentic Karol's, Vlado's and Marek's words in wrong contexts. It wouldn't fool any of us, but Mrs H. the caretaker and thousands like her would lap it up – it certainly wasn't 'neither here not there'. It implied that there were 'true' and 'untrue' members in the committee, leaving open to speculation who was who. The more I stared at the typescript, the more I was convinced that it was a product of my typewriter. Ugly thoughts began to swirl in my head; I could feel awkward suspicious glances on my burning cheeks, small whispers and little silences, and my own helpless tears. Why didn't I have that chain fixed to my door? Because Norma was all the safety I wished for, that's why. Because I still was a conceited unthinking brat, who – contrary to what Anton had said – never learned from her mistakes. But why would Anton . . .?

'So.' Major Fischer was facing me again. His face was redder and his fist was clenched. 'I'll say one thing for you, Miss Skinny . . . you don't whimper. Makes me want to make you – even though I am impressed. So be a Miss Smart and answer the question: what does "including the police force" mean? Have some of my "lesser comrades" become traitors? You know many of them, don't you; especially one? I never liked that two zero two: too dressy. Give me a clincher on him and I'll let you go scot-free. Like this.' He tore the sheet in half and then placed the pieces neatly together again. 'For all I know, he could have written this himself, the young Jesuit. Let me re-phrase it: would you say that – from your experience – he could have written this himself?'

Yes, I wanted to say. Why not? He likes this sort of thing. He succeeded in making you nervous, did he not? Never mind that it is my skin that gets burnt; I am standing in a pool of quicksand anyway, or so he believes. It could well be that had the question been put by anyone else but Major Fischer, I would have nodded in affirmation – I'll never know.

'Don't try my patience, Miss Bloody Nose.'

Anger, my blessed companion in times of dire fright, came to sit on my shoulder. My arms and hands were numb, the caked skin under my nose itched maddeningly, but I felt

110

fortified. Let them thrash it out in their own house: I wasn't going to be a weapon for either of them. Besides, one more blow or two and he'd have to let me go. He wouldn't have had me dragged out here if he were about to charge me with anything. Stupid, preposterous brute! I gave him a full blazing look, daring him to get it over with.

But the Major merely went to the door and called for a glass of water. The two men came in, one unlocked the handcuffs and the other held the glass to my lips, knowing well that my hands were usless. It had been so hot in the room; I drank greedily, forgetting – once again – to learn from my past mistakes. A glass of water had always meant trouble, one way or another.

Soon, I felt an urgent need to tell Major Fischer what I thought of him. But what I thought of him was too strange for words: I pictured him as the father of difficult contemptuous teenagers and the husband of an ailing, nagging wife. I felt enormously sorry for him.

'Don't worry, Major,' I mumbled. 'They won't scold you. They know I never talk. I can't, see, because if I do, I blab. Blab-blab-blab, like that. There is nothing to talk about anyway. I keep my nose clean.' I giggled and tried to rub off the dried blood, but my fingers were too soft. 'Listen, things have to get better. People are born free. Ouch, that sounds terrible. I mean they are not farm animals, you have to feed their spirits as well as the body. Or the spirit gets hungry and gobbles you up in the end. And that's that, Major, let's go home. How's your wife these days?'

Somebody shook me, somebody cursed, somebody else said that doctors were bloody charlatans and I was a tough bitch. After a long while, the fog cleared and I had a sudden vivid vision of Dr Burda and Anton bending over a game of chess by a tall barred window behind which the night sparkled like a black diamond.

I overestimated them. They were, in fact, playing checkers. It took me a while to accept the reality of it. The walls were white, the plants were poorly and the narrow bed I lay on had a hospital feel. I was in the city's lunatic asylum above the zoo, in Dr Burda's spacious office.

'Hello, gaolers!' I joked feebly. My mouth felt hellishly dry, but I was determined not to ask for water.

'Ha ha,' said Anton without a smile. 'You don't know how lucky you are that it's Dr Burda's night. You'd be pinned to a bed in a ward if it weren't. Certified.'

'Nonsense!' Dr Burda was smiling. 'This isn't Russia. My colleagues would have let her sleep it off and sent her home in the morning. Unless, of course, they suspected she was an addict. But I would have known she was here sooner or later, and made it as short a stay as possible. Don't forget I have a tape which proves that she is crazy, but sane. And I'd like to see anybody try to bully me – anybody at all.'

There was a little square of plaster on my forearm. Dr Burda nodded. 'I just counteracted the drug. You should be feeling fit as a fiddle by now. Why did your nose bleed?'

'I bumped into a major.'

'Are you saying he beat you up?' The doctor appeared horrified.

'Never mind what she's saying.' Anton walked rapidly over to the bed and searched my eyes. 'Are you well enough to get up and let me drive you home? Your pet moron must be worried.'

I felt my nose – it did not seem swollen. 'How do I look to you?'

'You look just fine. I wouldn't call you pretty, but then that's not what you're about. Let me see you walk.'

I obeyed: apart from the monstrous thirst, there was nothing wrong with me. 'Let's go, I croaked.

'Better drink a glass of water first,' said Dr Burda. He sounded more than a little offended. I shuddered and shook my head rather violently. 'Oh, for God's sake, woman,' cried the doctor, 'don't you know by now who you can trust?!'

'I think she does,' grinned Anton, 'but I would not be surprised if she didn't. Thanks, doc, I enjoyed the game. Should anyone ask, say she's absconded and that you've spanked the nurse. But I doubt anyone would bother. My colleagues know how to cut their loses. We must dash – don't take offence. The less you know, the better for you. Cheerio!'

'And just how do you propose to get out of here?' asked Dr Burda, mollified. He walked us down the stairs and unlocked the door for us. 'Buy her a beer then – she needs a drink. One pint, mind, and no more, or she'll up and dance on the table. The pub by the zoo should still be open. If they grumble, just mention my name. Doctor's orders!'

He bowed quickly and kissed my hand. 'Ouch,' I said, and meant it.

'You're not fair to the man,' protested Anton as we drove through the gate. 'The moment the chaps who brought you in cleared out, he phoned Dagmar. You owe her one too – she phoned me. Did it... the glass of water... make you talk? What did Fischer want to know? It was him, wasn't it? Where there is a nosebleed there is Major Fischer. You have to tell me, you know.'

'Why?'

But when I was in the middle of the pint, I told him all I could remember, down to the two buttons missing on my coat. They must have got torn off as they bundled me into the car. I felt much better when I had finished the story. That's what it felt like – a story, something which happened to somebody else. I did not even want to know whether or not Anton had written the fake committee statement. He wasn't telling, and that was fine with me. Everything was fine with me.

'Can't you get out of town for a while? Have a nice holiday somewhere with your pet?'

'Maybe.' I wasn't telling. 'Her name is Norma and you'd greatly oblige me if you called her just that.'

'Golly,' sighed Anton. 'I'd like to have a friend like you. Won't you at least give me a chance?'

'Sure,' I said. 'Why not?'

Back home, Norma thought I'd had one too many and fussed and fretted me to bed, like a drunkard's loving wife.

On December the twenty-third, we went to a hard-currency shop on the boulevard and squandered the fifty-dollar note on coupons that bought us instant coffee, boxes of chocolates, West German washing powder and fancy booze – all presents for my loving family. For ourselves, we bought a carton of Gitanes and a pound of dark coffee-beans from Brazil. We still had one coupon left: I spent it on a packet of chewing gum – as many flavours as there are colours on the rainbow, it said – for Norma. This isn't for Christmas, I said, pressing the packet into her hand; it's for that night when you gave me your last gum after I threw up, remember? But that was ages ago, she protested, I forgot. And then she whinnied and kissed me on the mouth, in front of the grumpy pushing queue. Merry Christmas to you all, I shouted, but nobody had the heart left to answer in kind.

In the afternoon, we bought a tiny tree from a street vendor who spread his thinning merchandise next to the vast wooden tub alive with fat carp thrashing about in agony. A huge fishmonger was selling them alive, or hammered and decapitated on the spot. Norma wanted to watch, but I dragged her away. You don't like dead people, I said, and I don't like watching things killed. But you eat sausage, observed Norma; you're funny, Funny; in giggles and arm in arm, we hurried through the frenzied streets towards Café Bohemia. Large pretty snowflakes floated in the air and laced shoulders and sleeves, but nobody, not even children, paused to admire them.

The Café was half-empty. At the usual table, there was only Dagmar engaged in an intimate conversation with Arnold. Pity you couldn't have come yesterday, said Arnold, we've had such a jolly time over the cakes! You two girls wouldn't mind sitting elsewhere for a while, would you? asked Dagmar. Arnold and I are discussing our respective sexual lives, she said.

'I don't like her,' whispered Norma when we'd seated ourselves at a small table in a corner. 'I think she's Uncle Herman's second wife, the one who read too much. Uncle Herman hates her too.'

Later, Robert walked in with Professor K. – whose face was fresh as a daisy but whose feet shuffled heavily – and we all sat at one table again. The conversation was rather flimsy

114

and melancholy until eventually I realized that Dagmar had not spread the news, that my ordeal of yesterday had passed unnoticed. Was she waiting for me to tell? How would I start? That is – where would I start? I longed for Vlado to join us, but time passed, Norma was getting fidgety, darkness fell and the lamps glared, and still there wasn't a sign of him. For an awesome minute, I actually felt the quicksand mounting up my thighs. Then Norma tugged at my sleeve again and I stood up resolutely, wished everybody a Merry Christmas and announced that Norma and I would be out of town for a few days – all that time waiting for some reaction from Dagmar, or somebody. None came, apart from the usual Christmas utterances and a whispered reminder of the New Year's Eve committee meeting.

Back home in Barley Street, Norma and I decorated the tree, lit a few candles and took turns in reading each other stories, a whole glorious batch of them, deep into the night.

I was learning to be happy and unhappy at the same time. Life!

We got up early on Christmas Eve, for we had a bus to catch. Norma asked the telephone what the weather was going to be like and then, as was her custom, opened the window to check. I saw her back stiffen. There are two dead men down there, come and have a look, she whispered. Apart from a ghastly pallor caused by the electric light, the men were very much alive, as was the driver of the black car – the same that had delivered me into Major Fischer's twitchy arms.

I ran downstairs and knocked softly on the caretaker's door. Mrs H., her mahogany-dyed hair on a hundred rollers, must have been up and waiting for me. She pressed her mouth against my ear: the men had been outside the house since five o'clock, she said, shame on them – so obvious, too. The back-door key was mine to keep, she insisted, shoving it into my pocket, but I wasn't to tell Rudi, as he was the one responsible for the back yard and a bit of a coward. What a piece of luck it was that she'd had a spare key he knew nothing about! Merry Christmas – and the same to you: she closed the door as noiselessly as if she didn't want to disturb a single spider sleeping in its cobweb.

Thus it happened that Norma and I caught the bus to the village of Broumy with only as much ado as was consistent with climbing over a few walls and fences dividing the crammed shabby back yards of the tenements. Three hours later, we alighted on the village green and were immediately surrounded by a mob of children, some of whom must have been my nephews and nieces, if somewhat removed.

They grabbed Norma's hands and set forth, leaving me behind to carry the two huge bags filled mostly with the hard-currency goodies. Bliss, pure as the village snow and rich as the smell of dung that hung in the cold air, descended upon me: this promised to be easily the best Christmas I had ever known.

Shush, I whispered down my chest, there is no reason why there shouldn't be a happy end to most tribulations.

IV

Christmas Eve was a big, panting affair in seven houses and under seven trees, each surrounded by a cloud of frenzied children. We had butterbrots and schnapps with my old aunt and youngest cousin, still a bachelor. For the traditional fish soup and fried carp with potato salad, we all moved to the house of my eldest cousin and his wife. But we also had blue-stewed carp in prune sauce; Viennese schnitzels; jellied eels; apple strudel; and – near midnight and at the southern edge of the village – a huge chocolate cake topped with whipped cream and cherries.

We were all sentimental and faintly religious at first, then giggly, boisterous and song-happy. Norma and the hard-currency presents went down extremely well and I was much marvelled at though nobody would say why. Shedding the children on the way, we returned to my youngest cousin's house – new and big enough to receive a bride – and stuffed ourselves silly on home-made Christmas biscuits and potent rum punch. We skipped the midnight mass which would have meant a trek to Kablov, a hamlet two miles to the north, and some nasty looks from the local member of the National Security Corps, Constable Pepan, whose mother – to his despair – was known to be a bigoted Catholic and a secret candle-lighter in that dreary little church.

Finally, all throats went hoarse and all eyes glassy. Norma and I were put up for the night in the attic of the new house, furnished in a bewildering Italianate style, where we soon fell asleep holding hands between our separate heavy-feathered beds.

'Your cousins are rich,' whispered Norma in the morning. 'My Uncle Herman is rich too, but he doesn't have so many houses and so many things to cook. Are you very happy? Do you love them very much?'

'I don't know.'

'But you are happy?'

'I am happy because you are here with me. I am happy because they love you.'

Norma giggled. 'That's because they know my Uncle Herman.' She mimicked my old aunt's croaking voice: '"Herman D. was a fine man. Pity he didn't live to see you all grown-up and strong. You may not be very clever but you sure are pretty."'

'You're making it up.'

'I am not, silly. She wants me to marry your cousin, but I don't like him very much. He'll soon be bald all over.'

'Oh, stop it!'

She gave out a chortling whinny. 'Have you seen the presents? I unwrapped them because you slept and slept. We'll never go hungry now, and we can even give some to Uncle Herman's poor children.'

Piled up by the door on the floral carpet were jar upon jar of village delicacies: bilberry jam, raspberry preserve, apples in cloves, pears in schnapps; lard with pork scraps and caraway seed, goose-dripping with chopped liver, soft black pudding; pickled red cabbage, gherkins and sauerkraut. And there was a whole string of smoked sausages!

'Whoops!' I said. 'We'd better give a party when we come home. These have to be shared, and shared quickly.'

Norma clapped her hands. 'We won't invite Uncle Herman,' she decided. 'He hates to watch people eat.'

Christmas Day was full of sunshine: the sparkle of the snow and ice crucified our town-lazy eyes. We were sent to skate with the children on the Bay, equipped with fancy gear that the big boys had outgrown.

The Bay, a mile and a half east of the village, was really the uppermost part of the Lake, only nobody liked to call it by that name. Sweet-singing rapids and a profitable wood-rafting business lay buried under the manmade flood. Worse still, the old cemetery was there on the unfathomable bottom, the graves held under slabs of concrete.

There was a patch of weak ice in the middle of the Bay,

marked by flag-poles on which red flags were flapping in the smart wind. If you knelt by those and peered real hard, maintained the children, you could see the spire of the chapel swaying to and fro so deep below that it made your stomach feel funny, but only if there wasn't any snow on the ice – so there, tough luck.

I was a fairly accomplished skater but Norma was marvellous, like one of those circus-trained penguins, so wobbly and yet so skilful. If I live to be a hundred, I thought, I shall never forget this Christmas.

The Christmas Day lunch had nearly had me killed: there was a rich clear soup with home-made noodles, God knows how many roasted geese with their livers braised in wine on the side, fluffy dumplings, spiced tender cabbage, freshly baked apple strudel, draught beer, egg-flip, elderberry wine and a thousand and one home-made sweets. Norma liked the tiny mocca-balls the most – she'd take four at a time and wallow them about her mouth, to the delight of the small children who gathered around her like bees around a honeysuckle. We ate in the largest of the houses, that of my middle cousin and her sturdy husband who spoke little but laughed the most.

When the coffee arrived on the table, the women and children vanished as if by a stroke of a magic wand; I was left facing the seven-strong male crew of my family boat, unsailed for so long that I still had trouble putting the right name to the right face.

It looked like a serious situation; short gold-tipped cigars were slowly lit. After some doubt-swopping, I too was offered one. Many minutes ticked off at leisure before my cousins, and my cousins-in-law, spoke their minds.

'You were always a rum kid, you were. Far too clever for your own good.'

'Mother always said you ought to have been brought up in the family. Maybe it's a shame you're a townie, and maybe it isn't. Maybe we're proud of you, and maybe you don't really know what's what.'

'There are always two sides to everything. What ought to be, and what is.'

'Hey, remember the cockchafers? Cor, you screamed!'

119

'She kicked my last milk tooth in!'

'We shoved them bugs down her neckline, ages ago. In the fun days. I mean we were just kids behind the chimney corner.'

'What ought to be, is democracy. We could do with an agrarian party, for example. A people's agrarian party. We could do without the bolshevik bureaucrats taxing away whatever extra profit the cooperative makes. They are like hungry wolves, never satisfied. What is, well... it's not so bad. I guess it's worse in the town. Down here, we have Pepan who's stupid and thinks he's a general, the local bolshevik-committee members who come out on May Day and on Seventh November with their bearded saints on placards and their red flag—'

'But they are good at funerals. Sometimes they do a better funeral than the priest.'

'True. What they did for old Kroupa was lovely, and he wasn't much of a communist. Then we have the bolshevik-chairman of the cooperative who doesn't know potato from beetroot—'

'But he is a bloody good mechanic.'

'So he is. Our machine park is spic and span. Still, he is a lousy agronomist and the young wench we got straight from school is too shy. Don't tell me we couldn't have had much better crop yields last year if he didn't push all that barley. Ours is an oat and rye land.'

'It wasn't that bad. You've bought yourself new wheels.'

'Not just any old wheels. He's got a Mercedes.'

'Well, I like the feel of it. Where was I? Ah – the worst we've got down here is the chairman of the socialist youth organization. Now he is a swine! He is a sneak and a squealer, and cheats at cards. Just like his old man, it runs in the family. But the young bum is married to some big-shot's daughter from the district town and has pretty sneaky connections, so avoid him like the plague. His name is Ivan – the kids will tell you which one it is. But you'd know him; he walks about in a lambskin cap, Russian style. What I meant is that on the whole, it isn't too bad down here. It used to be worse.'

120

'All we had was one crummy house, remember?'

'Two. We had two crummy houses for the whole family. And there were years when we ate meat only in winter.'

'We still could have kept her with us. It was a shame that the old grandmother was so strict. Nobody would give a damn nowadays. So a woman who was forty and unmarried and not much to look at got herself laid for once, so what? She paid for it with her life, so why take it out on the brat?'

'Shut your big mouth! Like I said, there are two sides to everything: what ought to be, and what is.'

'Maybe it was for the better. Now we have a celebrity in the family.'

'Don't hold your head too high though, or you'll lose it.'

'We're proud of you, but keep it to yourself.'

'Maybe you want too much from people. People are people; they'll always lie and cheat.'

'What ought to be, is democracy. In a democracy, people don't need to lie and cheat. Or if they do, everybody can see it and say it out loud and do something about it. What is, well... maybe it's time to speak up for democracy. You townies can do it better than us peasants.'

'We have our hands up to the elbows in dung so that you can eat.'

'Mind you, watch what you say. There was a bloke on Radio Free Europe who said that the collectivization was a tragic mistake and that the farmers of Bohemia would like to go private again. Who was he kidding? The state farms may be shit, but the cooperative is the best invention since the plough. We work eight-hour shifts, we have regular holidays like everybody else and if you ask me, we're rich. Who'd like to go back to the old round-the-clock, round-the-year slavery?'

'Grandmother ought to hear you now. She fought the commissars with a pitchfork when they came for the cows.'

'Jesus, remember when she burned a whole field of rye and the orchard caught fire and we ate baked apples off a tree?'

'You did; I wasn't even born then. It's history. Frankly, I don't give a damn. What screws me up is that we do all the work and the comrades do all the talking. Who needs them? That's what you should be saying: who needs the comrades? People have good heads on their shoulders, they can do the talking for themselves! I am not saying hang the comrades on lamp-posts; I am saying shut their traps, get them off their fat prebends and make them work for a living. We don't want them down here, but the state farm in Kablov could use a few. I am not talking revolution, I am talking common sense and ordinary justice!'

'Don't listen to him, he's had too much to drink. It's quite enough what you're saying already in those papers of yours. We only hear it on the radio and it sounds a bit like preaching to me, but maybe some preaching is what people need.'

'What people need is to keep their ears to the ground. The earth speaks in plain words. Plain language is what you should speak, not fancy declamations.'

'Aren't you scared, little cousin? The bolsheviks can't like what you're doing! We only have Ivan and Pepan in the village, but the town must be crawling with dirty dicks. I am surprised you're still walking free.'

'If you go to jail, we'll send you food parcels. But don't expect more; we have families to look after.'

'If I was a single townie like you, I might well join. But it's not for a family man on the land.'

'What we wanted to say was that we're proud of you, and that you can always come down here for a bit of a holiday, but not if there are cops on your heels. You may have nothing to lose, but we've got plenty.'

'You were always an odd one out, weren't you?'

'*Enough!*' I cried. 'Don't start all over again! I get the point. Thanks anyway. Listen, if... if anything happened, would you take care of Norma for me? I mean, could she come down here and stay? She hasn't got anybody, and she is the one thing in my life I'd hate to lose. She's a tremendous baby-sitter.'

They laughed. 'Townies! We've got a crèche and a kindergarten. They send delegations from the district to admire them. Of course she could come and stay! She is a strong girl, and even if she is a wee bit weak in the head, we do like her. Was she with you in the orphanage?'

'Yes,' I lied, 'but don't talk to her about it; she doesn't like to remember... nobody does. That's not a reproach,' I added quickly, 'it wasn't your fault. Maybe it was nobody's fault. Now you've got me talking the way you do – maybe yes, maybe no. But I truly thank you for the wonderful Christmas. I can't remember feeling so good, so warm, since... the cockchafers.'

'Cor, you screamed the roof off the house!'

'I swallowed that bloody tooth and had to pick the turds for a week, as mother had promised me a crown for it.'

'You were always a dirty miser!'

'We had loads of fun, didn't we, little cousin? Remember how you broke into a rash after each hay-making and we plastered you with mud from the Toads Pool and then went around the village singing "Here Comes The Bride"?'

'No wonder I never got married,' I laughed and backed out of the room and joined the women in the kitchen, where I found them shaping the dough into tiny kolache – flat round cakes topped with ground poppy-seeds and curd cheese – for tea. Tea! Have mercy, I begged and they all laughed and said that kolache were nothing but fancy nibbles and that we'd have chicken-paprikash for supper, which was so light a meal it could hardly be called food. Tomorrow, they promised, we'd have the last of the autumn's bacon, which is so tender you could eat it raw, with potato dumplings and the best of last year's sauerkraut. Go play with the children, they said; they'll give you enough appetite to eat a horse!

Norma did not budge. She was firmly seated at the large table, topping the kolache with nimble fingers and a dreamy smile on her face. A teeny pain tugged at my heart, or was it jealousy? All alone, as used to be my custom, I went for a walk.

I walked west. Past the snowbound hayfields of my youth, down to the brook, around the frozen Toads Pool and into the forest I went, following a path the villagers stomped out in the snow on their search for supplementary firewood and

123

Christmas trees. There were neat stacks of both in a sunlit clearing; the forestry and the cooperative were obviously trusting partners. Goodness swam in my chest like that rich clear soup my middle cousin had cooked; I walked off the path on to the untouched snow and carefully foot-tracked a huge heartshape, my message to the winter birds and possibly to God peering down from heaven. What was Evil? Where was Evil? Far, far away, if it ever existed.

Only it wasn't and it did. A sharp whistle brought me to my senses. A young man with a long nose and very little chin, sporting a Russian-style lambskin cap, stood on the path with his hands in his pockets and what was probably meant to look like scorn on his face.

'Can't you read, comrade? Or should I call you "miss"? I guess I'd better, hadn't I? There is a sign at the forests's edge – you couldn't possibly have missed it. It clearly says "Please stick to the path. Offenders are subject to a fine of fifty crowns." I have a good mind to report you. You townspeople think that the country is all yours, don't you? But you don't want any responsibility for it. Yes, I have a good mind to report you, and not just to the forestry.'

'Have you followed me or what?'

'Most definitely I followed you. I don't get the chance to see a real-life enemy every day, do I? Oh, we have plenty of petty-minded anti-communism around here, I wouldn't put my hand in the fire for half the village, but they keep their mouths shut and stick to the path, so to speak. Nothing to get my teeth into for real. You're meaty – I wouldn't have missed you for the world.'

I returned to the path below him and started to march towards the village, but he caught my sleeve.

'Not so fast, miss.'

'Take your hands off me!'

'Prissy missy dissy!' he tried to slip his arm around my waist.

I slapped his face and to my surprise, he snuffled like a little boy. 'What did you want to do that for? I was only trying to get acquainted! And if you feel like telling tales, and if my wife hears anything, I'll get you for it, I swear I will.'

124

He massaged his cheek. 'It hurts!'

'Oh, for God's sake, Ivan, I hardly touched you.'

'How d'you know my name?'

'How do you know who I am? Or what I do? Don't tell me you listen to foreign broadcasts, naughty boy!'

'It's one of my duties, if you must know. Always be on alert, is my motto. They talk rubbish. We've had an instructor down from the district, and he said that if some people think that the comrades in Moscow are ready to jeopardize seventy years of socialist achievements for some flimsy democracy, they've got another think coming.' But his voice trembled and squeaked. 'So if you people think you're going to take over, forget it!'

'We don't. We are not about power.' Briefly I thought of Vlado, and wondered. Quite missed him too, for a long second.

'Don't make me laugh. Who isn't?' He was obviously in a tizzy. 'He had me thinking, the instructor did. I mean, why would he bother to come down here if it was all rubbish? Listen, I want to make a deal. Fifty crowns must be a lot of money for somebody like you. I shan't report you if you promise... I mean if the time comes – which it won't, but still – and I am in a spot of trouble, you could say that I didn't report you. I mean that would prove I sympathized, wouldn't it. Promise?'

'Easily. If you won't report me, I won't say you did.'

'What I mean is that you actually step forward and say: Ivan had not reported me to the authorities when he could have done.'

'I'll step forward.'

'He said – the instructor – that some KGB comrades had been suspended, but that it only meant they had been promoted, taken out of public view so to speak. I ask you, does it make sense?'

'Maybe, and maybe not. There are two sides to everything: what ought to be, and what is.'

'Precisely. I mean, what's the world coming to?' He looked peaky, and so very old; yet he couldn't have been more than twenty-three. Pity, my treacherous companion on such occasions, nagged my heart. I held out a hand, he shook it and blushed crimson.

'Don't you get any ideas,' he hissed. 'It's me who's being generous, not you. One word about this conversation and I'll have you driven out of the village in a panda car!'

'The pitcher goes often to the well, but it is broken at last,' I said mystically and marched away. When I looked over my shoulder, he still stood there looking old and actually picking his nose.

The sky went pink with the shame of it.

It was getting dark as I walked through the village again, the packed snow squeaking underfoot, the street empty but for the dogs wagging their tails and licking my hands, the windows flitting with electric candles, the chimney-smoke quite incredibly blue against the purple sky.

On the green, in the shadow of the old linden tree, two figures were entwined in a heavy embrace; I coughed and they sprang apart – Norma and my youngest cousin Jarek, the bachelor. Where have you been, we've been waiting for you, they said over one another; you didn't even know which house to go to for tea, did you? That was perfectly true, and it was also true that a heavy frost had fallen and it was only natural for people to huddle together, but I still shivered with apprehension. I was becoming the genuine article, the old maid who felt tainted at the sight of a kiss! Or maybe it was just . . . fear: there loomed in my mind a perfectly natural way in which Norma could be lost to me – nothing sinister, nothing political . . . nothing to do with me. I had never thought that anyone would want to marry Norma; by the same token, perhaps, as I had accepted that nobody would want to marry me. Suddenly, violently, I didn't want to let it happen. Norma was mine: she blossomed in my company! They would only put her to work, and maybe even to breeding children who, if slightly afflicted, would not be much different from all the other village morons. I stood there, hating the snug village with a heart as black as the December sky on which not one star was showing; clouds came and obliterated all the sparkle of Christmas.

The tea and the supper, though taken in two different

houses, were one tedious television affair: there was a festive line-up of fairytales, comedies and Western adventure movies long past the expiry date. Everyone sat transfixed, shedding crumbs and laughter, dripping sauce and tears; bottles of Pilsner and Coca Cola were passed around from a crate by the set. Norma and Jarek held hands, and my old aunt had her toothless mouth set in a determined matchmaker's smirk. I had been less unhappy spending long hours in interrogation rooms...

Finally, towards midnight, Norma sensed my unhappiness and came to sit by my knee, her hot dry hand stroking my ankle: there, there. I longed for a stiff brandy; the hard-currency Courvoisier we'd brought stood intact on a mahogany cabinet, ribbon and holly still around its neck. Not that, said my plump cousin-in-law, scandalized; that would go to the doctor next time we have to visit the hospital, or to the greedy dentist. And she produced a demijohn of home-made sloe gin which everyone greeted with a cheer. Do me a favour, said manacled James Bond to a blonde; ease my belt. Everybody leaned forward to see what deadly device he'd had built into the buckle.

Five minutes to midnight, while James Bond luxuriated on inflatable cushions with the blonde pinned to the satin sheets so standard in a space capsule, and M. leered at them across the stratosphere, sleepy children were carried to makeshift beds and cosily inebriated adults huddled around a Toshiba wireless. Short cigars were distributed among the men and I was once again awarded the dubious honour of being one of the boys. I smoked hungrily though; all that food had starved my soul out, and I hated gin.

Curtains – laced nylon and velvety dralon in two shades of gold – were drawn tight; the broadcast began harmlessly enough, with *Stille Nacht, Heilige Nacht* and *We Bring You the News from Bethlehem, Rejoice*, played and sung my some tired, faraway Bohemians and coughed over by atmospheric crackle. There were Christmas greetings from directors, managers, producers, editors and presenters; then the jamming device began to hum. A sharp querulous voice was cutting through the drone, announcing the latest communication from Bohemia to Bohemia. With every discernible word, a part of me froze.

'Dear fellow... zens... this Christmas... time of reckoning... signs... evil empire is crumbling... bolshevik leaders are reaching... last resort... reforms... beloved country, many lesser comrades... including the police... people whom they have betrayed... let us stand up as one man... factories... farms... when the time is ripe... we are with you... true... zens committee.'

The jamming squealed up and hooted; too late. Jarek switched the wireless off and they all looked at me as if they'd seen me for the first time.

'We haven't written this,' I said feebly. 'It's a fake. A provocation.'

Nobody spoke.

'I'll leave here first thing tomorrow morning. There is a bus to town on Boxing Day, isn't there?' I was near to tears; there goes my wonderful Christmas, and God knows what else.

'Ten-fifteen,' nodded my eldest cousin, 'but it'll be better if I drive you to the district station for the morning train. It leaves at seven, so be ready by six. Jarek will wake you up; he's milking tomorrow.'

'What are you all fretting about?' asked my old aunt. 'Why do you all look as if you'd swallowed a fish-bone?'

'It's the girls, mother. They are leaving in the morning,' said Jarek wistfully.

'Nonsense!' cried the aunt. 'They've come for a week, haven't they?'

'I have... urgent business in town, Auntie. But...' I bit my lip to make myself say it, '... Norma can stay, if you'll have her.'

'Of course we'll have her, stupid! What kind of a question is that?! She is a sweet soul, she is more family than you are,' grumbled Auntie. 'Maybe it's our fault, but you're a strange bird. Fly away if you must, but we won't give you the child.'

Norma chuckled and clapped her hands. My cousins and cousins-in-law all kissed me ceremoniously on both cheeks. Take care; come back when all is quiet; it'd be better if you didn't say you'd been with us; nonsense, family's family, there is nothing wrong with that; make sure you eat properly, you're so skinny; get out of it if you can, leave it to men with more muscle; you must come in summer, you can earn yourself some money on the raspberry plantation. Raspberry plantation? That's right, they all laughed, we leave little to mother nature now.

'Maybe I'll be back the day after tomorrow,' I said hopefully. 'I mean, a fake is but a fake.'

But they all looked away and began to disperse.

'Are you angry, Funny?' whispered Norma from the depth of her Italian bed. 'If you're very angry, I'll come with you. I love you so, I really do.'

'I am not angry.'

'But you're very sad.'

'I am not sad. All right, I am, a little.'

'Do you want me to read you a story?'

'No. Besides, there are no books here.'

'I have a book in my head, did you know that?'

'I've had my suspicions, yes.'

'You're clever,' sniggered Norma. 'Will you listen?'

'I might.'

She scrambled out of her bed and snuggled in mine. A cruel pain of past and future loneliness shot through my veins. I remembered old Joseph and his wisdom and promised myself to go and see him first thing tomorrow night. Or as soon thereafter as events would allow, if any. Norma passed her hand over my eyes, making me close them. The darkness was the same – a village darkness, hushed and unrelieved.

'Once upon a time, there was a boy who lived in a pigsty. The pigs loved him very much and the cows too, but he had many cousins who laughed at him. They laughed at him because he was always so dirty and because he had very little hair and also because he thought he was a prince. He would not marry girls the cousins brought him because they were not princesses. So he was very sad. So one day, a tall ghost came to him and said: "I am your Uncle Herman and I shall bring you two princesses to choose from. One is very clever and very skinny, and one is big and pretty." And he gave him a golden-green fly and said to watch it because it would sit on the nose of the princess who was right for him. So the boy did this, but the fly kept buzzing about and would only sit down on the wonderful food the cousins had cooked. They did this on purpose so that the fly could not find the right princess, because they did not want the boy from the pigsty to become a prince. They loved him very much, but they were mean. Uncle Herman watched this from the window and he was very angry. So he sent men to take the skinny princess away, because' – she squinted at me mischievously – 'he wanted her very much for himself, as she was so clever. And the boy's mother was an old witch and she gobbled up all the food and the fly was very tired and it sat down on the pretty princess's nose and—'

'Stuff the fly!' I said wearily. 'Do you really like Jarek? You said you didn't! You're not in love with him all of a sudden, are you?' I felt dreadfully tired.

'No-o... but my Uncle Herman wants me to marry him. It was in the story, didn't you hear? Uncle Herman wants you for himself. He wants you to be his third wife—'

'Fourth. The third got herself killed by a vacuum cleaner. It sucked her soul out, remember? Stuff Uncle Herman once and for all, I am sick and tired of him!'

Norma whinnied. 'You're funny when you're angry. You're my funny Funny. I love you very much.'

'Oh, stop it.'

'You don't want to love me any more.'

'I don't...?! Norma, sweetheart, I am sorry. I am just very worried, that's all. Worried and miserable. I ought to have told everybody about the fake. I mean, I did not do what I ought to have done and now we may all suffer for it—'

'Vlado too?'

'Vlado too. It may not be so bad and it may soon be over, and maybe nothing much will happen anyway, but I have an awful amount of explaining to do. The worst is – will anyone believe me?'

'Vlado will believe you. He loves you very much.'

'I don't know... You see, dearest, if I had told what I

130

knew, we could have issued a warning about a provocation . . . it wouldn't have been broadcast, for chrissake! I can't understand what came over me, why I—'

'A spell. You were under an evil spell. I know, I've had them too. They had to give me an injection, and never mind if it killed me. I'll come with you and tell Vlado about the spell. There, now you can be happy.'

'No, sweet soul, I don't want you to. You stay here and enjoy yourself. For both of us. There must be some joy somewhere, dammit. I'll phone every day. If I don't, I'll be thinking of you anyway, so don't you forget me.'

'I forget lots of people,' Norma whispered, 'but I shan't forget Funny. Are you happy now?'

'A little.'

'I'll pray for you if you want me to. I'll say please God, take the evil spell from Funny. I'll say it every night.'

We snivelled for a while, wetting each other's cheeks; then Norma got out of the bed, brought over her pillow and placed it at my feet. Ankles to shoulder, shoulder to ankles we slept, toes to chin and chin to toes, cousins behind a chimney corner which did not exist any more.

The steel-grey Mercedes purred and slithered up the road through the black ink of the early morning, past the brightly lit milking parlour and several women on bicycles on their way to the animal farm; past the open fields with towering silos it swished, and along the Bay.

I thought, with brief sorrow, of the graves cemented to its bottom. What did the bones do? Scrape away in the soft soil underneath, doggedly escaping? My mother's bones, light as feathers, what did they do?

'It's a shame,' sighed my eldest cousin. 'Tell you what: you make it clear that you had nothing to do with that provocation, and come back for New Year dinner. Pig's trotters and all! How's that?'

'That's fine,' I replied, sprightly.

'You're a brick,' said my cousin and pushed a wad of banknotes into my coat-pocket, while his other hand caressed rather than mastered the elegant steering wheel.

'Blacksmith's mare and cobbler's wife walk barefoot,' remarked Professor K. while another tear formed in the corner of his eye. 'Half of my scholarly and artistic friends have acquired the qualifications and the skills of plumbers and stokers, and I sit here shivering amidst frozen pipes. I'd much rather be with them in a warm cell.' The tear slid down an unusually pale cheek and dropped on the floor strewn with brutalized papers and tortured books.

'Did they have a warrant, Professor?' I asked as if it mattered.

'I don't think so, my dear. But I didn't make a point of finding out. I made no point at all. I was paralysed by the violence of it. I am too old; I ought to have died ages ago, surrounded by my students after some rare seminar in which minds met minds in a true search for the meaning of history. I would now be lying in peaceful silence by the side of my wife, the roots of the yew tree mingling with my bones, oblivious to the suffering and indignities of life. Don't leave me if you can, at least not for a while. It is Christmas and God is busy, and there isn't enough faith or passion in my prayers to gain His attention.'

I put the drawers back, gathered the papers and heaped them on the desk, and began returning the books to their walnut shelves following the directions of the old man's finger. The upper and lower shelves had not been disturbed; it was clearly a case of vengeful vandalism rather than a systematic house-search. Some of the books had broken backs or torn ligaments; I concealed their injuries as best I could.

The small Christmas tree lay on the carpet in a glitter of smashed baubles and tangled tinsel. 'Leave it,' said the Professor. 'Or better still, take it to the bin, if you don't mind the trouble.'

I swept the carpet and poured out two glasss of port. There were many bottles on the side-table, some in Christmas wrappings: obviously this had been meant to be as much a festive gathering as an ad-hoc meeting. I hadn't found anybody anywhere when I arrived in town; on my cousins' money, I took a taxi and went all the way to Arnold's and then back to the foot of the Hill where Professor K. lived in his gloomy mansion, long divided into ill-proportioned flats. But I came too late; the meeting was over, ended by a massive raid at the finale of which, Professor K. said, eleven people had been herded out in handcuffs and kicked and shoved into the waiting police cars.

'Eleven?' I asked suddenly over the glass of port. 'Surely you meant ten, Professor? Ten people were arrested – though it'll probably soon be eleven. They must be waiting for me at my door in Barley Street.'

'No, my dear, eleven were captured. Arnold brought Dagmar with him; he said she had something important to tell us. We never got round to it; we busied ourselves refuting the alleged Christmas declaration of the committee. Although, I must say, many of us felt that we ought to have issued one, more or less in the same spirit if far less vindictive towards the government and avoiding terms like "evil empire" and "bolshevik". A word of hope, so to speak. I think,' he fumbled in his breast-pocket with mild surprise, 'that I have the text of the refutation on me. I now remember pocketing it when the door-bell rang and rang, and young Robert went to let them in. And so I have.'

He handed me the paper, a page done in Karol's ornamental handwriting, crossed and glossed in places by several different pens. 'What do we do with it, dear friend? I know there is an emergency procedure, but however hard Marek tried, my fussy old brain had not retained it. You must take charge, you know. I am tired.'

Reluctantly, I nodded. My stomach trembled at all the frost of this bewildering winter. 'I'll do my best, Professor, though I can't imagine that they'd let me walk about and keep Dagmar. They'll soon realize they've got the wrong woman who's not on the committee.'

The Professor coughed. 'As a matter of fact, she is. During the raid, she asked to be co-opted. It seemed to mean so much to her that even Marek agreed. It didn't make much sense, but it was an emotional moment, embracing a woman scorned while being thrown to the lions – that sort of thing. So there are thirteen of us now, a number deemed unlucky by most but lucky by an elitist few. She may well have taken your place in the cells, you know. You may have been left out in the cold just like me.'

'They'll all be back in forty-eight hours,' I said, not really believing it. It was only a few days since Vlado sat in my armchair talking politics and tactics with Norma on his lap, yet already it seemed to belong to a bygone era. The time might come when I would be needed, Vlado had said; was this It? What was I supposed to do? While Dagmar, in the waiting room at the police headquarters or in the cells, was spreading stories I should have told? I shuddered and forced myself into some constructive thinking.

'First things first, Professor. Let me try to get you a plumber. There must be some emergency services working.'

I reached for the telephone book, but the Professor caught my hand and held it as if I merited compassion. 'Dagmar did it the moment she arrived, she seems to have a plumber friend. He has promised to come as soon as the Boxing Day lunch is over. She is a very efficient lady, so very feminine and yet with a man's brain.'

I found the kitchen and boiled four of my cousins' sausages – leaving the rest in the Professor's fridge, empty but for a chunk of cheese – and warmed up a jarful of my aunt's sauerkraut. We had our belated lunch while outside a roll of thunder announced the approach of a winter storm. Fortified by the food, we drafted a telegram to the president, protesting at the arrests. By the time we had finished, the storm had come and gone, the snow danced playfully in the dusk behind the tall window laced with frost and the plumber arrived – a burly fellow with baby-blue eyes. It was time for me to face the streets. I promised the Professor I'd come back and stay the night. Bring your cousin, he said, but he appeared relieved when I explained that Norma was in good hands elsewhere.

The plumber caught me in the hall. 'There are cops outside. Plain-clothes and snazzy cars, but I could smell

134

them long before they stopped me. Buzz off, boys, I said, don't you know a plumber when you see one? There is an old man freezing to death; surely you don't want that on your conscience? A plumber is a king in Bohemia, but you'd better watch your step.'

I went to the loo and sat on the bowl for half an hour memorizing both the brief telegram and the page-long statement of the committee; then hid the sheets inside the roll of toilet paper and went back to tell the Professor where they were, in case I didn't make it. Finally, I put my coat on and stepped outside into three inches of fresh snow, a fallen night and a police extravaganza.

Nobody approached me, but six men followed closely on foot and three cars glided by like planes in formation. I felt eyes on my back and my knees went stiff, and my buttocks clenched. Grateful it wasn't summer and I wasn't naked under flimsy silk or a clinging T-shirt, I strutted with my thighs so close together I could hear my trousers swish.

They did not prevent me from entering a phone-booth, just stood outside lighting cigarettes, ostentatious yet uninterested in what I was actually doing. I dialled a number Marek had made us learn by heart. There has been an accident, I said to the young voice who answered the call; eleven people have been taken to a hospital and I am still walking, but not without a number of difficulties. Nothing more was said; the emergency procedure devised by Marek to the last detail demanded that in an hour's time from now, I would enter the public lavatory in the middle of the boulevard where I'd be met. If I couldn't make it, I was supposed to try three hours later, or again at seven in the morning, after which I'd be presumed arrested or otherwise incapacitated.

The natural way to the main post office led across the ancient bridge, recently made strictly pedestrian: the men kept in touch with the cars through walkie-talkies they kept in their breast-pockets. It was ludicrous. Look, mummy, cried a child, the gentleman's talking to his pocket! He's a creep of a policeman, I wanted to shout, but the mother looked so scared – she knew it anyway. Anybody could smell them, but who'd lift a voice or a finger if I fought them?

The main post office off the boulevard was full of shamefaced citizens sending belated Christmas parcels and telegrams to friends and families they'd nearly forgotten. I filled out the telegram form while queuing, addressing it to the President's Bureau, The Castle.

MR PRESIDENT WE PROTEST STRONGLY AGAINST UNWARRANTED AND BRUTAL ARRESTS OF ELEVEN FELLOW MEMBERS OF CITIZENS COMMITTEE STOP PEACEFULLY ASSEMBLED IN HOUSE OF DISTINGUISHED HISTORIAN PROFESSOR K. ON BOXING DAY COMMITTEE MEMBERS WERE ASSAULTED AND DRIVEN AWAY IN HANDCUFFS WITHOUT CHARGE STOP ILLEGAL HOUSE SEARCH WAS CONDUCTED AND PROPERTY DAMAGED BY POLICE STOP CITIZENS COMMITTEE HAS SENT ITS PROGRAMME DOCUMENT TO YOUR BUREAU STOP IT IS INFORMAL GROUP OF CITIZENS ACTIVELY INVOLVED IN MATTERS OF PUBLIC CONCERN FULLY IN ACCORDANCE WITH CONSTITUTION STOP WE BESEECH YOU AS HEAD OF STATE TO DEMAND IMMEDIATE RELEASE OF OUR FRIENDS AND BEGIN INVESTIGATION INTO THIS AND SIMILAR POLICE ACTIONS INCOMPATIBLE WITH CALLS FOR DEMOCRACY AND PEOPLES TRUST STOP.

I signed it in the name of Professor K. and myself, while the six men – or were they seven now? – watched with contempt from a distance. 'Do you need both the signatures?' asked the telegraph clerk, her eyebrows sweating. 'It's just that it's going to cost you a lot; the second signature brings it over the limit.'

'Too true,' I said, my eyebrows in similar sweat, 'but there

136

comes a time when you don't count the cost.'

The clerk blushed, took the money – my cousins were paying – and quickly murmured, 'Bless you. Happy New year to us all.'

The men now walked so close behind that I could feel their breath. I was beginning to wonder who they were, Major Fischer's goons or some murder squad waiting for a chance to push me under a tram? I remembered my cousin Jarek with sudden warmth and Norma with tender sadness, then pushed them out of my mind as I descended the stairs leading to the underground lavatory. Two of the men followed me to the door of the 'Ladies', but the attendant shrieked at them and they retreated. I tipped the old woman generously. Another gypsy, but that was hardly surprising – most of the city's lavatory attendants were gypsy women, brutally domesticated.

'My lucky day, madame,' she smirked. 'The first on the left is all yours, madame.'

I entered the cubicle and nearly screamed, as there was a young man in it, stubble and all. That was the beauty of it, he explained; he'd walk through the attendant's little office to the 'Gents' and leave from there, thus making detection practically impossible. It was costly for the old gypsy was greedy, but that was another beauty of it – in their arrogance the cops forgot about the power of money and she would not squeal for free; fear she did not know. Besides, she thought that this was a sexual encounter, very romantic.

But what if it had been a man who called? I asked, intrigued and curious. The young man, whom I now vaguely remembered from the meeting in the Old Tavern, merely smiled. Men had different instructions from women, no reason for me to know. Let's not waste time. We spoke in an almost voiceless whisper, reading each other's lips. I swiftly dictated the telegram and the refutation to him; he took it down in an accomplished shorthand. Dear Marek, I thought, how seldom we loved you enough! It'll go out as a package, said the young man, the report on the arrests, the statement

137

and the telegram, the domestic round tonight, the authorities and the foreign press tomorrow morning – if the correspondents hadn't all gone skiing in the Bohemian Forest. Tough luck for them if they did, because it will also be telephoned to emigré agencies in London and Vienna tonight, and they deserve a scoop. A scoop? Something's definitely happening on the top, he smiled, so we'll be interesting again. I nearly forgot to mention Dagmar's co-option. He frowned a little and said that in that case, we better mention in the report that others will volunteer and be co-opted into the committee if the eleven aren't released. He'd have the list of candidates by tomorrow night, so would I please go swimming in the city's public baths between seven and eight? Ladies' night, he smiled, so I'd be met by his girlfriend. Were I not there, it would be assumed that my luck had run out and the new provisional committee would start to function, hopefully with Professor K.'s co-operation. He kissed me on the lips, and though it was a kiss over a smelly toilet bowl and amidst nasty stains and graffiti, it was one of the best I had ever had. I left the cubicle and he stayed behind.

'Madame only took five minutes,' sniggered the attendant. 'That is not much with such a nice young lover!'

I didn't dare to hail a taxi, for fear that the driver might be one of the goons, so I walked back against the stream of the Christmas crowd – men, women and children in their best Sunday clothes on the way to the cinema or perhaps even a theatre. The men, definitely seven now, marched all around me, pushing through the crowd, never once giving me a direct glance. My teeth began to chatter and my feet walked so fast that my hips hurt and my heart thumped like a hopping rabbit.

When I reached Professor K.'s house, the three cars already stood there, waiting. Fear seized me in one anguished wave; somebody gave me a push from behind that hurled my body against the door and sent my mind reeling in anticipation of more pain. Then somebody laughed and in the next thirty seconds, they were all gone, the red rear lights of the cars flickering jauntily until they vanished in the last night of Christmas.

The Professor was glad to see me, but all I was glad about was the cold bed and a couple of sleeping pills he gave me. I hugged them in my palm while he lingered by the door to the spare bedroom. Still pale and fragile, he told me about the rather harassed hour he'd spent on the phone, warning friends and families that the eleven might not come home tonight. There was nobody at Karol's; Marta had taken the children to their grandparents in the country for Christmas, and he was grateful for that – he would have found it very difficult to be the bearer of bad news there. Six children! It ought to be a great blessing, oughtn't it, and yet...goodnight, he said abruptly and I swallowed the pills, washing them down with a pint of cool water, and fell into a slumber so heavy I might as well have been dead.

Having gone to bed so early, we were both up and in the kitchen at five. The air was lukewarm – the central heating was working again, and Dagmar deservedly got more praise from the Professor. We ate sausages for breakfast, without sauerkraut, and were drinking coffee in the study when the phone rang ... at six o'clock in the morning!

'They've let them go!' I cried and grabbed the receiver. 'Hurray!'

'Well, thank you,' said Anton's amused voice, 'but aren't you rather overdoing it? I merely wished to inform you that you will have regular operatives tailing you today, nothing to worry about, unlike yesterday. It's for your own protection, so give them a smile.'

'Have ... have charges been brought?'

'A measly agitation.' He sounded genuinely disappointed. 'But maybe we can push it up to subversion.'

I shuddered. 'What about Dagmar? She's only made a gesture—'

'Oh, Dagmar's clever! Use your brains, my scraggy friend,' laughed Anton, and hung up.

On the spur of the moment, I told Professor K. everything, from A to Z, from the spittle to the nose-bleed, leaving out nothing but Norma's bedtime stories and a few odd bits and pieces unrelated to the central problem of my guilt and my part in a game I still did not understand. I felt so much better when I finished, even though I soon saw that the Professor listened with about as much attention as an absent-minded don at a tutorial.

'Do not reproach yourself too much, my dear, we all have moments of weakness and vanity. You have a certain tendency to heroics which easily leads to trouble, but you also have a commendable, enviable, genuine courage. And you have done well not to succumb to whatever our *cher camerade* Vlado was plotting. I do not deny all moral qualities to all secret policemen, nor do I exclude the possibility of a moral conversion of some rare individuals amongst them, but on the whole I find it advisable not to corrupt our stance by entering into any negotiations with them. I do no agree with Karol that they are sub-human, but the truth is that even the most enlightened amongst them are still members of a repressive force fundamentally opposed to free, unlicensed thinking and its results. You have my full absolution, dear friend, if that's what you wanted.'

'But Professor, I could have prevented—'

'Vanity again! I do not believe for a moment that the arrests made had any connection with the Christmas forgery. Indeed, if there had been any firm reason at all, then it was to prevent the New Year's Eve meeting. I understand you haven't told anybody about that, have you?' I shook my head vigorously, and he sighed. 'Somebody must have done. I am afraid we've lost a very valuable draft of a substantial statement which had been prepared by that fine thinker, Dr Florian. He says it's a compilation of the more tenable and compatible theses we have been exchanging about the predicted democractic reforms and our place in them, but I suspect he wrote a brilliant synthesis rather than a mere catalogue of thoughts. I shoved it under the carpet when the police rang, all twelve copies of it, but it wasn't there after the raid. I should have thought of a better hiding place, but my mind is slow in such matters. So you see, everybody fails now and then.'

'Those who walk the tightrope can't help swaying. Sometimes they fall,' I said dreamily. 'Strange: if they live, they always climb back.'

140

'What a beautiful quote. How come I haven't read it?'

'You couldn't have done. An old barman said that, a couple of weeks ago, though it seems like ages. He caters for the underworld – he is very wise.'

'He sounds a worthy man. It's a pity I don't enjoy meeting strangers any more. What do we do next?'

'I don't know... Charges have been brought, but I suppose we'd better wait till tomorrow; there still may not be an indictment. If there is, I suppose we start a petition...' All I wanted, passionately, was to sit tight under the palm by the window and read a book; I was willing to contemplate scrubbing the floors or doing the Professor's laundry, anything to keep me off the streets. I did not wish to meet the 'regular operatives'. I did not want Mrs H.'s whispered comments and the emptiness of my home.

'Yes, indeed, but in practical terms, how do we...'

I took him to the bathroom, ran the taps and told him – leaving out all particulars so as not to lumber him with secrets – that the emergency procedures seemed to be working well and we were not alone. He looked rather childishly pleased with my bathroom prudence; I had not told him that if I don't want to believe in actual squealers, I'd better begin to believe in bugging.

It was half-past seven, the time for a grey winter dawn, when the black limousine arrived and stationed itself directly under the stuffy window. 'Are they yours or mine?' asked Professor K. nervously.

'Mine,' I breathed unhappily. 'Most probably so.'

'You'd better lead them away from here, then. My housekeeper is coming in today, she's back from her Christmas vacation and I'd much rather not have her upset. She is a loyal soul, but scares easily and drops the china.'

'See you tomorrow.' I smiled, hoping that the touch of bitterness wasn't showing, gathered my belongings, left the jar of pears in schnapps on the kitchen table and walked out into what promised to be a sunny day.

Two men in practically identical trench-coats but wearing different hats jumped out of the car and stopped my progress. Their faces were set in amicable expressions as they showed me the badges and informed me that they would follow wherever I went and that it would be much easier for everyone if I told them my destination. I declined and wished to see some kind of a warrant authorizing them to tail me. They laughed and hoped I wasn't going to be difficult, as this was very much in my own interest as well as that of the state. I rushed to cross the street and would have been run over by a lorry if they hadn't pulled me back. They laughed again, and said that I was definitely in need of protection. I walked on and they kept close behind me conversing loudly about the weather, obviously – if in vain – inviting me to join in. The limousine crept along the curb like a fat black slug.

Anton had been right, this was much less worrying. It was still illegal and preposterous, but it had an air of respectability and order and didn't inspire thoughts of rape and murder. Or perhaps I felt happier because the sun was shining and the darkness slept underneath the Earth.

The bag was too heavy for me to carry all the way to Barley Street: I hailed a taxi. The moment I climbed in, one of the men flashed his badge at the driver.

'Take the dame wherever she wants to go, but no fancy tricks and no speeding. We'll follow, so watch your wheels.'

'Jesus,' said the driver feelingly. 'Who are you, Miss? A bait to catch a drug-pusher? Or some comrade's naughty daughter? Or a famous dissident?'

'I don't know about the famous. I am on the citizens' committee, if it means anything to you. Barley Street, please.'

'Holy smoke, look, they really are following! Well, I'll be . . . ! Listen, this gets my adrenalin going – do you want me to lose them? There isn't a cop driver in town I couldn't lose! Bastards!'

'Thanks, but don't. They'll have your number by now.'

'Okay, if you say so. How come you're walking about? It said on the radio that you folks have been arrested. That was the Czech BBC broadcast; I couldn't get the others, they're jamming them like mad. Hey, you're not an *agent provocateur*, are you?!'

142

'No. I am genuine, I came too late to a meeting, that's all. Professor K. is all right too; I guess that's because he is so frail.'

'I get it! You've signed that telegram with him, you're the lady with a funny name.'

'I have a friend who calls me Funny.'

'You folks should have come up with something meatier. It's time for this old country to shake the lice out of the pelt. I mean, could you imagine the Ruskies having more freedom than us!'

'It's not all over yet. There are many more of us than just twelve or thirteen. But all we can do is to call upon you folks to stand up straight and speak the honest truth!' Shut up, clown, I thought, and added lamely, 'I mean it's us, isn't it? Us all, together.'

'Yeah... but there are always leaders, aren't there? We need good leaders, that's what we need. Good leaders. Mind you, they'd have to be damn fucking good to drag people out of lethargy. That isn't so much to ask – a bit of liberty, a bit of free enterprise, a bit of democracy – but the trouble is that people don't believe we can ever get it. So we're in a rut.'

'But we're good talkers.'

He grinned. 'Grumblers, more likely. We've all been through the grumbling university... in the corner pub! Barley Street coming up. Here is my card – call any time and ask for Franta. I'll drive you straight to hell if you so wish. I am not scared of them! The best of luck to you, love.'

'How much do I owe you?'

'Nothing. That's the least I can do. Just fumble with your purse, will you? We don't want the bastards getting any ideas, and reporting me to the boss.'

The two 'operatives' walked me to the door like polite gentlemen escorts. Mrs H., her hair on rollers, watched from behind her net curtains.

The telephone still worked. It took ages for the operator to connect me with Jarek's house, as if the village of Broumy lay somewhere in Siberia.

'Norma here. What do you want?' The curiously loving voice clutched at my heart.

'I want you to read me a story over the phone.'

'You're funny, Funny.'

'No, I am sad. I miss you. Can't you read me a story?'

'Of course I can't. Not in the morning, silly. I am going to the milking parlour with Jarek's elevenses.'

'What else are you going to do today?'

'I don't know. I've hoovered, she wanted me to.'

'Auntie? Oh sweetheart, weren't you scared?'

'No-o. My Uncle Herman came to the window and told me it was all right. His third wife was a bad person, that's why it sucked her soul out. But I am a good person. I was not always a good person, but now I am. You're good, too. Are you in the clink?'

'No, I would hardly be on the phone if I were.'

'Oh, you're clever. I am stupid.'

'You're nothing of the sort. You're a cunning little witch. Norma, are you really happy there?'

'I am happy. When will you come?'

'Do you miss me? Is Jarek boring?'

She whinnied merrily. 'He loves me very much. I must go now, or he'll be hungry and all his hair will fall out.'

'Remember I love you too, will you?'

'Listen for the kiss.' She smacked her lips loudly, and hung up. I had a long weep and a hot bath and spent the rest of the day reading *The Brave Soldier Schweik* and nibbling on my cousins' apples in cloves, while the three men lounged in their black limousine making everybody nervous.

Marta phoned towards the evening, her voice gruff with a cold, and said she was leaving the children with her parents and would be in town tomorrow morning; could I come over then? Of course, I replied, but I'd be bringing a tail. As if it mattered, said Marta drily.

The limousine looked the same, but the three men were different. Another shift, noticeably less amicable; or perhaps it was me feeling more apprehensive in the dark. I boarded the bus and the two had to talk to the third on the walkie-talkie; people stared and I felt shamed. Clearly they didn't like it when they saw where I was going and that it was a ladies' night; I paid my fee, didn't wait for the change and ran through the doors before they could make a decision or get an order.

While I was changing into my old bikini, a wet short girl with flaxen hair slipped through the plastic curtain of the cubicle. In a melodic whisper, she recited twelve names to me, until I too learnt them by heart. They were easy to remember; I knew them all. Twelve people ready to be co-opted into the committee if need be, declare themselves and possibly share the same fate as the eleven. I felt strong enough to swim across an ocean. A meeting – only if need be – had been prearranged for midnight tomorrow at Robert's, his father being one of the new candidates. I was not to come if I were shadowed, but the 'regular operatives' were unlikely to work nights. There'd be a car for Professor K.; would I please tell him to expect it, at quarter to midnight, if need be. She said she'd had her swim and slipped out again, leaving a faint smell of chlorine and youth.

I swam a good thirty lengths while the two sat frowning in a cafeteria on the balcony overlooking the pool – the only two fully clothed male persons amongst the glistening women, some teasing, some indignant. I enjoyed myself, even though the water was rather murky, the smell of chlorine quite strong and the want of Norma's company hardly bearable. In summer, I promised myself, I'll take Norma swimming in the Lake. She won't be married, she can't be.

There was an unpleasant woman ostensibly checking the locks in the changing room; she even peeped into my cubicle. Too late, comrade, I thought underneath a grin; too late.

My tails walked me to the door like a couple of disgruntled uncles, and at ten p.m. sharp the limousine departed with all of them on board. I toyed with the idea of going to see old Joseph, but the swim had tired me out; I went to bed and dreamt of him instead. He looked like a very old Jesus Christ on a pale horizon of a desert or a yellow sea, and now and then threw a leg of chicken or a handful of chips to where I was sitting in a sandy hole, my left foot in an iron trap but otherwise strangely contented.

'My parents are in a state of shock,' said Marta. 'Poor dears! If the worst comes to the worst, Auntie will move in with us to keep house. She's tough. You will let Norma come and help her with the children, won't you? Your cousin's taught me a lesson or two about the mentally handicapped. I've been too . . . clinical. Insensitive is the word. Dismissive. Un-Christian. Let's go, and God be with us.'

We walked from Peace Square to police headquarters arm in arm, closely followed by the morning shift. The black limousine had been washed; it glistened majestically. One of the men suddenly ran forward, produced a camera, grinned and took a picture of Marta and me and his colleague lurking in the rear.

'You poor dear,' Marta whispered. 'Don't you wish you were behind bars with my Karol, rather than walking about with these creeps?'

There was quite a crowd on the pavement outside the police headquarters, friends and families of the eleven waiting for news: the forty-eight hours were up. They'd either come out any minute or be served with indictments and transferred to a regular prison pending trial. It was another sunny day, but the street lay in a dark frosty shade. Nervous policemen in plain clothes or winter uniforms pottered in and out of the building, while both my tails now busied themselves taking pictures of the tense, murmuring expectant crowd. Even Dr Burda was there, though he pretended not to know me or anybody else and stood slightly apart. Then Anton appeared in the door, flanked by two uniformed guards. With a boyish grin on his face, he informed us that the Prosecutor-General had decided to prolong the preliminary detention of the eleven members of the so-called citizens' committee for another forty-eight hours to allow the police more time for preliminary investigations. The charges stood, but there was no indictment. So far . . . His eyes sought mine and he shook his

146

head merrily before asking us to disperse in an orderly and peaceful manner unless we wanted to be fined for obstructing the pavement, or worse.

In an uncertain mood, we shuffled towards Café Bohemia. 'I think,' Marta said abruptly and loudly, 'that this is very hopeful. Take heart, everybody, chins up!'

I didn't go with the crowd to the café. Robert's father, blushing painfully, had asked me not to. So I took my tails to Professor K.'s instead. On the corner of the street, I turned to speak to them, my stomach clenched. Would you mind, I muttered, parking two houses below? You make the old housekeeper nervous. They laughed and said that when invited to cooperate, all I did was be haughty, so why should they ... but they did as I asked.

Professor K. was pleased. 'I've had a most peculiar telephone call today.' He spoke after the housekeeper had served us with fragrant jasmine tea and left the study. 'Most peculiar. A former student of mine, whom I never particularly liked and who is now an assistant professor at the faculty of history, has asked me if he could come and discuss a matter of utmost importance with me, preferably tomorrow but certainly before the New Year. It would be a tentative discussion, but there were definite possibilities. He kept hinting at the New Year as some kind of a milestone. What can happen on New Year's Day, for God's sake? It's a holiday.'

'The president's speech?' I offered. A strange hope seized me, though it felt like fear. Shush, I breathed down my chest.

'I wouldn't mind ending my days in a lecture hall,' the Professor sighed and withdrew into a wistful silence. I used it to write a note about the car coming to fetch him before midnight and bring him to the meeting with the new twelve committee members whose names I listed; I didn't want to alarm the housekeeper by a conference in the bathroom. He read the note and tore it up, nodding absent-mindedly.

'But maybe you shouldn't,' I ventured, suddenly hesitant. 'If there are chances—'

'Nonsense!' He snapped out of the dream. 'I can't stand by when ... We'll get them out. The time has come for some

147

resolute if polite pressure. History doesn't serve anything to anybody on a plate. I have never been a mere observer, and I do not wish to become one now.'

I spent the afternoon in a cinema on the boulevard, which was showing a continuous programme of Disney cartoons. My two shadows and I were the only adults amongst a couple of hundred fidgety schoolchildren spending their holiday money on lollipops and ice-cream sold up and down the aisles. I felt utterly and desperately friendless. The two enjoyed themselves tremendously, quacking with laughter like Donald Duck.

'There is a foreign gentleman waiting for you upstairs,' whispered Mrs H. hurriedly. 'I told him you weren't at home, which was easy to know as the watchdogs weren't around, but I don't think he understood a word I said. He's been there for an hour now, poor thing. You'd better let him out the back way, when you're done with him. Oh Miss, everybody says that things are going to get better like, is it true? I do hope so, for your sake as well as anybody's! But judging by the way they treat you, it doesn't seem very likely, does it?'

The man's name was Peter Sanders; he said he was a freelance working for the *Guardian* and the *Observer*. A mutual friend – Anna's sister-in-law – had given him my address and told him to watch for a black limousine with three men in it; if it wasn't anywhere near the house, it would be safe to come in and wait. Mrs H. had him scared a bit – he thought that having recognized him as a foreigner, she might turn informer. Not at all, I said starchily; people sympathize.

He produced a half-bottle of whisky and four packets of Rothmans; I was grateful, for I had left the Christmas Gitanes with Norma and was pining for a good smoke. Poor man, he kept shivering though I thought it was quite warm in the apartment, the radiators were almost hot. How can you all live in such a cold climate, he complained. It's quite hot in Bohemia in the summer, I told him, and put the kettle on to make him a toddy.

'What do you people aim to achieve?' asked Peter Sanders, restored by the hot drink. 'Let me be blunt with you: unlike some of my colleagues, I have always sympathized with the dissidents, but I was never sentimental about your lot. I find that patronizing. I am well aware that you know your risks and take them whether or not there is help forthcoming from Western public opinion. But are you aware that the greatest risk, right now, might be blocking the reformist tendencies at the top? Have you taken into account that by persisting in your active criticism and in broadcasting your idealistic view of human rights through advocating policies independent of the party, you may actually strengthen the position of the hard-liners? I know you have denied the Christmas declaration, but tell me, was it really a police provocation or has a radical wing in the opposition momentarily gained the upper hand? Do I speak too rapidly for you?'

I fought an urge to throw him out, the front way. Maybe they'd take him to Major Fischer; maybe he'd learn to be a little sentimental after that. I took a long swig of the Scotch and a long breath.

'I can cope with Queen's English, thank you. I happen to know it was a police provocation. I happen to know that there are at least two factions of the secret police fighting each other. I have been kidnapped and brutalized by one, trying to make me say that the declaration was a product of the other; that's how I know. You may quote me on that. As for what we're aiming to achieve... it's not the achievement that counts. It's the continuing presence of conscience. Whatever is happening on the top, it is the citizens who are the actual creators of the society. Without their conscious partici- pation, shabby tyrannies will flourish and reforms will fail. Listen, Peter Sanders, you have two choices. Either I take you out the back way now, minimizing the risk that you'd be caught – for all I know, there may be a bug in the ceiling – or you sit tight till 10 p.m. – which seems to be the end of their working day – and leave the front way; you'd be risking more, but perhaps I could make you understand a thing or two. What's it to be?'

He twisted the tumbler in his fingers and gazed at its

149

bottom. 'I don't know ... tell me, what are your plans now? Our mutual friend mentioned that you might want to start a petition which, given the present possibilities, could well reach beyond the usual dissident circles. Any comment on that? Do you sincerely believe that you can get the eleven out by making their plight a public concern? Will your message to the authorities be that once they are released, the citizens' committee will exercise moderation?'

'You speak like somebody dear to me – only he has more right to his views. Our message will be that prison, both in its strict and its metaphorical meaning, is not the place for citizens to be in. You can't have a prospering state without a prosperous people. Listen, let me take you out the back way.'

As we climbed over the walls and fences, I actually took a liking to him; at least he didn't care about the fate of his fur-lined coat and flannel trousers. He wanted more details about the kidnapping, so I spared Major Fischer nothing, not even the vodka, but left Anton's name and number out, shrouding him in mystery. For Vlado's sake.

Peter Sanders shook my hand and said he was driving to Vienna tonight, but he hoped to come back for a few more days; could he perhaps contact me again? I shrugged my shoulders and we wished each other the best of luck.

Climbing back, I felt like a bearer relieved of his burden, or a chestnut tree that has shed its prickly fruit. Come what may, I'd had my say. It even rhymed.

'Norma here. What do you want?'

'Do you sit by that telephone or what?'

'I was wanting you to call. I love you so much, I really do.'

'Are you all right, my soul?'

'A man has been nasty to me, but Jarek punched him on the nose. If you see Uncle Herman, will you tell him to send men to scare the goon? His name is Ivan.'

'That shitty prick! Don't mind him, sweetheart, just... avoid him. What did he do?'

'Jarek says not to tell you,' she whined.

'Okay, dearest, as long as Jarek looks after you, that's fine

150

with me. Did you do anything nice today?'

'I went skating with the little people.'

'The children?'

'Ye-e-s. Some other little people too.' She began to whisper. 'I did not like them very much, I thought they were dead. Can't you come? Please, Funny?'

'Norma D.,' I said severely through an aching lump in my throat, 'pull yourself together. I'll be there on New Year's Day, that's only three more days to go.' And if I have to shoot my way out of this town I will, I thought savagely.

'Listen for the kisses.' She sent a whole series of them and hung up – without waiting for me to send her some back.

At 10 sharp, I heard an engine cough and looked out of the window; the limousine had taken off and the coast was clear. A cold coast, covered in dirty snow, whipped by a rising December gale, scarcely lit by swaying, flittering street lamps – yet homely; mine.

The wind in the back pushed me into an effortless run and I soon landed at the bar of the Three Bears. In a cosy corner of the dim parlour, the afternoon shift – the two tails and the driver – were supping on fried liver with tartare sauce. My heart sank, but they only nodded a casual greeting at me, as three friends in a bar would at an acquaintance with whom they didn't particularly wish to spend an evening. As if after ten p.m. we were in a different play, or perhaps in the same tired show but playing different parts – far less dramatic, with no conflict involved.

Joseph seemed genuinely pleased to see me. He warned me against tonight's liver and had a toasted sandwich made for me, oozing with melted cheese. I chatted about Norma and the village Christmas as if nothing else mattered; he listened with that sad smile of his.

I leaned forward and held his yellowed eyes for half a minute. 'You were wrong, Joseph. She does need me. She needs me badly – I kept the dead people at bay. They frighten her so when I am not around. She wants me with her.'

'Then why are you sitting here? Why don't you go? I am a

151

man chained to this smoky hole, or maybe it's a root I grew over the years that only death will wither, but you're young and vigorous and free – why not follow the heart?'

I glanced at the three secret policemen now flirting with a couple of hookers. 'I am not free, Joseph.'

'Bah!' he sneered and lowered his voice. 'Those are only the blunt instruments of a quaking institution. Easy to fool, as they are not eager. I hear many a whine these nights. And if you are talking loyalties, then remember that a group of wronged people commands a large support and one voice less would hardly be noticed; but a lonely human being could perish without one extra heart at hand. If you really think she needs you, I can show you a way through the cellars and the dustbin alley that nobody knows about since the war. If I die behind the bar, which is the likeliest of my deaths, I wish to be carried out that way; I wrote the instruction into my testament which is kept in the till.'

'I'll go on New Year's Day. I'll let nothing stop me then.' I couldn't bear the deepening sadness of his smile; I drank the glass of wine he gave me and left.

Nobody followed; just to be on the safe side, I decided to push against the wind back home and then go straight out again through the yards. Very few people walked the streets; a gust of the gale threw a woman into my arms. It was Manon, as in Lescaut, on her way to the Three Bears.

'Hi there, skinny! Have they let you out?!' she cried with sincere joy.

'I missed the boat. They never took me in.'

'Poor sweet, and now you're lonely.' She gave me a light kiss on the cheek, wrapping me warmly in a scent of furs and roses. 'What a shitty world.' Then the wind took her and she hopped and floated on it, and I watched her until she cut a corner and disappeared. Aching, I pushed towards Barley Street and then to May Day Crescent off the boulevard, definitely and securely on my own.

The meeting was brief and efficient. Some twenty people were packed in the living room, each holding a tiny glass of

152

home-made Moravian slivovitz. The girl with flaxen hair and the boy from the public lavatory, Martin by name, were also there, their faces earnest and eager. Professor K. and I held the place of honour; the meeting was chaired by Robert's father. In ten minutes, a decision was reached that while we would start the petition first thing the next morning, the identity of the candidates for an enlarged citizens' committee would be kept secret until the additional forty-eight-hours detention was over and the outcome was known.

In the meantime, we should regard ourselves as a provisional and completely clandestine cell. To the world, and especially the secret police, the members should appear merely as an informal ad-hoc group of petition-carriers and signature-collectors. A draft of the petition was read and speedily amended, and twice twelve carbon copies immediately made on one of our new typewriters; many more would be typed during the night. We ought to be able to get the first 500-1,000 signatures by midday; Professor K. and I would carry the sheets to the National Assembly, while more signatures would still be collected. University colleges should be a cinch, but we'd need workers too. Leave it to me, said Martin, I'll get you a whole factory.

I went to bed feeling surreal. The tot of Moravian slivovitz lay heavy in my stomach and I dreamt a succession of collages that would have made Salvador Dali envious – some jolly, some distressing and some, like the one I woke up with – a mountain of snow-white apples in a red-painted stately hall – extremely beautiful. I decided to write little stories around them, a bedtime read for Norma straight from my soul.

But I overslept by ages and the writing had to be postponed. All there was time for was a quick cup of coffee: I was supposed to spend an hour pretending an interest in the post-Christmas sale on the boulevard before entering the public lavatory at a quarter to twelve, to collect the signature sheets. Professor K. and I were to meet by the entrance to the National Assembly at the top of the boulevard by twelve

153

o'clock, precisely. While the kettle hummed, I re-read the
text, marvelling at its brevity and wondering who drafted it:
'To the honourable members of the National Assembly. We,
the undersigned citizens of Bohemia, demand immediate
freedom for eleven members of the citizens' committee held
in police cells on trumped-up charges. We demand that laws
defining "agitation" and "subversion of the republic" be
reviewed urgently, as they are a complete travesty of
democratic rights and liberties granted to citizens by the
constitution. With this petition, we claim our right to
influence actively the decisions of the Assembly which
should lead our country on the path to a true socialist
democracy.' The kettle boiled and I let it whistle while I
printed my name and address on the sheet.

'Lucky you,' said the trench-coat with the brown hat,
'sleeping late. Not like us working people! We were
beginning to feel lonely without you. Where is it to be today?
Come on, a job's a job, we're not lepers or something! It
won't kill you, talking to us.'

'We're going to the sales,' I chirped. 'A girl's got to get a
few rags now and then.'

'You could have fooled me,' smirked the black hat. 'I've
never seen a drabber woman. It's the boulevard then, is it?
Maybe I should get the wife a little something.'

Thus we browsed, including the driver, through un-
attractive piles of Bulgarian sweaters, East German brassières
and Hungarian blouses, like four country cousins willing to
part with one penny, until it was time for me to have a pee.

'Don't sit,' the brown hat advised, 'or you'll catch
something nasty. There is a lot of VD around; the chaps on
the vice squad are quite worried.'

Martin was shedding sunshine all over the cubicle. 'Nine
hundred and twenty-one signatures, in one morning! On
fifty-two sheets – we've photographed them, so don't worry
too much. Listen, when this is all over, will you let me take
you out? I am not as young as I look, you know.'

He kissed me warmly to prove it and then helped me to

154

fold the Hungarian blouse around the signature sheets; albeit heavier, it hardly increased in bulk.

'Oy oy,' sang the gypsy. 'Love is so beautiful, so sad!'

At twelve precisely, I was walking towards the pillared entrance of the National Assembly, but there wasn't a sign of Professor K.. I went past as if heading for the Main Station – that sent the walkie-talkies buzzing – and turned back three minutes later, mumbling that I'd forgotten something. By six minutes past twelve, Professor K. still wasn't in sight. I had to brave it alone.

There was quite a fuss after the lady in reception understood what it was I had in my hand. She frowned at me furiously, but I stood my ground. My two tails were shifting their weight unhappily by the magnificent stained-glass door, discreetly talking to their breast-pockets. A youngish comrade came running down the stately staircase and took me to a plush room marked 'Public Relations' which looked as if it'd never been used before. The flowers and the pots were plastic, the ashtrays glittered. Was this a wise step, he wanted to know; wouldn't the Prosecutor General be a far more suitable address for such a petition, since it had already been unwisely undertaken. I would not comment on the wisdom of it, merely stressed that it was urgent, well within the constitution, and that we'd had copies made of the signatures; more would arrive tomorrow. An imposing woman of about fifty entered the room and wanted to know who really was behind this, and did I realize I was allowing myself to be misused? Two more comrades joined the chorus, suggesting that the petition should be withheld until tomorrow, pending the Prosecutor General's decision on the arrests. I pointed out that the petition contained wider demands and that I wasn't empowered to hold it; they read the text and nodded, the woman with a sneer, the men with nervous smiles.

In the end, there was little they could do but promise that the petition would be brought to the attention of the appropriate committee of the Assembly. To my great surprise, they all shook hands with me and walked me to the door. I wished them a happy New Year and they shuddered perceptibly, but wished the same to me.

Heavy snow-clouds had gathered again over the wintry city; it was so dark that cars, trams and buses had to switch their headlights on. Something was missing; after a minute or two I realized that I no longer cast a double shadow, nor was there a black limousine creeping along the kerb. I kept looking back but apart from a self-absorbed man with a plumber's tool-case, nobody walked in my tracks. I ought to have rejoiced; but I was scared, quite beyond reason.

Marta, her hair wrapped in a scarf and a duster in her hand, let me in with little grace. 'I wish people wouldn't call all the time. Sympathy is a fine feeling, but all I want to do is scrub and dust and polish, not to entertain guests. I never get a chance to do any housework with Karol around; can't I be left alone to enjoy it? All right, it's time for a bit of lunch anyway: you certainly look peaky. Listen, have you had your blood count done recently? Come over to the clinic after New Year and I'll do one. You may well be anaemic.'

We ate thick slices of home-cured ham which a sympathizer had brought, and each drank a bottle of Karol's beer. I told her how I delivered the petition and how they all smiled and shook hands in the end. 'I have no patience with the likes of you and Arnold,' scolded Marta. 'You'd be nice to anybody. And yet there are times when the Lord, merciful as He is, wants us to take to the sword and slay the worshippers of evil, not make peace pacts with them. How can there be a real change if people shrink from pointing the finger at the wrongdoers and punishing them? Those people you shook hands with were basically of the same kind that beat you up!'

'How . . . how do you know?'

'It was on the Austrian radio, the news at ten. It was a big item about the citizens' committee; I didn't catch it all, my German's rusty. Why haven't you told me? Has your nose been bleeding since?'

'No . . . you weren't in town when it happened. You'd

already gone with the children for the holidays. Are they all right?'

'Apart from snotty noses, yes. The baby's got a touch of bronchitis; she's prone to it, poor darling. The village air should be a benefit. How's Norma?'

'I don't know. I am worried, Marta. My cousin Jarek's sweet on her and she seemed to enjoy it, yet ... yesterday, she sounded queer on the phone. Jesus! I completely forgot! May I ring Professor K. from your line? He was supposed to ... oh God, how could I have forgotten?'

The Professor was asleep, said the housekeeper. He'd had visitors all morning, they ... they wanted to know all sorts of things, and he was very tired. He said that if a young lady called, he was very sorry and hoped that all went well.

Marta shooed me out of the flat. She wanted Karol to be green with envy when he came out of gaol tomorrow, he'd always maintained he was the best house-cleaner of them all; and if he didn't come out, well, she'd better get used to the work, hadn't she? Her pretty face was set in determined lines; it was I who was green with envy.

There was another plumber outside the house in Peace Square, complete with overalls, a padded jacket and a toolbag. I met two more on my way to Barley Street, and wondered how many kings did Bohemia have?

I stopped briefly in a telephone-box, dialled a number and announced that apart from an old teacher who couldn't get to the library because there was too much traffic around his house, there hadn't been any accident and I was walking much better, thank you, without crutches, and would see everybody tomorrow before the show. Somebody said fine, and I hung up.

At home, the phone rang a minute after I'd shaken the snow off my coat over the bath-tub. I picked it up and my aunt said curtly, 'She wants to talk to you.'

'Norma here. What do you want?'

'It's you who's calling, you twit. Funny here, what d'you want?'

157

She whinnied, but if I hadn't known her I would have sworn it was somebody weeping. 'Oh, you're clever! I've found a book. Do you want me to read you a story?'

'I'd like nothing better.'

'Will you listen?'

'I am all ears.'

'You mustn't laugh. It's a sad story.'

'I won't.'

'Once upon a time, there was a witch called Norma. She was born very old and very sick, but she was also very pretty, so nobody knew. One man wanted to marry her and she liked him, but not very much. And this witch had a sister who was also very old but very wise, so she called her on the telephone. But the dead people stood all around and made funny noises, so this witch couldn't—'

'Norma, dearest, is Auntie there with you?'

'No, silly. She hates the telephone. Why can't you listen?'

'I am sorry. I will.'

'The dead people were terrible. One said this and others said that, and so all day. They tugged at her arms, one this way, one the other way, until this witch you-know-who had lost all power. The sister knew this, but she was married to a dead man called Uncle Herman and he—'

'Stuff Uncle Herman! Norma, my love, what's wrong?'

'Hallo?' This was Jarek. 'Listen, can't you come? I need to talk to you. Maybe you should bring some pills. Doesn't she take any? I am quite sweet on her, you know that, but—'

'I'll come on New Year's Eve. I can't possibly travel tomorrow, but I'll be there first thing the day after. Let me speak to Norma some more, will you?'

'She's run out of the house. Listen—'

'I'll see you soon, Jarek. I can't talk now.'

I couldn't. The lump in my throat was throbbing painfully. The blasted telephone rang again the moment I put it down and a woman's voice asked me to come to Café Bohemia on urgent business. It didn't sound like anybody I knew, but I was getting used to new voices and cryptic messages; I was also glad to leave the house, which was filled to the brim with the enormous unfinished sadness of

Norma's story. Maybe I could travel tomorrow, there might not be any midnight meeting and even if there were, maybe I could be excused... I'll talk to whoever is waiting in the Café, I thought; I'll tell them that one lonely human being could easily perish without an extra heart at hand.

It was still early afternoon, but the clouds sat on the roofs and the twilight was darker than dusk. Through the dim air, the snow was falling so densely that it blinded the eyes and made breathing difficult. Another hour of this, and the city would come to a standstill again.

I saw yet another plumber, and still took no warning. It happened on exactly the same spot as the last time: a car pulled up, a sack came over my head, somebody shouted in the distance as I was bundled in, the car jerked forward and my hands were tied behind my back with my own scarf twisted off my neck. I bit and bit my lip to stop myself from useless howling.

'We warned you, didn't we, you stupid cunt? We wrote to you, that's how much trouble we took with you, you ugly bitch! Leave off, we said, didn't we? Now you'll eat your own fucking shit!'

We must have been going up the Hill for I felt the tilt of the car, but perhaps it was the weight of my own fear that was pushing me against the seat. If it was the Hill, then we would soon be passing by the president's Castle. I pictured the man in his slippers pacing up and down the priceless carpets, musing about what kind of speech his aides were writing for him, sighing heavily and polishing his steamed gold-rimmed spectacles with a corner of his pricy shirt... and giggled. It came out as a sob.

We couldn't have gone far, yet when the car stopped and the engine was cut, there was a stillness such as could be found in a winter forest. The park above the Castle, I thought, as they dragged me out of the car. God help me, nobody ever comes here in winter!

'Beg for mercy, slut!'

'Here goes, missy dissy!'

The first blow was the worst. My stomach reeled with it, my mouth filled with bile, flames shot through my brain. After that, while my body was thumped and hurled from one blow to another and my throat let out strange thin wails, I concentrated on not wetting my pants. If I were to die, I didn't want to... oh, Lord, no! Please, stop! I screamed, please! I must get to Norma! The sack got into my mouth and I choked. Suddenly they threw me to the ground and there were no more blows, just one piercing kick in the side. Feet ran and engines screeched and I tried hard to live, but could not...

Swaying arms cradled me gently. Anton's face swam above mine, tears swam in his eyes and sweet warm blood swam around in my mouth. An engine purred a lullaby. Am I...? I wanted ask, but I choked on some darkness that was spreading all over me.

V

Leontes: Where's Bohemia? Speak.
Lord: Here in your city...

William Shakespeare
The Winter's Tale, Act IV, Scene I.

The world becomes inhabitable. She who creates it daily is
either being interfered with by evil powers, which she thinks
unlikely, or else produces the poison herself. It attacks every
pattern on every surface: stripes, dots, scratches, smudges,
dents and blots, they all assemble whenever the eye's
frightened focus falls upon them into unknown, living faces.
Decorporated, yet moving, twisting, lifting, turning, rarely
smiling but frequently grinning, young men, old men,
ageless women, never children. There is no escape for the
tortured eye; even under the cover of the shut eyelid, specks
of light and shapes of colours perform the same trick; a face
forms, gazes, turns away, its features dissolve and rearrange
themselves into yet another unfamiliar ghost. Not one of the
faces comes from the portfolio of famous people; not one has
a name; and they never repeat themselves.

Who are you?! she cries into the palm of her hand,
gripping her mouth. Do tell, or go away, leave me alone! But
the faces are silent, and they don't go without being followed
by more and more. Sometimes two or three at a time, as if
those belonged to some inseparable family. Long dead,
perhaps.

When sleep approaches, the faces fade. But four, five, six
times a night the peace is broken by a voice or another human
sound like a heavy footstep by the bed or a loud breath in the

hall. These are sounds of men, menacing strangers. Stiff with fear, she awaits molestation or murder; she bites and chews the sheets until long dead minutes tell her that what she hears must have been unreal, a hallucination. Sleep comes and the knowledge is forgotten – the next sound or voice will frighten her as much as the one before.

But she overhears true conversations too, late evening or early in the morning, when Peter and Serena are having whispered talks in their bedroom, bathroom or kitchen. She doesn't eavesdrop, but her ears are terribly sharp.

What's to be done, Peter? I can't bear this; the woman is impossible. She doesn't go anywhere, she doesn't try! She just slouches around my guest-room; it gives me the creeps.

Have a heart, Serena. Give her time, you know what she's been through. She's frightened of the streets.

This is England, for Pete's sake! I don't want to be mean, but she'll just have to settle in, she'll have to try!

Give her time.

I think she's sick, Peter.

Oh God, oh no. Just give her time.

I am sure she is sick, Peter.

Oh Serena, what's to be done?

I feel so terribly mean, Peter, but we did our best, didn't we?

I don't know. I suppose so.

Tomorrow then.

We'd better tell her it's a routine check-up. She won't know the difference, poor darling.

We did our best.

She needs professional help. They'll know what's to be done.

I didn't want to tell you until . . . we'll soon need the room for a nursery, Peter.

What? What?! Oh, Serena! Oh, darling!

You see, we have to be firm tomorrow.

Tomorrow she is stiff, heavy and cold like a slab of foreign marble. Silent, eyes shut, she won't budge; she sits on the floor clutching her knees. They have to call an ambulance.

162

She opens her eyes briefly to see the brilliant tears streaming down Serena's face. Forgive me, she wants to say, but the words won't come; she is transferred to a stretcher still clutching her knees but now lying on her side; they sway and bump her down the stairs, the world collapses and shuts in on her – a sheet over her face with a clump of earth weighing it down.

Faces, yes, but how mutilated! Blank white skin where the eyes should be, or the whole lower part missing, the red messy hole of the throat gaping wide, a stump of the tongue perhaps, and quivering tonsils. Pain, what pain! Unrelated to body; tormenting the being. The being, alive and conscious though inarticulate, cut to ribbons: cuts itself to ribbons. Remember! Remember! she screams into the palm of her hand, but the memory is going, going, gone. She opens her eyes briefly to see who's bought it – a gentleman in plainclothes with a kindly frown upon his brow.

She weeps feebly and trembles violently; she won't be touched. Peter and Serena, so close together that their voices seem to come from the same mouth, are telling her story, as much of it as they know, as beautifully as they know how. She listens on the sly, but recognizes nothing. Goodbye, doctor, we'll phone tomorrow.

The next day, she is so sleepy she might as well be dead. The day after, a nurse says 'Good Morning' and it gives her the shakes; she waves her arms ferociously to protect herself from being touched.

This is England, remember? says the nurse. Good old London, none of your foreign wilderness.

She tries to remember England, good old London; she likes the sturdy sound of the words. But all that comes into focus is a department store. A sweet stink of soap and perfume and the clothes, the clothes! Thousands of them suspended from black plastic hangers like dry-pressed human skins which have had their bodies starved out of them. Touched, fondled, unwanted – what happens then? A pyre – she can smell it, she chokes on the thick foul smoke wallowing about the burning nylon and smouldering wool. The escalator slithers down past the dummies with dainty

163

fingers and into the food hall, the promised land of biscuits, steaks and winter grapes; but her hunger is insatiable like the hunger of the world, her stomach is huge and she howls with a craving that has a name to it, but it is written in Chinese signs and she can't read it, she can't and she howls... a doctor is summoned and soon she is so sleepy she might as well be dead.

Flowers arrive. Far too many to gladden the heart. From Peter and Serena, remember us! Get well soon, darling, things will sort themselves out. We love you!

Bianca, a large woman with fierce brows who walks about with one breast bare and the other neatly covered, grabs the huge mixed bunch and runs away with it, shrieking abuse. It appears that she believes herself to be royalty and demands that all tributes, floral or otherwise, be delivered to her.

The eerie faces do not visit any more – she almost misses them. The doctor is pleased with the drug. The drowsiness, he promises, will ease and cease over a couple of weeks. You and I, he says, must soon have a long talk.

Nothing happens. Nobody minds if she draws the curtains around her bed and lies there, missing the meals. A cup of tea, toast perhaps or a biscuit, and certainly the pills arrive at times that mean nothing to her.

She remembers Serena first. Serena has heard the car and stands on the doorstep under the white portico, tall and slim, arms gracefully at her sides, long-faced and corn-blonde, quietly welcoming. The whole house is white, as are all the others, an entire street of identical houses with identical – grand – porticos and small front gardens turned into parking lots. The cars are large and they glimmer and shine.

That's Kensington for you, smiles Peter. Anxious to please, she remarks to Serena that of all the countries Peter had driven her through en route from Bohemia, England seems to be the one most bent on uniformity; towns and streets may vary, but nowhere has she seen row upon row of the same houses... Nonsense, says Serena, instantly displeased, just the opposite is true; no other country can compete with England in architectural richness and variety. But come on in, the tea is ready and waiting.

164

But you can't walk around in these rags! cries Serena and gives her two fifty-pound notes. You can pay me back when you get yourself a job – no hurry. There is, for a change, true kindness in her smile. I would go with you, but I work for a living. Serena is a teacher in the American school of London, only a few blocks away.

In the blonde-blue kitchen, Serena whispers to Peter: She brought nothing. She came home crying like a baby. Don't they have department stores over there? But of course they do, says Peter. It's the scale of things that's so different, I suppose. She may find the choice on offer here . . . aggressive. Give her time. For Pete's sake, cries Serena, isn't choice what freedom is all about? Isn't freedom what she wants?!

Serena is drinking her fifth gin and tonic. Filthy stuff, she sighs. Sometimes, you see, I think that Peter doesn't really love me. You're not after him, are you? I warn you, he only loves a good story. Besides, I want him and I'll keep him. You're not his type anyway, so don't get any ideas. Sure I am drunk, and why not? It's well past midnight, my husband hasn't even had the courtesy to phone me, and I am bored stiff with tales from behind the Iron Curtain. Why don't you forget it, darling, wipe the slate, start a clean new life? I bet you haven't answered the ads I clipped out for you, have you?

Give her time, says Peter, coming through the door, his tie askew. Serena weeps.

Here, try this on. Serena holds out a peach coloured cashmere dress. It's shrunk a bit, it should fit you just fine. Gro-o-vy! Hey, you do look lovely in it – it really does go better with dark hair. You want to impress those Home Office people as somebody who can stand on her own two feet . . . eventually.

On your feet! says a nurse. Hop hop! Time for a bath. I ran your bath for you, nice and hot.

But the bathtub is already occupied. Noreen, a sturdy Asian girl, sits in it with all her clothes on, sucking a wet fag between loud shrieks.

You filthy cow! screams the nurse. Filthy-cow-you – it echoes under the sky-high ceiling of the bathroom. One tub, three wash-basins and one shower for twenty women. The lavatory next door, however, has five fairly clean cubicles. A habitable world.

The nurse scrubs her back in the trickling shower. You mustn't let the other patients push you around, you sweet little thing. If they try anything, come and tell the staff, all right? This is a mean ward sometimes; if things get real rough, run and hide in the office, all right? Do you want me to get a hospital gown and some shirts and trousers? It's a sheer waste to wear your own nice things around here.

Night falls and Bianca comes through the curtains wearing a hospital nightgown, both breasts decent. She has taken her teeth out and her face looks less furious but more wicked. She is bringing the freesias. Here, honey-bee queen, the servants tell me you're a minor royalty yourself, so I bring you the minor flowers for your minor sufferings, while keeping the grand flowers for my graceful major pains.

Bianca is an educated woman, says a nurse peeping in; she used to be a university teacher, but she is a pest, so don't let her get too close.

I am a great lover of women, declares Bianca. The toothless mouth swoops down and presses hard, the sharp gums grinding the lips. She chokes and kicks under Bianca's body while a couple of curtains to the right, Noreen shrieks and shrieks and shrieks.

Listen to her, says Bianca, sitting up; it's the drugs, they make you a raving lunatic, the stupid bitch swallows them. I hope you palm yours, honey-bee queen? Intelligent people do, you know. I am writing a book. Do you want to be in it? I'll make you a price – a packet of fags a week.

Go away, please.

A foul smell is spreading. Oh no, not again! yells the voice of the big black girl who thinks she's Princess Diana, Nurse! Nurse! The fucking fucker's fucking fucked again!

She should be in geriatrics, for fuck's sake, bloody old cunt! That's the voice of young Maria, a child really, a prostitute and a glue-sniffer, homeless and very pretty.

She is beginning to know them all – a pleasant thought. Having successfully palmed the last dose of pills, she obediently pictures Peter, knowing that there must be more to him than she can recall. He drags her out of the car when they are barely twenty yards into West Germany, the Bohemian borders still visible in a not-to-distant haze.

Look back, won't you? That's where the prisons are, and the bastards who hurt you so. You are free, my dear friend! It may not be easy to start with, but Serena and I will help you as much as we can – remind me to phone her when we find a hotel. Are these tears for joy?

She nods and perhaps they are, though the heart is in a strange, numb agony.

Memory, she whispers into the palm of her hand, best you don't come back.

I don't like Germany, says Peter. Would you mind if we drove straight through to Switzerland and found ourselves a little 'pension' there for the night?

Wake up, we're nearly there. Why are you trembling? You can't be cold, the heating is on full blast. Oh, the borders? Silly, they'll just wave us through. This is freedom, remember?

Did we or didn't we? asks Peter next morning, in bed. An empty champagne bottle lies between them and there are two more on the floor.

I don't think we did, she says, and hopes it's true.

Gosh, sighs Peter. Listen, whatever happens Serena must never know we shared a bed. We'd better not do it again. She is terribly fragile ... vulnerable.

Don't you love the scenery? I adore Switzerland, especially in winter. Glorious! Listen, we'll do the interview in France. I loathe France at this time of year.

French borders coming – smile! – gone. So what do you think of freedom, eh?

It's a tall word. It scares me. I am scared, Peter. Let's not do any interview. Give me time.

It's the shock. It's been observed before. Okay, we'll do it on the ferry. Do try to dig out some euphoria, will you? For my sake?

I don't get this. Why do you want to go all soppy about the old Channel? It's nothing but a grey bad-tempered stretch of sea-water! Come on inside, you'll catch your death of pneumonia out here. Gosh, it's rough tonight. And dark!

In a minute, she shouts. I can still see the lights on the coast . . . of Bohemia, she whispers down her chest, the desert land near the sea. I shall soon forget it and live happily ever after.

You'll have to see the immigration officer on the boat. Don't worry, I'll come with you; it'll be over in a jiff. All the paperwork's been done, you're a political refugee and that's that. It's gratifying when things go smoothly for a change in the old Britain.

They did. The officer is polite and in a couple of minutes shakes hands for a welcome. Please, sir, says a darkish man sitting on a bench in a corner with his wife and child, please, what about us? I told you – the officer's voice narrows into a bark – you'll have to go back to France. How many times do I have to repeat this?!

Bangladeshi, whispers Peter. Or Tamil. It's a sad story. Let's go and eat. The cafeteria food is uneatable, but the restaurant doesn't look too bad.

How do you feel? Two black irises surrounded by shining white circles peer through the curtain. It's Selma, a dark depressed beauty from the Seychelles. She wears her silks even in bed.

Peculiar, she answers. Actually rather dreadful. It's true – her limbs begin to tremble, even jerk, her head is ringing, her heart beats fast.

You haven't palmed your medication, have you?

She nods.

Have the pills about you?

She nods again.

Then eat them quickly, silly. You mustn't listen to that lesbian cow; she's completely bonkers, she's been here for years. The drugs are good for you. Look at me, I hardly spoke a word when I came, I couldn't do nothing, they took my daughter from me. I'll soon have her back. I was even better last week, but that fucking Noreen drives me mad. She stole all my fags, did you know that? You haven't got one on you, have you? Oh well, I guess I'll go beg in the office. It's male nurses tonight – they can't resist me.

Tomorrow, she is so sleepy she might as well be dead.

The world becomes small and explorable in a madhouse. She who inhabits it now ventures further afield; she conquers the smell of the dining room, the gloom of the hall, sometimes even the noisy drabness of the day room. The sexes are mixed in all these, but although there is some surreptitious necking going on amongst the young, most of the mumbling men and women waddle past each other without a sparkle of recognition. Bianca's bare breast means that she is on a war-path, not a hunt. Nigel, the angry Irish boxer, shaves twice daily to recover some of his shattered dignity, not to please or be pleased. He still loves his wife who divorced him and changed addresses like gloves to prevent him from finding her.

A tentative friendship is developing there – Nigel takes her for a boy or a creature nearest to one, and pours out the scorn that sits in his boxer's chest. She flees after a while, frightened, but comes for more a few hours later – perhaps because her own anger is sadly missing, forfeited, stranded on some tide-swept coast, unreachable.

Nothing happens. The doctor promises a long talk every time he rushes by, a harassed man following the call of his bleeper. She rummages through a dilapidated chest of drawers in the hall and finds a few sheets of yellowed paper; a perceptive nurse unlocks a cupboard which yields a set of unused pastels and a few sharpened pencil stubs. Nigel sits by her side while she draws; he smokes in hungry puffs, still angry yet strangely comforting.

The story of the drawing is about saving a fieldful of hay from a brewing storm. It happens every July of childhood: the sun is hot, the hay has been turned over for the last time and lies strewn about the field, crackling dry. From behind a wooded hill, moving with a slow inevitability, a fat white-edged cloud begins to mount the sky. Thunder rumbles softly in its belly; the air gets hotter, swallows swoop low in pursuit of frenzied flies. She stands in the middle of the field, a book limp in her hand – waiting, excited, pleasurably scared.

169

Aunts and cousins come running from the village armed with sun-bleached rakes, and the dance begins. Sweep and pile, sweep and pile, carry; sweep and pile, sweep and pile, carry. A mountain of hay grows at the edge of the field by the dirt track above a lazy brook. Thunder rolls louder and louder, lightning begins to show against the blackening cloud. Sweat trickles and pours.

Uncles arrive swearing and waving their pitchforks, driving a creaking hay-wagon pulled by a team of stout dappled horses. Arms, rakes and pitchforks swish through the sea of sweat; children spread and stamp the hay on the wagon, mounting higher and higher, until there is precious little left between them and the flashing sky. Wind now comes in sudden gusts, eyes burn. The horses pull: the children fall flat on the soft swaying hay-top, daring each other to lie face up, to glare at the dazzling darting snakes. The thunder roars, the wagon sways and tilts down and up a slope, threatens to keel over on every bend; the uncles swear and whip the horses, the village cheers and the dogs leap and howl, large hot raindrops begin to fall. The barn gapes open on both ends – the beams miss the children's heads by inches. The race is won. Outside, rain pours in solid splashes. Laughter fills the barn, and slaps of sweaty hands on sweaty shoulders. The world dims and swings away into a long drunken sleep in which she is so happy she could cry.

She cries. Nigel takes over the drawing, blackens the cloud some more, adds a splash of blue sea next to the fields and pencils himself in, astride the dappled horse. Also in the barn, lifting the hay with an enormous pitchfork. And, after some deliberation, among the children on the heaped wagon. Then, while she still cries, he tears up the drawing and walks off, swearing and kicking whatever furniture stands in his way.

A kind nurse takes her for a short walk in the grounds. Crocuses and snowdrops, few and far between, grace the timid grass. Crows perch on an old cedar, while pigeons and sparrows gather expectantly around a bench. A young woman with Chinese eyes sits there, eating a giant-sized sausage roll, the crust scaling on to her lap.

Don't even smile, says the nurse, or you'll never get rid of her; she'll be walking behind you like a dog.

Peter comes to visit. Serena is pregnant, he says, far too fragile and vulnerable to face this place again, but she sends her love. Presents, too – a pretty set of toiletries: cleanser, moisturizer, talcum powder, perfume and a toothbrush with an ivory handle. Bianca hovers in the distance, ready to seize them.

You don't look very cheerful, I must say. Still, much better than the other morning; gosh, you had us scared. What went wrong, darling? England isn't such a bad place, is it?

It's lovely.

You'll be okay. It's the shock – you've had it worse than most, I should imagine. You'll be fine. There is a monitoring job going in Reading... but I mustn't get your hopes up too soon. Rest. Talk to the doctors. Get well. It isn't too awful here, is it?

It's lovely.

Oh, come off it, you don't have to... Listen, I am still sore we never did that second interview. I still think you're special. Sleep on it, will you? Come to think of it, you might even find it therapeutic! There is no hurry; I won't be seeing you for a week or so, I am going to the Falklands, there is some nasty story there about devaluation of property...

Peter doesn't stay long after that. Bianca swoops down but she only wants the perfume, immediately pouring it all over herself.

You fucking pervert, screams Maria, get your stinking arse out of here!

The night falls, the lights go out and she can't sleep. She paces up and down the dimmed hall until a night-nurse calls the duty doctor on the house-phone and gets permission to give her a couple of sleeping tablets. She breaks into a black and white nightmare, the same she had in Switzerland and then every night in Kensington until it drove her out of her mind.

A battlefield heaving with explosions, strewn with bodies. She crawls, inch by inch, towards a barbed-wire fence: if she can get through there, she'll be safe, out of it for ever. She is surprised at how much she wants to live, breathe, have a swim in some cool clean river, hold a warm hand. The shells scream, the din is unbearable until suddenly she is on the other side of the fence in an untouched meadow overgrown with tall silent grasses, poppies and cornflowers. She looks back and recoils: under the tongues of smoke and flames, the bodies move. They are not dead at all, just injured, in urgent need of help; every face is that of a friend calling to her. But she can't return; where there was a fence is now an abyss. Hollow voices echo from precipice to precipice: traitor! deserter! The pain of the shame, like a hot iron, carves up her brain, her heart, her intestines; only the skin of her life remains unblemished, uncharred, breathing.

In the morning, she can't speak but nobody notices. As they queue for breakfast, Nigel stomps the floor, a boxer dancing on the ropes before a fight. When an orderly offers him a ready bowl of porridge with a skin on it, he forms a – reasonable – suspicion that it sat in the heated trolley waiting for him, doctored with the drugs he is so reluctant to take. Give us a fresh one, he demands. I want to see it bloody ladled out like everybody bloody else's! The orderly perseveres; the staff nurse looks on with a supercilious grin.

Fury mounts in Nigel – at the speed of an earthquake that's been long in waiting under the crust. His muscles tense, a rumbling sound comes from his chest: now he grabs the trolley in his outstretched arms, lifts it and throws it against the wall, the whole half-ton of it. It could have killed: blessedly, nobody was hit. The wall is plastered with slow-dripping porridge and there are steaming cowpats of it on the floor, while rashers of fried bacon still slither forward leaving greasy tracks on the lino. The nurses gape helplessly, everyone's paralysed but Maria, who gives a rebel's yell and starts beating her spoon on the table. It's catching: the inmates pick up the rhythm and the dining room resounds with the drums of momentary victory.

She too wants to join in, but just then Bianca screams and leaps at Nigel with all the wrath of an upstaged prima donna. The nurses move on them and more orderlies come racing in, bulky men summoned from other wards. It takes ten strong men to subdue the two raging adversaries.

Spellbound, she watches. Bianca is screeching with joy, but there is enormous sadness in Nigel's roar. Traitors! he shouts. English bastards! Trash!

Strait-jackets, syringes, two dark windowless cells with nothing but a mattress on the floor; the punishment is so spectacular that soon the entire ward is steeped in such silence that they all might as well be dead.

Maria lies face down on the slimy carpet in front of Nigel's cell. Noreen's shrieks are noiseless, just an awful gaping mouth. Selma fiddles endlessly with the buttons of the TV set in the day room – it has been unplugged, as a punishment for the spoon-rebellion. Most of the others slouch on their beds – and so does she.

But she is almost happy: it is as if a balance has been restored, some emptiness filled; she lets her mind float.

What do you miss most? asks Serena in one of her kind moods.

The police, she answers; it is and it isn't a lie. There is a limit to what she can say, or think of.

I don't think I like this particular kind of humour, frowns Serena.

She complains to husband Peter when he comes home, whisky on his breath. Nothing that a twice-weekly trip to the Wapping pickets can't cure, he laughs. Or Greenham Common, but that's a beastly place, best left alone. It'll die a natural death. Speaking of death, must I starve?

There is a smear of lipstick on the lobe of his ear. Serena takes his supper out of the oven, opens the kitchen window and flings it into the garden, baking tray and all.

It wasn't quite true what I said the other day; she tugs at Serena's sleeve as she is leaving for school. Every time a car brakes and stops outside the house, I go stiff. I am glad I am where I am.

Listen, says Serena, why don't you go out more? I hate to think of you sitting alone in the house, brooding. It interferes with my teaching. Now that you have your social security money, why don't you treat yourself to a few sight-seeing tours? We'll take you to Windsor on Sunday, Peter and I.

173

Serena tells me you have been sight-seeing, smiles Peter, fresh mint on his breath. So how do you like London?

It's lovely.

Is that all?!

What more do you want, laughs Serena; she is tipsy and there is a ladder in her stocking. From what she keeps telling me about her city and the whole of bloody Bohemia, you'd think she came straight from Eden and could only find fault with the rest of the world!

You've been drinking, says Peter accusingly.

Surprise surprise, giggles Serena, and cries.

The big black girl who thinks she's Princess Diana comes through the curtains, her face flooded with tears.

The cunt Noreen tore up all my press-cuttings, she whines; how am I to prove to my rescuers who I am? Would you like to be my lady-in-waiting?

She merely stares – she still has no voice to speak with. Sleep on it, says Princess Diana magnanimously. I'll ask you again tomorrow, unless there is a revolution. If there is, you mustn't tell them who I am.

The doctor comes in the afternoon and takes her to his office, a tiny white cubicle next to the punishment cells. He is very young and growing a moustache. Sorry I didn't have time for you earlier, he said, but this hospital is a madhouse. He coughs and blushes: I mean it's severely understaffed. Mind you, it's the same nearly everywhere. The government doesn't seem to understand the needs of national health. But enough about us – tell me about yourself. How do you feel?

She shakes her head.

Okay, let's start at the beginning. Tell me who you are.

Tears well in her eyes. She grabbed a pencil and scribbles on a piece of blotting paper: I can't talk.

Let me guess, the doctor smiles kindly. You feel that you're being persecuted. There are some people or some other creatures who are after you, so you feel you mustn't tell who you are. But you see, I am on your side. I am here to protect you. Tell you what: I won't ask any questions. You talk about whatever's on your mind, okay?

She lets the tears go. They pour and pour, washing her face

174

clean and peaceful. For long minutes, the doctor waits patiently, looking out of the window. Then he tries again, and fails. At the end of half an hour, he sighs and shuts the folder with her notes.

The nurses tell me you've done a lovely drawing. Pity it didn't survive. Would you like to go to art therapy? I don't know how soon I can get you there, but I'll certainly try. There should be occupational therapy on the ward, I am painfully aware of that, but we simply don't have the staff to do it. You deserve better than to sit around the ward all day; I'll get you to the art therapy if I have to cut through the red tape in this hospital. We don't often have patients like you. And don't worry about not talking to me today – I understand. You'll soon be telling it all in pictures. What about pottery? That's easier – I can get you there by tomorrow. Would you like to start with pottery?

She nods: why not? The night falls and her tablets change – there are more of them, and different colours. She is soon so sleepy she might as well be dead, but she wakes up quite early in the morning with a clear empty head and a restless body. Nigel, pale as a ghost, passes her on his way to the gents' showers; he does not know her.

The pottery is housed in a low prefabricated shed in one of the yards. It has snowed in the night – the light powder is melting rapidly in the morning sun, but it still evokes some recent joys and pains that are best kept unremembered.

A rather glamorous young woman explains kindly and with pleasure the simple secrets of working the clay. It has to be battered like apple-strudel dough to get the air-bubbles out, an aggressive procedure that some dread and some find helpful. Don't you be timid, smiles the woman; take a big chunk and beat the hell out of it. Then shape it any which way you want – ignore the wheel, that's for unimaginative souls like myself. It needs certain skills and quite a bit of strength too, and you're so tiny. Enjoy yourself – snap your fingers if you need any help.

The kiln is on – the room is filled with a dry pleasant heat and the humdrum murmur of a dozen patients wearing shiny blue aprons or purple overalls. All around the walls and

175

windows, on tables and shelves, bizarre creatures and objects – fired, painted or brightly glazed – seem to be muttering to themselves in crackling little voices. She still has none in her throat, but it doesn't worry her and bothers nobody.

Blissfully absorbed, she is shaping a child, a naked girl with a bare little fanny, large head and skinny limbs, kneeling on a bed of hay. Soon, however, she dresses her in bulky winter clothes, smoothes the base to make it look like snow, and adds a little snowman and another small girl with her mittens on and with slanted Chinese eyes in her little face.

You're really clever with your fingers, aren't you, says the young woman, whose name is Vicky. That girl with the mittens reminds me of someone, though I can't quite remember who. Somebody rather nice, I should think.

Come lunchtime, she squashes it all into one big lump. Pity, says Vicky cheerfully, but no harm done. You can start all over again in the afternoon, and maybe by that time I shall remember who your little girl reminded me of.

She cries into her soup and for some obscure reason, palms her midday medication. Shush, she whispers down her chest, you're only thirty-three and you'll live for a long time yet.

From half-past one to half-past four, she works on a head the size of a big man's fist. The face is broad and smooth, without features, the unvisited half of the moon. The hair is a thick wreath, the hair is all that matters. She takes a long pin in a wooden holder and begins to separate the curls, frantically, obsessively, prickling the clay against the hasty time.

That's it, I am afraid, says Vicky, but you'll be back tomorrow, won't you? What you want to do is to wet a rag and wrap it around the clay, then cover it with plastic film: it'll be as fresh and soft as you want it in the morning. Who is it going to be? Somebody you know?

She nods, but it may not be true. If it is true, her heart, already beating faster, might burst.

Maria is running up and down the ward, stomping her slender feet like an enraged elephant. Get out of my way, cunt, she screams, you're no better than the rest of the fucking cows! Nine months I've been here, nine months, and all they want is to get rid of me! The shitface of a doctor is sending me home. Home! I phoned my dear mother – piss off, she says. Keep away! I am cured, says I, the shitface says so. Go and be cured some place else, says mum, I don't want you around the kids. So what's it to be, eh? Some fucking bloody hostel for difficult juveniles? Fucking bloody thank you, I am not moving out of here before they find a decent place for me to live in, a bedsit or something. Is that so much to ask? What do you stare at me for? I bet you have a place, all you bloody foreigners do!

I used to have a friend who called the doctor a shitface, she whispers in a voice that seems all new.

Yeah? Good for her. Or was it him? Mind you, you don't look like someone who'd have boy-friends. You look like a fucking nun. Don't mind me, sweetheart, I am in a bloody awful mood. I hate this place! They bugger you up and throw you out. You know what it used to be called? A nurse told me: a paupers' lunatic asylum! And that's what it bloody is, a fucking paupers' lunatic asylum! What are you doing here? You have class, don't you? Don't you know what class is? I mean you're educated and all that, aren't you? You'll soon have the doctors dancing around you, mark my words. Fuck off, will you? I want to stomp their brains out!

During supper, Nigel comes to sit at her elbow. Don't eat the mash, he mutters, that's how they get you.

Shut up, yells Bianca, I am saying my prayers!

Noreen shrieks for a while, and then all is quiet.

Please, can I have a sleeping pill? she whispers and gets a couple, for the price of having to eat all her tablets while the nurses watch. She soon feels hazy, but wakes up at dawn. A furious wind is lashing the window behind her bed with ropes of wet, heavy snow. Under her gaze, it opens like a curtain and lets the memory in.

Anton sits by her bed, playing with her fingers, twisting and squeezing them one after the other as if he were counting his sins on them.

*

177

'Who is he?' asked Jarek darkly. He took great pains to avoid a look at my swollen, bruised face.

'Tony's my name,' said Anton. 'Don't mind me, I am just a driver. But I wouldn't say no to a drink. The roads are beastly around here. What are they like under the snow?'

'Fair enough.' Jarek poured out two schnapps – I did not want any. 'Where is Norma?' I enquired casually, although my heart was pounding. It felt as if I hadn't seen her for a month, as if I had a very urgent message to deliver, a word or a touch that couldn't wait a minute longer. 'Your phone's dead,' I added accusingly. 'I would have said when I was coming.'

'The wind has pulled the lines down. Nobody could be bothered to do anything about it over the holidays. Pity you didn't come yesterday. That was some New Year feast we had, we went through a whole pig. She missed you. We told her you were probably too sick to make it, but you know how stubborn she can be. Mother said she wouldn't hoover to save her life, though she'd oblige with everything else. Perhaps if she took some pills now and then, she wouldn't get so stubborn. She is as sweet as a pie most of the time . . . She just stood on the porch all day yesterday. But she is out skating with the kids now.' He shot the first direct glance at my face. 'You look awful. If anyone did this to a woman around here, we'd . . . Listen, mister, I suppose you're a friend. Couldn't you have taken better care of her or something?'

'I tried,' said Anton earnestly, 'but she wouldn't stop running around on her own. Stubborn.'

'Women,' sighed Jarek.

Impatiently, I waited for them to finish the drink. I needed Anton to drive me to the Bay, I couldn't have walked fast enough with the pain from the cracked rib stabbing my side. Norma, you silly liar, I thought, so you've hoovered, have you? Why would you want to make me believe you have? Did you think I'd be on my aunt's side? Don't you know you are all the family I'd ever want? I'll take you home, sweetheart . . . as soon as I can. Even tonight, if you want me to.

178

It was still warm inside Anton's car, but I wouldn't have minded had it been below zero. I took the skates with me, despite Anton's protestations. Slow skating could only be better than slow walking, I argued, for the motion was that of gliding instead of heaving and jerking. Women, laughed Anton, and concentrated on driving along the snow-covered track furrowed by heavy tractor wheels. It was a bumpy ride, but I was hardly aware of the pain. The day, the second of January, was as pretty as a picture in a children's book, and the air by the Bay vibrated with jolly cries and echoes.

Anton stood by the car smoking a cigar – as if he were already in Major Fischer's shoes – while I slid down the bank and sat down in the shade of an old willow tree to put my skating boots on. Through the curtain of leafless osiers sparkling with frost I could see the bright winding snake of the skaters circling the Bay, each clutching the other's waist from behind, with Norma at the head of it and the smallest children at the laughing, shrieking tail. I had laced up one boot and was about to pull the other on when Norma spotted me. She opened her mouth in a wide smile and her perfect teeth flashed in the sun, sending reflections across the ice like tiny mirrors. She detached herself from the line and waving her arms made straight for the bank.

Straight through the flag-poles and over the patch of thin ice. Shouts failed to stop her. No! I yelled and lurched forward with the dreadful, incredulous knowledge that it was too late. For a couple of seconds it seemed that she was going to slide across like only a penguin could, but then the ice crumbled and she went under, a slab of marble, with one dull splash. There was no fight, she just vanished without even pushing up a hand or a finger through the white crush. Screams splintered the air, screams filled my mouth, screams were pulling me back by the waist until I fell, feeling no other pain than that of drowning, of cold dark water flooding my lungs, of cold dark fire consuming my life. Norma, you twit, spit it out, swim, come back!

'Stand back! Nobody move! Stop yelling!' It was Anton's voice shouting and it was Anton's knee my head was up against. In the sudden silence, the disturbed ice creaked,

179

heaving slightly but not cracking. I began to slide forward towards the still bubbling but fast-freezing hole, feet first; if I could stretch them over, Norma might grab them and hoist herself up. Anton pulled me back by the hair.

'Don't be an idiot! There is nothing we can do but get the hell off the ice. Okay, everybody, skate slowly to the bank one by one, the little ones first. Keep well away from the poles. Go!'

I struggled with him for a while, but grew weak rapidly. Finally, he pulled me up and together we shuffled to safety, two feet in brown suede boots, one in a woollen sock and one on a skate, like a strange slow animal. I knew then that even if I had jumped through the same spot of treacherous ice an instant after it swallowed Norma, I would never have found her. She must have gone to a far better Heaven than I could ever hope to reach.

Back by the willow tree, I sat down heavily, my temple against its rough indifferent bark. 'It's all your fault!' cried a small girl, my middle cousin's youngest. 'We were having such fun. What did you want to show your ugly face for? You look like somebody dead. You've scared Auntie Norma, you've made her go stupid! I hate you!'

Anton slapped my screaming face and the pain brought me to my senses. 'Sorry,' he mumbled. 'Still, remember you owe me your life.'

I nodded. What was it I owed Norma? Something enormous, too large to see. A cold numbness overwhelmed me and after a while I followed Anton into the car like a frost-crazed lamb. We soon caught up with the trotting children and followed slowly, a hearse in which I was the coffin.

Jarek wept openly like a little boy. My old aunt fussed around the kitchen and soon all the cousins and cousins-in-law trickled in, some in house clothes, some in smelly overalls. By and by, a funeral meal was laid on, cold meats and fat gherkins, and schnapps was drunk in befitting quantities. I was the one who was dead, though they mourned me not.

'There won't be a funeral, you know,' said my eldest

cousin. 'Not until spring, there won't. They might find her by the dam then, that's what sometimes happens when somebody drowns around here; there is a strong current underneath. But mostly they never come up. Too deep.' He patted my shoulder heavily. 'There are two sides to everything: some die, some live. You should count your blessings. If it hadn't been for your friend here...'

Anton held a glass to my lips. 'Bottoms up, little soldier. People die a worse death every day. Hers has been quick and easy. Just hold on to a few sweet memories. You too, my friend,' he turned to Jarek. 'It wouldn't have worked, you know.'

'Thanks, chum,' muttered Jarek. 'I guess you're right. I don't know what it's like in the town, but village people can be swine. I mean she wasn't stupid or anything... just too easy to get at. Yeah ... I guess you're right. Poor sweet thing, I'll miss her.'

Savage pain and fury were tearing my skull. It wouldn't have worked for you, but Norma and I have had it made, we were the perfect sisters... now I am an orphan for ever. I have lost the beat of my heart: on whom do I revenge myself? Who will have pity on me?

'You'll be all right,' said my aunt, the sour juice of a gherkin dribbling down her chin, 'you look just like Jarek when he fell off the roof, and he was driving a tractor a week later.'

'We're so glad you aren't in jail,' whispered a plump cousin-in-law, squinting at Anton. 'Like Auntie says, you'll be all right.'

I put my head down among the plates and wept – tired, meaningless, lukewarm tears. The sunshine still danced around the warm kitchen, but the world inside my eyelashes was dark and empty.

A hand fell upon my shoulder. 'Pepan's coming,' said my eldest cousin. 'Why don't you just leave, by the back door? The children can tell him all he needs to know. It'd be easier that way for everybody. I mean, you don't want to—'

'Leave the constable to me.' I could hear Anton smile. 'No need to trouble the children. Where do I take him?'

'The front room, I suppose,' sighed Auntie. 'But make sure he cleans his boots on the mat. He is not a bad lad, but don't get too cosy with him. We don't want him hanging around.'

Jarek squeezed my hand. 'I like your friend. He's cool.'

'Pity he's far too young for her,' murmured the aunt. 'High time she was married. It's not natural for girls to live alone. No wonder she gets herself into trouble.'

After that we sat in silence, waiting for Anton to return. I never lifted my head: it was as if I slept, only much heavier, without a flicker of a dream. The tears kept wetting my face, still meaningless, coming from nowhere in particular.

The goodbyes were long, ceremonious and final. My brief encounter with the family had not been a happy one, and nobody was suggesting a second helping. Perhaps in the spring, if... but they shook their heads.

Anton arranged the seat-belt carefully across my chest. I shuddered under his touch, though I was quite grateful for his presence. It held me together.

'I would like to go to a cemetery... Tony.'

'Wow,' he breathed. 'That was worth waiting for. Sorry, my friend, I didn't mean to be frivolous.'

'It's in New Village, not much out of the way. I have to tell somebody there that Norma's dead.'

He didn't ask questions and when we arrived at the cemetery gate, he stayed in the car, puffing at that cigar again. I walked slowly to Uncle Herman's grave, preparing a speech, but when I reached it I merely felt absurd. I had nothing to say to anybody, dead or alive. The packet of coffee wasn't there any more, only the discoloured ribbon and a scrap of the wrapping paper lay half buried in the snow under the gravestone. I picked them up and threw them into the bin by the gate – worthless litter.

I cried for two nights and two days. It had little to do with Norma and me; the tears continued to flow from that vast unknown, independently grieving source. After that, I turned into a stone, just like Queen Norma and the girl Funny and the entire wishing well on the coast of that big sea in the middle of the snow. I thought of writing down all of

182

Norma's stories before I forgot... and didn't. I could never forget! A stone keeps its inscriptions for ever... but cannot read them.

The doctor visits her in the pottery, where she works – with a peaceful obsession – on a head of a woman, the size of a small curly cabbage. The clay lips are drawn upwards at the corners and half-open in a coquettish little laugh, the forehead is flat and broad, the blunt nose and the slanted eyes aren't finished yet – they look blurred as if by sleep.

No more tears? teases the doctor. We'll soon have our chat, won't we? My, aren't you good at this! Somebody you know?

Yes, doctor, she says in that quivering new voice. Somebody I love very much, I really do.

Somebody you left behind perhaps? he prompts.

No, doctor. Somebody who left me behind. She couldn't help it. The bleeper squeaks and he has to rush on.

You must be very special, marvels Vicky. The doctors hardly ever pop in here, even though they should.

A black boy moulding a foot-high garden dwarf spits on the floor. She is foreign, they don't give a fuck about us Brits. Why do I have to sit next to him, complains a thin old woman with a chalky face who rolls one tiny clay ball after another; he is dirty.

Now now, says Vicky, I won't have any of this; we are one big family here, no bickering. Everybody's welcome as far as I am concerned, as long as they don't start any trouble. I want you all to watch carefully, I am going to show you how to work the glazes.

She finishes the head in the afternoon, adding a hand on which to prop the heavy chin.

Oh! cries Vicky, but it looks just like Jo! Have you met her? She comes and goes; nobody can keep her in one place for long, and she can be quite a nuisance, but she is sweet. I wish she could see this, she'd be awfully pleased! Maybe she'll pop in if she's around. I haven't seen her for some time. I've fired an ashtray she's made for her, do you want to see it? It's very pretty!

No, she says through a lump in her throat. And she carves 'Norma D.' on the side of the hand, Norma's hand under Norma's chin. It goes straight to the kiln, now ready for another batch of ashtrays, dwarfs and merrier creatures.

Nigel, Maria weeps, has been transferred to a closed ward. Everybody who's any fucking good around this bloody place gets treated like a piece of shit. I'll be glad to be rid of it, but I am not going to any bleeding hostel! Oh, look at that cunt, look at her! Nurse!! Old Hilda has peed on the floor and the nurse makes her mop it up. I was not always like this, sobs Maria, I was the poshest-spoken girl in the whole school. It's this bloody place that's fucked me up. Mind you, I learned a thing or two in the squat, but I wasn't that bad, really I wasn't.

A kind night-nurse offers her a cup of Nescafé instead of the pink-grey cocoa she can't really drink – for the price of seeing her wash down the night-medication with it. Everyone says, you were quite a hero in Hungary; do you want to tell me about it? She laughs until she shudders with hiccups. I am sorry, Nurse, it's just that I am as Hungarian as I am a hero, so you see there is nothing to tell.

The wind is up again tonight, throwing the white sleet at the window-panes. It is the coldest first week of March England has known in umpteen years, or so they say. She thinks warmly of the clay head in the heat of the kiln.

Selma is singing her prayers on her bed behind the curtain. It sounds very much like: Oh Lord, would you buy me a Mercedes Benz. Shut up, cunt! shrieks Noreen merrily. Shut up yourself, you noisy cow! Maria screams, Jesus, I can't wait to be rid of you all! Do you hear me? I can't wait! Old Hilda is counting the sheep in a loud, querulous voice. Bianca thrusts her head in, a smouldering stub in the corner of her mouth. Blessed are the poor in spirit, she grins, for theirs is the kingdom of Heaven. If you want to be in my book, you'd better pay quickly, I am running out of fags.

Hallelujah, she whispers. I have hardly any spirit left; does it mean that after all, one day, I may join my love in Heaven?

You're mad as a hatter, scowls Bianca.

She slumbers away and wakes up in the dead of the night.

The window is completely plastered with snow, it looks like flocks of new lambs' wool glued to the glass; the glow of good old London is reduced to a few feeble sparks. Her stomach turning, she goes to beg the nurses for a fag.

They are fast asleep in their brightly lit, glass-panelled office, but wake up at the sound of her bare small feet. It's against the rules, says the kind nurse, but have a couple by way of apologies. I looked into your file, now I shan't forget that you're from Bohemia. Is it far from Hungary?

It depends, she says sagely, on how fast you walk.

Hey, here's a letter for you. Now why didn't you get it sooner?

I am in the pottery all day. I am easy to forget, she smiles. She would be nice to anybody; it's a curse.

The envelope yields a note from Serena, a week-old newspaper cutting and a postcard. I thought you might like to pin these on your locker, writes Serena; I hope the postcard says something nice too. You were right, it looks a beautiful city. Love and all the best, Serena. P.S. Peter hasn't phoned, so I can't give you any message from him.

The news item states briefly that now that the eleven members of the dissident 'citizens' committee' have been released from gaol in Bohemia and the charges against them withdrawn, the reformist tendencies in that wintry country can and should be taken more seriously by the West, even though there were no major changes in the party leadership.

The postcard pictures the Castle on the Hill, the steep roofs and spires underneath, part of the old bridge flanked with baroque statues and the quicksilver of the river. The stamp portrays the president with his gold-rimmed spectacles. Come back, all is forgiven. That's a joke, stupid. We think of you fondly. Dagmar and Vlado. Underneath, some twenty more signatures, more or less illegible.

Which is the joke? she wants to know. The invitation or the absolution? Or both?

This winter, it seems, will never end, unless she faces up to it. The smoke helps.

*

185

'You shouldn't be unfair to the plumbers,' said Anton's mouth, which seemed too big for his face. 'They were my men. How else do you think we found you so quickly? Spared you quite a lot, too, by the look of things . . . not enough, I know. We've expected Fischer to move once I took the operatives off you, I must say we wanted him to move, but we didn't anticipate that he would go for such sheer brutality. I admit, we've made you into a bit of a scapegoat, you were just such an obvious candidate, giving that interview and walking all alone into the National Assembly with that petition – that really took everybody by surprise—'

'You've shaved the moustache,' I whispered through lips that felt like raw meat. 'You'll soon be promoted.'

He blushed, or so it seemed to my badly focused eyes. 'We thought it'd be like the last time. We'd have busted in and forced Major Fischer to resign. You weren't meant to be a sacrifice . . . just a bait. Listen, Fischer's had it. On a grand scale, much more grand than we'd hoped for. We'll let him simmer now, we'll make it known what happened to you, but leave his name out of it for the time being. He'll panic, he'll push his chums in the Prosecutor's office to have new charges shifted up to subversion; our friends will spend a few weeks in the West Prison and then we'll make our move. The president's speech, half-baked as it was, will have sunk in by then; your petition might catch a good few thousand signatures. The Major will fall deep, and drag quite a few nasty characters with him. Your friend Vlado will be awfully proud of you when he comes out. It won't be long, I promise you.'

'Excuse me,' I mumbled politely and retched into the white-enamelled pan Dr Burda had provided me with. 'Concussion,' nodded the doctor. 'Plus, I should think, a general revulsion, which I would be inclined to share if it weren't all so exciting. I wonder what Dagmar will be like after a few weeks in jail. Unbearable, I should think. Taller than ever. To be fair, she couldn't have known all this when she took your place. Hers was a serious gesture.'

Anton sniggered. 'Dagmar's got a nose. The day can't be far away when she'll get herself appointed as the minister of information.'

She'd really get her revenge then, I thought, and shuddered violently. 'What if...' I croaked, 'what if everything goes wrong?' I retched again and couldn't stop shivering. I hurt and I was tired to death: why wouldn't they let me sleep...?

'Don't sleep,' said Dr Burda sharply. 'Why do you think we keep talking to you? To keep your brain awake! Concussions are tricky, you know. There is not much harm done otherwise, you'll ache from the cracked rib and you won't be pretty to look at for some time, but there is no internal bleeding and no serious injury. Still, you are evidently concussed and I'll have to keep you here for a few days.'

'No! I've promised—'

'Listen, my dear, I am doing you a favour. I am playing with the devil on your behalf, so be grateful. You can't go home for medical reasons, and you're much safer here than in any general hospital. For all we know, some nasty boys might be scouring them by now. This an infection ward and you're suspected of rabies, that's why you're in isolation. You've fallen off a horse and been bitten by an urban fox, how's that?'

'Tall,' laughed Anton. 'But I suppose that in a madhouse, everything's plausible. Dr Burda's right. After your plight's been publicized, you'll be fairly safe, but not before. You know,' he drawled dreamily, 'I've always wanted to ride a horse. There is a riding club near where I live. I used to watch the riders taking the horses across the street and trotting away into the fields or down towards the Wild Rock park... they looked so elegant. But my parents maintained that it was a bourgeois occupation. Do you think I am too old to learn?'

'Could I make a telephone call, please? I've promised—'

'Not just now. Tomorrow. Give me the number and I'll phone Norma for you. She'll call me names, but she'll take the news from me better than from anybody else, including you. Don't forget I've been her doctor for years.'

'She isn't in town,' said Anton. 'Maybe it's better not to disturb her.' He grinned at me. 'I'll drive you there when you're better.'

'How . . .?' The blasted telephone, I thought wearily.

'I am not giving all my secrets,' laughed Anton. 'Besides, I wouldn't want to spoil your trusting nature. We wanted to turn you into a Mata Hari, but you're a much better agent the way you are. You think so little of yourself, yet you move hills, if not exactly mountains.'

'I only do what others want me to . . . friends, I mean. If I think it's right.'

They both laughed; I barely heard or saw them, I was so infinitely weary, so . . . sad. Finally, I was allowed to fall asleep and instantly drifted to the village of Broumy, where Norma and the children and some other little people were making a snowman taller than the walnut tree in Jarek's yard. They used kolache for eyes and buttons; flocks of greedy crows and gulls were circling in the sky and I wanted to shout a warning, but had neither a voice nor arms to wave. A sack came over my head and body and I squirmed and choked till morning.

Then Norma died and it was all my fault. How gladly would I have . . . but maybe I was right, maybe there was little togetherness in death and her Heaven would not admit me.

Anton drove me home from the village of Broumy and returned the spare keys to me before letting me out at the corner of Barley Street. He said he would not be seeing me for a while, for I needed a rest and he needed free hands to wrestle with. Mrs H. greatly lamented the death of Norma, my appearance and the general fate of Bohemia – which to some might look a little lighter like, but she had her doubts. Despite Rudi's protestations, she kept house for me during the two days I did nothing but weep, feeding me with chicken broth. I split the village delicacies I couldn't possibly touch between her and Marta, who came to tell me that Karol and the others had been transferred to the West Prison accused of subversion. Marta had understandably little patience with either my grief or my physical torments; she looked me over and announced drily that I'd live to be a hundred, in considerably more comfort than her Karol or the fatherless children. As for Norma, she was blessed – but I wouldn't understand. I was glad when Marta departed, so abrupt were her manners.

Martin has visited me briefly, spending most of the time writing notes and tearing them up. I gathered that the new enlarged citizens' committee was in full operation and the New Year declaration will be ready in about a week, based on Dr Florian's draft – the original of which had been found by his nephew inside the television set in his flat. I would be excused from meetings and work in general for some time, as was Professor K., still ill after the prolonged interrogation which prevented him from joining me in the delivery of the petition; apparently the police returned to his house in the afternoon and stayed until the small hours. Was there anything I needed? Anything at all? He appeared sincerely concerned about my well-being, but it seemed to me that now and then, he shot a curious, suspicious glance at either myself or the typewriter.

On the third of January, when the swellings had all gone and the bruises could have been mistaken for birthmarks, I called on my employer in Foreign Trade. Work was what I needed most, unless the answer to Arnold's question – do we want to go on living – was a resolute 'No'. Which it wasn't: the will to live which my aching scraggy body kept generating surprised me greatly each morning. But my hitherto kind employer turned me down, rolling her eyes to hint at higher powers and asking me to come back in the spring. She pronounced it The Spring, and sighed. Thank you for all you've done for us, but I do wish you really were a Veronika Nowak, you'd have a much better life, what with your linguistic talents and all... Not once did she look straight into my eyes.

In the morning of January the fourth, the door-bell rang, and rang. Two young policemen in winter uniforms informed me that thenceforth, I had been placed under a twenty-four-hour 'protective surveillance'. Two folding chairs and a portable table complete with an ashtray and a pack of cards were already placed firmly outside my door in

189

the corridor. For my own safety, my visitors would be intercepted and undesirable persons, foreigners in particular, would not be allowed to enter the apartment; I would be escorted to the corner shop once a day, if I so wished. They sneered at my expostulations that this was like establishing a mini concentration camp, but I could see that they were bothered and uneasy. What a job for youngsters who were lured into the force by romantic visions of catching dangerous criminals on jolly good pay! Money isn't everything, is it, I said and they blushed and ordered me to close the door and stay quiet, unless I wanted to go shopping right now. It sounded like a threat.

In half-hourly intervals, I phoned the police headquarters and asked for two zero two, but was repeatedly told that the comrade wasn't available. I gritted my teeth: Anton, you bastard! I called the Prosecutor General's office and wished to lodge a complaint; they said they'd call me back. When they did, it was only to say that they'd checked and there wasn't such a thing as 'protective surveillance' the way I described it, and that I should contact a psychiatrist. My emotions were quickly exhausted; my anger was a poor specimen to start with, and I couldn't spare a sorrow. There was still half a cauldron of chicken broth left, bless Mrs H., and a few eggs in the fridge; I took Marcel Proust and James Joyce off the shelf and went to bed with them, after having phoned a few people to tell them what was up. The first day passed slowly in gentle agonies; at night, I put *War and Peace* under my pillow, opened in the middle where Norma's palms had been. But it did not soothe my dreams; they were all about the orphanage, rough and lonely, full of hostile little people and creepy adults and that terribly hushed breath in the middle of the night. Norma, sweetheart, I whispered in the morning, haven't you punished me enough?

Visitors started to arrive at half-past nine – none were allowed entry. I would hear them arguing; open the door, join the protests and exchange greetings. It soon became clear that it was a solidarity campaign, and my cold heart warmed up considerably – at least, the one chamber that wasn't frozen for all eternity. Every day, I had ten to fifteen would-be visitors, including a few foreign correspondents; I didn't have to be escorted to the corner shop, as people brought me butterbrots from the delicatessen on Peace Square or hot sausages from a stand on the boulevard; unwrapped and poked about, they were passed on to me by the bewildered policemen. Long chats weren't allowed, but the hellos and how-are-yous between helpings of Proust and Joyce were nourishing enough. Peter Sanders, back from Vienna, threw me a carton of cigarettes over the surprised heads of a particularly young shift; the two of them pushed him down the stairs rather unceremoniously, but made no attempt to retrieve the parcel. They clearly had no brief to enter my flat.

Each night, I wedged the armchair into the hallway and said my prayers: please God, be good to Norma. I forced myself not to think of her body floating with the current down the Lake, nearer and nearer the dam. I hoped that the weight of the skates and her winter clothes, perhaps with some help from those dead little people, had dragged her straight down, and that her body was resting on the slab of concrete that covered my mother's grave. Her soul I believed to be happy, a little sad perhaps, but happy. How could God not be good to Norma?

The worst part of those days and nights was going to the bathroom. Through the bathroom wall, I could not only hear the two policemen talking to each other or to their walkie-talkies: I heard the soft thumping of the cards and every louder breath they heaved, every shuffle of their feet or creak of a chair. Which meant that they too were involuntary listeners to every little sound I made. I suffered acute shame and inhibition; yet it occurred to me only on the fifth day that I could take my old radio in with me and play loud music while I was peeing or worse. But at night, even that didn't help much; in the general peace and quiet, it felt like announcing loudly what I was doing. I wished I were a man, I really did.

Only once did I attempt to listen to a Bohemian broadcast from abroad. I was unlucky, I caught them just when they were talking about me; I switched the radio off after a few seconds, startled, flustered, unable to enjoy the flattery of it, appalled by the nakedness of my name. Something was definitely wrong with me; I had little reason to be frightened, yet I was perturbed, trembling with trepidation. Without Norma, whatever the world was saying, I was a small scared nobody, loaded with guilt only she could redeem. Had done; couldn't do any more.

On the sixth day, nobody came to see me. In the early afternoon of the seventh day, the police guards suddenly vanished, leaving behind only a pile of old newspapers and chocolate-wrappers. Mrs H. came up to tell me – she saw them loading the chairs and the table into a police van, and deduced it was all over and done with. All troubles come to an end, she cooed soothingly, and all mourning. Somebody told them off, I shouldn't wonder. They say that soon, like, people will have more rights than the police, is it true? You'll feel better in the spring, when... when you can give your cousin a funeral. People are not properly dead without a funeral, are they?

I dressed up in my best things as if I were going to the doctor's and set off to Café Bohemia. The sky was clear and white with wintry sunshine, the snow lay smooth on the roofs and the air was still, yet I nearly didn't make it. My eyes darted from man to man; they all looked capable of turning into assassins, they all seemed to snarl as I passed. I kept to the houses, away from the kerb; my stomach somersaulted whenever a brake screeched; at one point, my knees gave and I had to squat, pretending that something was wrong with my shoe. Then I braced myself and passed the spot of the assaults with stiff dignity.

The afternoon ladies were sipping their coffee and dabbing at the cakes with miniature forks – neat, elderly, unruffled. I was ashamed of the bruises that were now sickly green and yellow and could not be mistaken for birthmarks; I was ashamed of bringing my bruised life into their cosy haven. But they hardly gave me a glance; theirs was a different world. I sat down at the usual table facing the panoramic window, watched the dark mute river and waited for somebody from my world to come and keep me company.

192

If only I had never gone! If only I had stayed home, healing quietly, waiting for spring!

Professor K. arrived, accompanied by Martin who'd clearly taken young Robert's place, and we had a pleasant slightly tired chat about the quality of coffee in Café Bohemia, and why it stayed so good. Many an excellent mind, many an extraordinary poet has sat here over the decades, offered Professor K.; their combined spirit must have acted as a preservative. Martin appeared terribly nervous; he fretted and fidgeted on his chair, his eyes avoiding mine, spilling the coffee.

'What's up with you?' asked the Professor irritably.

Martin glanced at me unhappily. 'Maybe you should know that the relatives were granted a visit yesterday. A typical West Prison visit, short and strictly supervised, but it was still possible to whisper a thing or two which wasn't about prison food and family. Your name was mentioned by nearly all eleven.'

'Not in vain, I hope,' I joked feebly; my hand trembled with apprehension, spilling the ashes of Peter Sanders' Rothmans. A helpless anger made my tongue heavy, unwilling to move much. 'Come on, Martin, what did they say?' Even my voice tasted like ashes.

'There is a strong suspicion that you were the author of the fake. Some believe you were drugged into doing it, others say the drug may have been a cover-up after the event.'

'Nonsense!' barked Professor K. 'I know all about it. Good heavens, who would want to spread a rumour like that? Our dear friends the police, I should think. Spreading mistrust is their speciality.'

'Vlado and Marek might share your opinion, Professor, at least they didn't say anything about it, but the others ... You see, Dagmar said it was positively done on your typewriter and that you more or less confessed to Dr Burda while you were still drugged. She came to warn the committee on Boxing Day, but—'

'Why, then' – Professor K. pointed his finger dramatically at my bruises – 'why then would they do this to her?!'

'Don't ask me,' sighed Martin. 'I am the last who ... but

193

some people are saying now that it was because she went too far in that interview she gave to the Englishman, which they think might have been a face-saving device, talking about factions within the police and actually naming Major Fischer . . . I think people are bothered by the fact that she wasn't arrested with the others; it seems to confirm—'

'Neither was I!' Professor K. was angry. 'I've had enough of this, Martin. Send the gossipers to me. As for our friends in prison, they may be excused for forming suspicions, the place must be seething with them; but next time they should be told to concentrate on their own and our collective innocence. We have all been weak as individuals, at one point or other, but together we stand strong and proud. Let nobody forget this, or we may just as well give up.'

Martin squinted at me. 'Why don't you say something?'

'What could she say?' Robert's father spoke behind my back. 'Our little hero has been found out. Now we know that her friends the police were truly protecting her, just like they said. Maybe from some other policemen, maybe from us. Excuse me, Professor, for not sitting down at the same table. My son is in prison. For all I know, our little hero here might have helped to get him there.'

I leapt to my feet and ran, sobbing wildly, through and out of Café Bohemia, never to return.

The snow is slowly shifting down the cold glass of the window, revealing a few stars flitting amongst the rugged clouds. She is sobbing, both hands pressed against her mouth, listening to the small sound of her grief, allowing a small door in her soul to open and let in the peace, step by step. It is all right, she muses, it is only a matter of changing places, Dagmar has taken my place, so that I could take Norma's. I shall stay quietly mad and live in this place, straying away when summer comes, returning for warmth in winter. I shall mould the clay with Norma's hands, paint pictures of all her stories and perhaps, if I am lucky, dream her dreams. I may send a postcard to Vlado now and then, if I don't forget the address: love from Norma and me, remember us?

194

Noreen laughs in her sleep, Selma moans and old Hilda in the corner begins to snore thunderously. Shut up, cunts, she whispers. Calling the doctor a shitface might be much more difficult, but she'll learn.

She lights the second fag at the end of which, who knows, a dawn may seep in and find her smiling.

There were far too many plumbers around again. Paranoia seized me and held me fast. I've barricaded myself in the flat for two days and nights and shivered in bed, fully clothed. The telephone rang a few times, but I wouldn't answer. Then came the door-bell, loud and persistent.

'Is it the police?' I shouted eagerly. 'Have you come to arrest me?' Hastily, I began to dismantle the barricade.

'Yes,' said a laughing voice. I opened the door and it was Anton, not laughing at all. He banged a bottle on the table.

'I brought you a present. Cuban rum, white as the air above a hibiscus bloom and all that.' He sounded nervous, almost angry, unscrewed the top with more force than was needed and filled the glasses to the brim. 'Down the hatch!' He drank his in one go, and I followed suit. This looked like another blow, and I was so weak. 'I brought you something else as well. I can't have you endlessly protected, but I can't let you upset the plan. It's working beautifully.'

He took a brand new passport out of an envelope. The photograph showed my face, though I never had it taken; not knowingly. 'Just sign on the dotted line and get yourself a visa to Austria. With your pedigree, that should be a cinch. They love dissidents. Tell them your life is in danger – you won't be so far from the truth. I had to pull a whole curtain of strings, so don't look so queasy. Others would pay a fortune for this little book. When was it you last had one? Ages ago, I should think.'

I nodded, walking my fingers over the smooth green covers. Oh, I'll go, I thought, and I'll never look back twice. But I'll have to wait for Norma's ashes.

'Listen, if you're thinking what I think you are . . . she may never come up, you know. On the other hand, you may be back by then. And it isn't that she's only got you, is it? If the body's recovered, your cousins will give her a lovely funeral, I'm sure. Besides, you haven't got much choice, not with Major Fischer still around. He's really got it in for you now. Do you want him to grab you again?'

I shuddered. 'Why did you do it?'

'Do what?'

'Use my typewriter?' ·

'Who says I did?' He grinned almost as merrily as he used to in the old, bygone times. 'I told you I am not giving away any secrets. But you see?' he spoke gravely again. 'Next time around Fischer will beat it out of you that I did, and that wouldn't do at all. Even if I did it – which, my dear friend, I strongly deny.'

'Who, then?'

'Don't ask questions the answers to which you'd hate. Who asks too much, suffers too much.'

'Vlado? But why?! Why would he write what amounted to a call for an uprising? He wanted to slow things down at the bottom so that changes can take place at the top, didn't he? Why would he use my typewriter? Why—'

'Enough's enough,' said Anton severely. 'And talk is dangerous. Think about the word "catalyst" . . . while you're on a train to Vienna.'

I put my head down on the table and wept bitterly. Anton stroked my hair with a tenderness that made me cry even more. 'I'll see to it that you're safe until then, but hurry. And don't go out more than necessary. That barricade was fine, keep it up. I'll miss you. I'll miss you quite a lot. I am not so young as I look, you know, we could have . . . Still, the way things are progressing, we may yet go places together. I've never been to Leningrad, for example, and mother says it's breathtaking . . . So long, love,' he said abruptly and walked to the door. 'I'll be seeing you, but you won't be seeing me . . . for some time.'

He let himself out and practically collided with Peter Sanders reaching for the bell. 'Hey,' cried Anton merrily, 'maybe Mr Sanders can get you a visa to England if you'd rather; why don't you ask him?' And that was the last I saw of two zero two, alias Tony, alias my youthful tormenter and a dubious friend.

'Did he actually speak my name?' asked Peter Sanders. 'How would he know me? I've never met him, I am pretty sure of that, I've got a good memory for faces. Quite an asset in journalism, if I may say so.'

'Somebody must have pointed you out to him. Bohemia's a gossipy place.'

Mercifully, no nasty rumours about me had reached Peter Sanders yet. I was still 'our little hero' to him, without the sarcasm. He was full of guarded yet pronounced optimism; obviously, he said, as long as there were political prisoners in Bohemian gaols and such beastly things happened to people like me, one had to be sceptical. But there were definitely changes in the air, he had a good nose for them. The president's speech wasn't much, but there were other indications. Bohemia might be the wintriest country in the whole of the East, but spring was coming at last. Suddenly, passionately, I wanted to go to England where, it seemed, one could cherish all the hopes without paying a penny of the price.

I was through paying. I was broke. I told him that my life was in danger and that some sympathizers in high places had organized a passport for me. Peter Sanders was nonplussed at first, then enthusiastic. He leaned heavily on the British Embassy and within exactly one week he got me a visa and the status of a temporary political refugee. I phoned Professor K. but the housekeeper said that he was tired and had asked not to be disturbed. I wrote a hasty letter to Jarek and asked Mrs H. to mail it, while Peter Sanders was loading the typewriter, the large suitcase filled with books and the small one containing the rest of my possessions into his car. Mrs H. cried and said that there was never a better tenant in the whole of Barley Street, and that she certainly hoped I'd be back soon. Two plumbers, complete with tool-bags, stood solemn guard, averting their faces from an amateur photographer interested in the proceedings. A momentary hatred passed hotly through my body like molten lava, but soon I hung my head in the disgrace of it all.

Followed by two cars that kept at a respectful but never changing distance, we drove towards the borders. Past the Lake we went, and so near to the frozen Bay that I had to dig

197

my nails into the plush of the seat; I found it difficult to breathe. Memories? asked Peter Sanders sympathetically, and began to tell me about his childhood holidays in a place called Lake District. I liked the man; he droned on and remained calm and composed, only a few beads of sweat forming on his forehead. The two cars now hung on to us very aggressively, one in front and one behind, the snowbound landscape offering no relief. But I decided never to tell him about Norma, never to tell anybody about Norma, except perhaps under extreme provocation which – if Peter Sanders was anything to go by and everybody in England was so outspoken in political matters and so considerate about not probing in to the personal life and emotions of others – seemed unlikely. I felt like somebody in the final stages of moving house, checking the landscape for things I might have forgotten, and would miss, and finding none. The removal men, and women, had been thorough. But then perhaps I possessed little to start with; and Norma was dead.

We drove through the last shabby town of Bohemia and straight into the reddening sun, setting in the West as if that was its home. The checkpoint approaching, announced by watchtowers and barbed wire cutting across the fields on both sides of the road, both cars shot ahead and vanished behind the barracks of the border guards.

Don't worry, said Peter Sanders, glancing nervously at me. I am not carrying anything... dangerous; I sent it out with the diplomatic mail. The chaps at the embassy were most understanding, they'd followed your plight with sincere sympathy. I liked the way he asked. Neither am I, I assured him, I am as clean as a whistle. Even my books should be kosher, I've left the samizdats under lock and key. He smiled and pinched my cheek rather awkwardly, like a boy who's never done it before. For that one little moment, I pined for Vlado's manly, tender, self-assured warmth and intimacy, the brandy on his breath... maybe he'd come out a cured alcoholic, a boring comrade... with a marked propensity for using the likes of me as tools to shape the world with. Disposables. I winced and Peter Sanders apologized.

198

We were asked to drive out of the small queue – mostly West Germans returning from a cheap dirty weekend – and left to simmer for three frosty hours. The lavatories were closed for winter; we had to have a pee in the snow under the weak protection of a cluster of birches, and were photographed on the way back to the car. A shuttered sausage-stand looked forlorn and desolate, yet I thought I caught a whiff of hot grease, smoked meat and mustard; I knew then that my lot might be one of eternal starvation.

In the end, there was little to it. We weren't even searched. A small group of plain-clothes men watched as a passport officer in a smart uniform stamped 'INVALID IN BOHEMIA' over the front page of my passport. Anton, you bastard! Tears flooded the inside of my head, but my eyes were dry. Nothing really mattered.

A steel bar painted bright red and yellow lifted up smoothly, giving us the freedom of the road.

The dawn does not find her exactly smiling, but dry-eyed and peaceful. Shortly after breakfast of toast, hard-boiled egg and porridge, Peter comes to visit, straight from the airport. Ghastly place, the Falklands, he complains; can't see what the fuss was all about. Brought you a present though, three hundred duty-free cigarettes, a special allowance. I'll get you a padlock, says a kind nurse, so that you don't have to carry them on you all the time. There is little else we can do about the thieving, she smiled at Peter; they can't help it. We don't provide padlocks as a rule, they have to go out and buy them, but she is such a sweet little thing that one wants to do things for her.

It isn't too awful here, is it? Peter wants to know again.

It's all right, she chuckles. Thanks for the fags. Hurry home to Serena.

I can't get her to stop drinking, whispers Peter. The child will be born an alcoholic.

Be around, and she won't drink.

He opened his eyes wide. How can I? You of all people should understand! Hey, isn't it exciting about your friends having been released and all that? Maybe you won't need that job in Reading after all. Just concentrate on getting well; maybe you'll be able to go back before the year is over.

I am not a merry globe-trotter, Peter, besides, I've swopped places with two women and it's rather final, I am afraid.

There, there, says Peter soothingly, and goes home to Serena. The doctor, his face pink with satisfaction, takes her to the art therapy. They walk along an endless, dimly white corridor, past clattering heels and shuffling feet, office signs, shops, kitchens, staff cafeteria, patients' clubs, workshops, trolleys, pharmacy, next-to-new boutique, spittoons and ashtrays, moans, curses and giggles, an entire habitat of despair and brisk care attempting to put a bright face on things. I'll live, she smiles to herself, if that's what Norma wants.

Mrs Patell, the art therapist, is an overbearing woman with aquamarine shadows applied heavily to her eyelids. But she is kind in her own strict way and generous with the supply of artists' tools. There are twelve seats in the well-lit room, now all taken. Twelve seats for eight hundred patients, says Mrs Patell, so use your privilege for what it's worth. I want you to paint your feelings, don't worry about the form; later, you may find that the form is as important as the content, but it takes time. Don't worry.

She dabbles the paper with water-colours all shades of the sunset, none of ice or cold blue. She isn't going to hurry.

The time passes slowly as if it were a lazy cloud. Just before lunchtime, the strange peace is disturbed by a young woman with Chinese eyes who bursts in and demands to be accommodated. Now, now, Jo, says Mrs Patell sternly, you know very well that you have to go to the patients' bureau and wait for a referral. I'll be glad to see you here when your turn comes.

Silly cow, says Jo. Wait till Uncle Pedro comes back from Australia! He hates you, he really does.

After tea-time, her breath wheezing, she walks into the pottery. It's come up a treat, smiles Vicky, handing her the head of fired clay. Give me ten pence and it's all yours. It

200

does look uncannily like Jo, you know; have you met her yet?

No, she lies. Shush, she whispers down her chest, things will sort themselves out. This is England, remember. Good old London, none of your foreign wilderness.

Where, pray, is Bohemia?